PRAISE FOR A LIFE REWRITTEN

"This story captured me from the start and surprised me with every emotional plot twist."—*New York Times* **Bestselling Author Lenora Worth**

"A heartfelt and uplifting novel about finding the courage to open your heart in extraordinary ways and discovering who you are in the process. I couldn't put it down!"—**Amazon top-5 Bestselling Author Miranda Liasson**

"Lauren writes a story with an ebb and flow that feels like sitting by the ocean—relaxing and engaging."—*USA Today* **Bestselling Author Kari Trumbo**

"This tender story of resilience, found family, and the unexpected grace of second chances will stay with you long after the last page."—*USA Today* **Bestselling Author Nancy Naigle**

"With impeccable storytelling, strong writing, and compelling characters, Laura Ashwood has crafted a masterpiece of hope and healing in *A Life Rewritten* that I haven't been able to stop thinking about."—*USA Today* **Bestselling Author Elana Johnson**

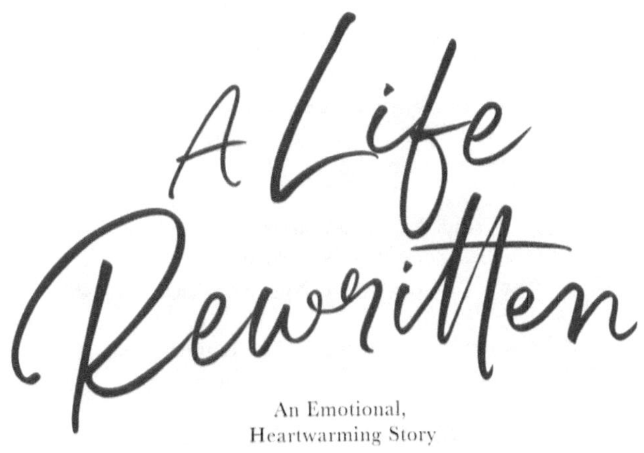

A Life Rewritten

An Emotional,
Heartwarming Story

USA TODAY BESTSELLING AUTHOR

LAURA ASHWOOD

HARPETH ROAD
PRESS
Nashville

HARPETH ROAD PRESS

Published by Harpeth Road Press (USA)
P.O. Box 158184
Nashville, TN 37215

Paperback: 978-1-963483-46-8
eBook: 978-1-963483-45-1
Library of Congress Control Number: 2026931952

A Life Rewritten: An Emotional, Heartwarming Story
(Based on the novel *Summer at Bluefin Bay*)

Cover Design by Sarah Hansen
Cover Images © Shutterstock

Harpeth Road Press, March 2026

A Life Rewritten

To God, for guiding every step of this journey.
To Nancy and Kari, your friendship and support mean more
than you know. Thank you for being on this journey with me.

CHAPTER 1

People always said that Manhattan glittered at night, but even in the lights, Abigail Whitney had never felt so invisible. She watched Michael's fingers curl around the stem of his wine glass, his gold wedding band catching the light from the crystal chandelier hanging above them. The band was a perfect match to her own, although she sometimes wondered if the matching set was the only thing connecting them anymore.

"And then," Michael said, leaning in toward the table of rapt listeners, "I told the board they were making a catastrophic error. We're talking millions in potential revenue, just waiting to be claimed, and they were balking over regulatory concerns." He chuckled, swirling his wine with practiced elegance. "Regulatory concerns that I had already addressed in the proposal they clearly hadn't bothered to read."

The assembled group—two investment bankers, their wives, and their attorney and his wife—erupted in appreciative laughter. Abby forced a smile, sipping her wine and letting her gaze drift across Le Bernardin's elegant dining room. Across the table, Elaine Harrington caught her eye and gave her a cheerful, conspiratorial wink. Abby's smile turned genuine. She and Elaine went back to their debutante days, and she was grateful their friends had been included in the invite, it made it feel slightly less like the networking dinner it was.

Michael had been home for just two days after his last trip to Los Angeles, and tomorrow he'd be gone again. Most of his time at home had been spent behind his office door, taking calls and preparing for his return to the West Coast. She had looked forward to this dinner out with him . . . until she realized it wouldn't just be the two of them.

"You always did know how to close a deal, Michael," Benny Rubinski said, adjusting his glasses. As Michael and Abby's attorney for the past decade, Benny had witnessed first-hand Michael's meteoric rise as a mergers and acquisitions specialist at The Vandermeer Group, eventually leading to his promotion to Chief Operating Officer. "Remember that Jenkins' acquisition? I thought we'd need the Jaws of Life to pry those concessions out of them."

"That was all Michael," Marcia Rubinski chimed in, her diamond bracelet sparkling as she gestured. "Benny came home that night saying he'd never seen anyone negotiate like that."

"You're brilliant, Michael," gushed Elaine. "The Vandermeer Group is lucky to have you."

Abby watched her husband bask in the praise, his shoulders straightening almost imperceptibly. She felt the familiar mix of pride and unease—pride in his accomplishments, unease at how much he seemed to need the validation. Her father had handpicked Michael as both his successor and son-in-law, recognizing in him an ambition that matched his own. But did that ambition leave room for anything else?

"Abby's father knew talent when he saw it," Michael replied, raising his glass in her direction. "To Robert Vandermeer, may he rest in peace. He gave me not only a career but my beautiful wife."

The rest of the table followed suit, and Abby dutifully lifted hers, her smile automatic. Her father had indeed introduced them, practically orchestrating their courtship from the beginning. At nineteen, she'd been dazzled by Michael's worldliness, his stories, his confidence. It'd been easy to get swept up in the romance of it all.

Michael was handsome in a sulky James Dean sort of way. He wore his straight, light brown hair slicked back, and a neatly trimmed beard accentuated his chiseled cheekbones. He had an imposing Romanesque nose that was slightly crooked from an overzealous game of football with his brother, Jack, when they were in their teens. He stood at an even six feet, just two inches taller than Abby, and while he'd been muscular when they were first married, he'd recently started getting a bit paunchy. His true charm, however, was his eyes. They were slightly narrow and an ordinary shade of hazel, but it just took one look from him to make you feel as if you were the only person in a crowded room. Abby used to joke that he could sell ice at the North Pole. Now, nearly fifteen years later, she watched him perform for their dinner companions with a practiced ease that seemed almost rehearsed. Where had the romance gone?

"Speaking of beautiful," said Stephen Harrington, Elaine's husband, "I heard you just returned from Los Angeles, Michael. Perfect weather as usual?"

"Perfect everything," Michael replied with a wink. "Closed the Peterson deal, played a round at the country club, and still made it back to New York in time for this lovely dinner."

A commotion near the entrance drew Abby's attention. A young couple were being escorted to a table, their daughter—perhaps four or five years old—trailed behind them in a frilly dress, her patent leather shoes clicking on the polished floor.

"Honestly," Elaine muttered, following Abby's gaze. "Who brings a child to Le Bernardin? Some people have no consideration."

"Mmm," Stephen agreed. "I can already hear the inevitable meltdown when she doesn't like the foie gras."

The group chuckled, and Abby watched as the little girl carefully climbed onto her chair, her mother helping her arrange her napkin in her lap. There was something so tender in the gesture, so loving. Abby felt an ache bloom in her chest.

"Michael," Abby said, seizing a momentary lull in the conversation, "I was thinking I might join you in Los Angeles this trip."

The reaction was instantaneous. Michael's hand jerked, wine sloshing dangerously close to the rim of his glass. He recovered quickly, but his eyes flashed a warning, his expression shifting to one of mild surprise. Abby couldn't remember the last time she'd accompanied him to Los Angeles—it had been years, certainly. The trips had gradually become his alone, with her staying behind in New York at his and her mother's insistence.

"Darling," Michael replied, his voice tight beneath its veneer of charm, "you know how boring those business trips are. All work and no play."

"I don't mind," Abby persisted. "I could explore the city while you're working. We could have dinner together in the evenings."

"What about your committee meeting for The Metropolitan Museum gala," he said. "And didn't you mention something about the hospital fundraiser needing your attention?"

Before Abby could respond, Elaine jumped in. "Oh, Abby, you can't miss the committee meeting! We're finalizing the seating arrangements, and you know how that goes. If you're not there to defend your territory, you'll end up seated next to that dreadful Cunningham woman all night."

The table laughed, and Abby felt the moment slip away.

"You're right, of course," she conceded, her smile firmly in place. "Perhaps another time."

Michael's shoulders visibly relaxed, and he smoothly steered the conversation toward the upcoming charity auction at Sotheby's. Abby picked at her perfectly prepared sea bass, her appetite gone. Across the restaurant, the little girl was giggling as her father pretended to steal a bite from her plate. The mother caught the father's eye, and they shared a private smile that spoke volumes about their connection.

When had she and Michael last shared such a moment? Abby couldn't remember. Their relationship had become so performative, so focused on appearances, that she sometimes wondered if there was anything authentic left between them.

The sommelier appeared to refill their glasses, and Abby placed her hand over hers. "Just water, please," she said.

"Everything okay?" Michael asked, his eyebrows raised in concern that didn't quite reach his eyes.

"Perfect," she replied, echoing his earlier assessment of Los Angeles.

By the time the dessert menus arrived, Abby found her resolve hardening. She'd been thinking about this for months, during lonely nights in their Upper East Side apartment.

"I've been volunteering at the Children's Aid Society," she said, her voice stronger than intended.

The table's attention swiveled to her, perhaps surprised to hear her speak unprompted.

"How charitable," Stephen said, clearly unsure how to respond.

"It's been incredibly rewarding," Abby continued, her eyes fixed on Michael. "Working with the children, seeing how resilient they are despite everything they've been through."

Michael's jaw tightened almost imperceptibly, a tiny muscle jumping near his temple. "Abby has always had a soft heart," he said, his tone indulgent but dismissive.

Across the restaurant, the little girl had fallen asleep in her father's arms. He cradled her gently while her mother paid the bill. The image burned into Abby's mind—the tenderness, the completeness of their family unit.

"I've been thinking about adoption," she blurted out. The words falling into the conversation like stones into still water.

The ripples were immediate. Elaine's eyebrows shot up. Her husband suddenly became very interested in his dessert menu. The other couple exchanged glances.

Michael's smile never wavered, but his eyes had gone cold, like glass frosting over. "We are not having this conversation here," he said, his voice low but firm.

"Why not?" Abby challenged. "You're barely home long enough to talk there."

A heavy silence fell over the table. Michael cleared his throat, his business smile firmly in place, though a vein now pulsed visibly at his temple.

"My wife has an extraordinary sense of humor," he said smoothly. "Now, who's interested in the chocolate soufflé? I hear it's transcendent."

The tension at the table eased slightly as everyone seized on the change of subject. Abby's cheeks flushed. She'd gone too far, and she knew it. She lowered her eyes to her plate, nodding mechanically when Michael ordered a soufflé for them to share.

For the remainder of the evening, Abby remained quiet, speaking only when directly addressed. She could feel Michael's displeasure radiating toward her like heat from a furnace, though his outward demeanor remained impeccable. By the time they climbed into the back of their town car, the silence between them was thick with unspoken words.

"That was inappropriate," Michael finally said once the privacy divider was up.

"I know," Abby replied softly. "I'm sorry."

"The Harringtons are key investors. What were you thinking? That kind of talk makes them uncomfortable."

"I didn't realize our marriage was part of your investment strategy."

Michael's head snapped toward her. "Don't start, Abby. Not tonight."

The rest of the ride passed in silence. When they arrived at their apartment building, Michael nodded to the doorman while Abby walked ahead. They rode up to their floor without speaking, the soft hum of the elevator the only sound between them.

The apartment was dark and quiet when they entered, their maid, Muriel, having left hours ago. Abby slipped off her heels while Michael hung up his coat.

"Would you like a nightcap?" she asked, offering a peace gesture.

"No," Michael replied curtly. "I have an early flight."

Abby watched as he loosened his tie and headed toward his office. Another night, another closed door.

"Michael," she called after him, surprising herself with her persistence. "Can we please talk about this?"

He paused, his hand on the doorknob. "There's nothing to talk about. We've been over this. I don't want children, Abby. Not now, not ever."

"But I do," she insisted, her voice small but steady. "I've always wanted them. You knew that when we got married."

Michael turned to face her, his expression weary. "And you knew I didn't. I was very clear about that."

"People change," Abby said, taking a step toward him. "I thought maybe you would."

"Well, I haven't." He ran a hand through his hair. "Look, I

have work to do before my flight. We can talk about this when I get back, if you insist."

"Will we?" Abby asked. "Or will you find another reason to avoid it?"

Michael's eyes narrowed. "What's that supposed to mean?"

"It means you're gone more than you're here. It means when you are here, you're locked in your office. It means we don't talk anymore, not about anything real or meaningful."

"I'm building a career, Abby. For us. For our future."

"What future?" she asked, the words escaping before she could stop them. "A future where we live in separate cities? Where we only see each other a few days a month? That's not a marriage, Michael. That's a business arrangement."

His expression hardened. "You knew what you were signing up for when you married me. Your father certainly did."

The mention of her father stung. "This isn't about my father. This is about us."

"No, Abby, this is about you suddenly deciding you want to upend our lives by bringing in a child. A child that isn't even ours." His voice had risen slightly, and he took a deep breath to compose himself. "After your miscarriage, we agreed—"

"No, you decided," Abby interrupted, her voice trembling. "You decided it was for the best." The memory of that loss still ached somewhere deep inside her.

She remembered how devastated she'd been, lying in that hospital bed eight years ago, while Michael had seemed almost relieved. He'd patted her hand and told her it was probably nature's way of saying they weren't meant to be parents. She'd been too grief-stricken to argue, too numb to fight for what she wanted. It had been easier, at the time, to defer to Michael's certainty than to face her own grief.

"You decided adoption was off the table. Just like you decide everything else in our lives. I just . . . went along with it."

Michael's face flushed. "That's not fair."

"Isn't it?" Abby challenged. "When was the last time you asked what I wanted? What would make me happy?"

"I've given you everything," Michael shouted, gesturing around their luxurious apartment. "This home, your social standing, the freedom to pursue your charity work. What more could you possibly want?"

"A real marriage," Abby said quietly. "A family. Love."

Michael sighed, his anger seeming to deflate. "I'm tired, Abby. I have a flight at six in the morning. Can we please not do this tonight?"

She wanted to push, to force the conversation, but the resignation in his eyes stopped her. This was how it always went—she would try to talk, he would deflect, and nothing would change.

"Fine," she said, her shoulders slumping. "Good night, Michael."

He nodded, then disappeared into his office, closing the door behind him. She stood alone in the hallway, the click of the lock echoing in the silence.

With a heavy sigh, Abby made her way to their bedroom, the familiar ache of disappointment settling in her chest. She changed into her nightgown, removed her makeup, and slipped under the covers, knowing Michael wouldn't join her until she was already asleep.

Morning came too quickly, gray light filtering through the curtains. Abby opened her eyes to find Michael's side of the bed barely disturbed. He must have come to bed very late and risen very early. She could hear him moving around in the bathroom, the familiar sounds of his morning routine.

He barely glanced at her as he emerged, already dressed in one of his impeccably tailored suits.

"My car is here," he said, checking his watch. "I should be back in two weeks. I'll call when I land."

"Like you did last time?" The words slipped out before she could stop them.

He paused, briefcase in hand. "I was busy."

"You're always busy."

Michael sighed. "Let's not do this now, Abby. I have a plane to catch."

She sat up in bed, drawing the sheet around her. "When, then? When are we going to talk about the real issues in our marriage?"

"When I get back," he said.

They both knew it was a lie.

He crossed to her side of the bed and leaned down to kiss her cheek, the gesture as perfunctory as a handshake between business associates.

"Have a safe flight," she said, the words automatic.

Michael straightened, adjusting his tie. "I'll call," he repeated, and then he was gone, the bedroom door closing softly behind him.

Abby listened to his footsteps receding, the sound of the front door opening and closing. Then silence, the kind that seemed to fill every corner of their spacious apartment whenever he left.

CHAPTER 2

The next few days passed in a blur of committee meetings, charity lunches, and social obligations. Abby moved through them on autopilot, smiling when expected, making small talk when required. Michael hadn't called when he'd landed, nor had he called since. She wasn't surprised.

Brunch with her mother loomed on her calendar like a dark cloud. Abby knew exactly what to expect—Marilyn Vandermeer would have heard all about the dinner at Le Bernardin by now. The Upper East Side gossip network was nothing if not efficient. She glanced at her watch. The driver would be there in just a few minutes. She wandered to the large windows that overlooked Central Park. A man sat alone on a park bench, feeding bread to a crowd of hungry pigeons. He looked as lonely as she felt.

Stepping away from the window, Abby started for the door, but stopped at the tall, black, and stainless-steel shelving unit. She lifted an elegant silver picture frame off its shelf and studied the image under the glass. A much younger version of herself and Michael smiled back at her. They made a handsome couple. The photo was taken on their wedding day. She wore a delicate, diaphanous white lace off-the-shoulder Giorgio Armani dress studded with Swarovski crystals. Her dark, wavy hair had been tamed into an elegant chignon, with the exception of a few loose tendrils that framed her face. Michael, also in Armani, had his arm around her, holding her close. Claiming her. They looked so happy. She ran her finger across the cool glass over Michael's face. They were so happy. Weren't they?

Abby, you have the perfect life, her friend Elaine had just told her the day before at lunch.

She supposed she did. She had a handsome, successful husband, and they shared an elegant apartment in a posh high-rise on Manhattan's Upper East Side. They were part of the "in" crowd that could always get a table at any restaurant of their choice, and their names were on permanent guest lists at nearly every club in Manhattan, allowing them VIP access. Social events and lunch dates at the country club and bottomless mimosa brunches at places like Pardon My French filled her calendar.

She should be content with her life, but a hollow sort of emptiness settled in her chest.

"Mrs. Whitney, your car is ready."

Abby's gaze snapped up, and she forced a smile. "Thank you, Muriel." She placed the frame back on the shelf. "If you could grab my bag, I'll be right there."

"Of course." Muriel nodded and disappeared around the corner.

Muriel had been their housekeeper since shortly after they were married. At first, Abby had objected, pointing out that since it was just the two of them, she could easily keep the house up herself, but Michael had overruled her. He wasn't about to have his wife cleaning and cooking when their friends all had housekeepers. Some even had live-in help.

When she'd broached the subject with her mother, her mother took Michael's side without hesitation, having a full staff of her own. Abby had to admit that having Muriel around made life easier, and she was an amazing cook, but Abby often felt as though she had no purpose of her own. And Muriel wasn't the friendliest person either.

She gave herself a mental shake. It was time to snap out of the melancholy mood she'd been in for the last few weeks. A glance at her watch told her if she didn't get moving, she'd be late for her weekly lunch date with her mother, and she did not want to be late.

"Enjoy your lunch, ma'am." Muriel met Abby at the door with Abby's brown leather handbag and stepped aside.

"Thank you, Muriel." Abby went through the door into the hall, looking over her shoulder as she pressed the button for the elevator. "You can take the rest of the afternoon off if you wish." She gave the woman a genuine smile this time. If she remembered correctly, Muriel's daughter was in town visiting, and she was sure they'd appreciate some extra time together.

Muriel's pinched mouth curved into a rare smile. "Thank you, Mrs. Whitney."

The elevator arrived with a soft chime, and Abby stepped inside, smoothing a hand down the front of her dress before fidgeting with the gold bracelet on her wrist. When the doors slid open, she walked into the marble-floored lobby, the familiar faint scent of lemon polish hanging in the air as she hurried beneath the gleaming chandeliers and out to the waiting car. The restaurant her mother had chosen was predictably exclusive, tucked away in a corner where old money spoke in hushed tones over poached eggs and mimosas. Abby arrived precisely on time to find her mother already seated, her posture perfect, her hair swept into an immaculate twist that made her cheekbones look even more chiseled.

"Abigail," Marilyn Vandermeer greeted her, offering her cheek.

Abby gave the requisite peck and slid into the chair across from her. "Mother."

"Please send for the server," her mother told the maître d' with a dismissive flick of her wrist. The man nodded and hurried off.

The knot in Abby's stomach twisted a little tighter at the tone in her mother's voice. She was used to it, of course. Her mother had been using that tone with those she deemed "beneath her" as long as Abby could remember. Now that she thought about it, Abby realized that many of her friends acted the same way. Including Michael. She made a mental note to be extra kind to the waiter.

Abby studied her mother for a moment, trying to read her mood. Marilyn Vandermeer was a formidable woman who stood nearly six feet tall. Her hair, once the same rich brown as Abby's, gleamed silver now, every strand disciplined into place. Not a fleck of makeup out of place. A sleeveless black dress skimmed her elegant frame, accented only by a thin silver chain. Her arms were tanned and toned, her face too smooth for a woman in her late-sixties—late-fifties if you asked her—which Abby suspected had more to do with Botox than good genes.

Marilyn placed a great deal of importance on appearances, and Abby found herself self-consciously adjusting the neckline of her own dress.

A waiter appeared to take their drink orders—a Bloody Mary for Marilyn, coffee for Abby.

"No mimosa?" her mother asked, one perfectly sculpted eyebrow raised.

"I'm not in the mood for champagne," Abby replied.

Marilyn studied her daughter for a long moment. "Elaine called me," she finally said, her tone carefully neutral.

"That doesn't surprise me."

"She was concerned about you. As am I."

Abby met her mother's gaze. "I'm fine."

"Are you?" Marilyn tilted her head slightly. "Because bringing up adoption at Le Bernardin is not the behavior of someone who is 'fine.'"

"I didn't realize there was a proper venue for discussing family planning with one's husband."

"There is when your husband is Michael Whitney," Marilyn replied coolly. "And when the Harringtons are present. Really, Abigail, you know better. Your father would be mortified."

Abby glanced at her mother, then busied her hands by straightening the silverware alongside the gleaming white plate in front of her. The invocation of her father was a familiar tactic, one her mother deployed whenever she wanted to ensure Abby's compliance. Robert Vandermeer had been dead for over a decade, but his expectations still loomed over her like a shadow.

Their drinks arrived, providing a momentary reprieve from the conversation. Abby took a sip of her coffee, suddenly wishing she had ordered something stronger.

"Children change everything," Marilyn said once the waiter had departed. "Your life, your marriage, your identity. Everything becomes about them."

"Maybe I want that change," Abby replied.

Marilyn reached across the table to pat Abby's hand, her touch cool and dry. "You're better off without, believe me. You have a good life with Michael. Don't jeopardize it by chasing some maternal fantasy."

"Is that what you thought when you had me? That I was a fantasy better left unchased?"

The question hung between them, sharp and unexpected. Marilyn withdrew her hand, her expression tightening.

"That was different," she said after a moment. "Your father wanted an heir for the business."

"And what did you want?"

Marilyn's gaze drifted past Abby. "What I wanted wasn't relevant. It rarely is, in marriages like ours."

The admission struck Abby with unexpected force. Had her mother been just as trapped as she felt now?

"It doesn't have to be that way," Abby said softly.

Marilyn's focus snapped back to her daughter, her expression hardening. "Of course it does. We are Vandermeers. We have obligations, responsibilities. Your father built a legacy, and it's our duty to honor it." She leaned forward, lowering her voice. "You think I don't understand what you're feeling? I do. But I learned long ago that the appearance of a perfect marriage is far more valuable than the reality of a passionate one. In our world, Abigail, stability and social standing are everything. Love is a luxury we can't always afford."

"By being miserable?"

"By doing what's expected of us," Marilyn corrected sharply. "Now, shall we order? I hear the smoked salmon Benedict is excellent."

And just like that, the subject was changed. They settled into the familiar rhythm of Upper East Side small talk, a dance of carefully chosen topics that revealed nothing of substance.

"The Kimballs are divorcing," Marilyn said, delicately cutting into her eggs Benedict. "After thirty years. Can you imagine the scandal?"

"How unfortunate," Abby murmured, pushing her untouched toast around her plate.

"Unfortunate is putting it mildly. Caroline has already been dropped from the hospital board." Marilyn's lips thinned with disapproval. "One simply doesn't air one's dirty laundry in public."

Abby recognized the warning beneath her mother's words. She nodded mechanically.

"The gallery is featuring that new artist next week," Marilyn continued. "The one who uses trash in his sculptures. Very avant-garde." She pronounced the French with perfect inflection, though her distaste was evident.

"Yes, I received an invitation."

"You should attend with Elaine. Show everyone that ridiculous dinner conversation is behind you." Marilyn dabbed at her lips with her napkin. "And wear your black Dior. It photographs well."

Abby smiled tightly, hearing the command beneath the suggestion. As her mother detailed the latest bridge club drama—something about suspected cheating and a decades-long friendship now in tatters—she found herself studying the woman who had raised her. The perfectly manicured hands, the subtle but expensive jewelry, the posture that never relaxed even in repose. Had her mother ever wanted more than this carefully cultivated existence?

When brunch concluded, they parted with the usual kiss on the cheek and promises to speak soon. Abby watched her mother walk away, her back straight, her head high, her silk Hermès scarf fluttering slightly in the breeze. Three separate acquaintances stopped Marilyn before she reached the door, each greeting returned with the perfect blend of warmth and reserve—the practiced social choreography of a woman who had spent decades perfecting the art of being a Vandermeer.

Instead of heading directly to her next appointment, Abby found herself strolling through Central Park. The day was warm for late May, with cherry blossoms still clinging to some trees while others had already leafed out in fresh spring green. Families strolled along the paths, children laughed on the playgrounds, and the scent of newly mown grass hung in the air.

Her phone buzzed in her purse. Abby ignored it, knowing

it was likely Elaine wondering where she was, or perhaps her mother with some afterthought from brunch.

She found an empty bench and sat, watching a young mother push a toddler on a swing. The child's laughter floated through the air, pure and uninhibited. Abby felt a familiar ache in her chest.

Her phone buzzed again, more insistently this time. With a sigh, she pulled it out, expecting to see Elaine's or her mother's name on the screen. Instead, she saw an unfamiliar number with a Los Angeles area code.

Frowning, she answered. "Hello?"

"Is this Abigail Whitney?" an unfamiliar male voice asked.

"Yes," she replied cautiously. "May I ask who's calling?"

"This is Peter Walsh. I'm a nurse at Cedars-Sinai Medical Center in Los Angeles."

Abby's heart stuttered, and she gripped the edge of the bench with her free hand. *A hospital. Los Angeles. Michael.* "Yes, this is Abigail Whitney. What's happened? Is Michael okay?"

"I'm afraid there's been an accident."

CHAPTER 3

Nine hours later, Abby stepped off the airplane at LAX and hailed a cab to Cedars-Sinai Medical Center. She was grateful to have gotten on one of the first flights out, but it seemed to take forever to reach Los Angeles. A tangible reminder of the distance she felt between them. Her stomach rolled, and the ache in the back of her throat grew and grew until she could hardly swallow. Her fingers tapped an impatient rhythm on her knees as the cab crawled along the wide, busy interstate toward the hospital.

Michael had been involved in a terrible car accident and was in the ICU in critical condition. The nurse had told her she was listed as one of Michael's emergency contacts and that his other contact had also been involved in the accident. Abby couldn't think of who else he would have had listed as an emergency contact. Perhaps a work colleague from the Los Angeles office? But it didn't really matter right now. The only thing that mattered right now was getting to Michael's side.

Please let him be okay, please let him be okay, she repeated, as much a calming mantra as it was a prayer.

The cab finally reached the hospital, and Abby raced

through the hallways toward the intensive care unit, her haphazardly packed carry-on bag bouncing along behind her. As she drew nearer the unit, she noticed the grim expressions of the staff in that area and slowed.

Abby recalled seeing the same bleak looks when her grandfather had had a heart attack and her parents had taken her to the hospital to see him. Her grandfather had been a big man with an even bigger personality, but Abby could still picture how small and frail he'd looked in the bed with the metal rails. Bags of fluids hung on a stand with tubes that ran into his arms as the *whiz-bang* of the ventilator breathed for him. Cold sweat prickled on the back of her neck, and she stopped. She couldn't do this alone.

Whiz-bang. The sound came from the room to her left, echoing in her head until it was all she could hear. *Whiz-bang.* Her grandfather had never left the room he'd been in. What if Michael . . . Abby's fingers began to tingle, and her feet felt as though they were welded to the floor. Her throat tightened, making it hard to breathe. Her gaze darted along the hallway, desperate to find a way out. She didn't want this, couldn't have it. *Whiz-bang. Whiz-bang!*

"Ma'am? Are you all right?"

The voice broke through the sounds whooshing through her head. A hand touched her arm, and Abby turned to meet the concerned gaze of a young woman in vibrant purple nursing scrubs.

"I . . . No . . . Yes . . ." Abby stuttered, her mind scrambling to find the right words as the strap of her purse slipped off her shoulder, catching on her elbow. The walls of the hallway seemed to be closing in on her, and she wobbled a bit as she tried to keep herself upright.

"Let's get you to a chair." The nurse's grip on her arm tightened, and Abby felt herself being led to a set of chairs near the nurses' station.

She sank gratefully into the chair while a deep flush crept up her neck and bloomed in her cheeks. *A lady always holds herself together in public.* She could hear her mother's voice admonishing her as she tried to slow her breathing.

The nurse held out a paper cup filled with water, and Abby released the grip she'd had on her luggage and reached out a shaking hand to accept it. She closed her eyes and brought the cup to her lips and drank deeply, feeling the cool liquid as it moved down her throat, through her esophagus, and into her stomach. She took a deep breath before opening her eyes.

The young woman crouching in front of her gave her a small smile. "Are you okay? Do you want me to call a doctor?"

Abby shook her head. The last thing she wanted was to create a scene.

"No. Please." Her gaze drifted down for a moment to stop on the name tag affixed to the front of the nurse's shirt. "Megan. I'm fine." She paused and took another deep breath, pressing her fingers under her eyes, then smoothed her hands down the front of her light tan chinos. Abby took another deep breath. She needed to focus. Michael needed her. "I'm here to see Michael Whitney," she said, her voice breaking just slightly. She felt like she was somehow trapped in a waking nightmare.

Megan blinked, then slid a glance at the nurse behind the desk and gave a slight nod before returning her attention to Abby. "Let's get you to the waiting area," she said as she helped Abby to her feet and led her toward the small waiting room. "I'll have someone come out to talk with you."

Prickles of cold sweat broke out on the back of Abby's neck again. She'd seen the look that passed between the nurses —what could it mean? *Was he . . .* She stopped. "Why can't I see him? I need to see him."

The nurse stared back at her, and Abby could see the

sympathy in her eyes. Her throat closed and her eyes stung with tears. She backed away from the woman and put her hand over her mouth. *No . . . No . . .*

"Ma'am." The second nurse stood and walked around to the front of the station. She put her hand on Abby's shoulder and gently steered her through the doors into the waiting area. "Please have a seat. Dr. Thomas will be with you in just a moment."

Abby nodded and did what she did best. Followed orders. She perched on the edge of a cushioned burgundy chair next to a small round table, with her purse in her lap and the carry-on bag on the floor next to her. An older gentleman with rheumy eyes slumped in a chair on the other side of the room, his head bobbing listlessly as he struggled to stay awake. A television mounted on the wall in the corner of the room blared with the cheering sound of an invisible audience as an overly exuberant game show contestant spun a colorful wheel hoping to win some big prize. Abby scowled at the cheerful sound and tried to tune it out as she waited. And waited. For what seemed like forever as her fingers ran back and forth along the zipper of her purse.

She did her best to hold back her tears. Her mother had always been adamant about never making a scene in public. Even when Abby's father had died, Abby couldn't recall seeing her mother shed a single tear. Not even at the funeral. Abby had been a mess, but not her mother. Marilyn had been crisp, cool, and collected, as she always was. At first, Abby was sure that her mother was just cold. But later that night, after everyone was gone, and long past bedtime, Abby had gotten up to get a drink and heard sobs coming from her mother's room. It was the only time she'd ever heard her cry.

"Abigail Whitney?" a man's voice called from the doorway of the waiting room.

Abby snapped her head up and met the gaze of a man who

looked to be in his sixties. He wore rumpled turquoise scrubs with a stethoscope draped across the back of his neck.

Abby stood. "I'm Abigail Whitney." She tried to read something, anything, in his eyes, but he stared back at her with the practiced detachment of a doctor who had delivered difficult news many times throughout his career.

"I'm Dr. Seth Thomas," he said. "Please come into the family room so we can talk."

Abby dutifully followed him into a small room that contained a desk with a computer and a wide-screen monitor, and several chairs identical to the ones in the waiting area.

"Have a seat." He gestured toward one of the chairs, and Abby sat, gripping onto her luggage handle like her life depended on it.

"What's wrong? What's happened to Michael?" She tried to keep the panic from her voice but was unsuccessful. "All they told me on the phone was that he was in an accident. Is he going to be okay? How badly is he hurt?" The words tumbled out of her mouth as tears pooled in her eyes.

"The car Mr. Whitney was driving rolled several times. He wasn't wearing a seatbelt and was thrown from the vehicle," Dr. Thomas said.

Abby gasped and placed a hand over her mouth. Michael had always hated seat belts. He was used to riding in the back of a vehicle and told her he felt so restricted the few times he needed to drive. It was generally a moot point because they used a car service or cabs in New York. Abby never gave much thought to him driving in Los Angeles. He must have been using one of the company's cars.

"Is he . . ." She trailed off, fear of the answer stealing the rest of the words from her lips.

"Mr. Whitney sustained very serious injuries. His liver was lacerated, and he has a fractured skull, which caused some intracranial bleeding. He also sustained a number of fractures on his vertebrae and ribs."

Abby's chest constricted. She tried to slow her breathing and focus on what the doctor was saying. *Michael is still alive.*

"We were able to stop the bleeding on both the brain and the liver, but the damage was extensive," Dr. Thomas said.

The doctor's words jumbled in her brain. "What does that mean?"

Dr. Thomas rubbed his jaw, then crossed his arms over his chest. "The surgeon removed a portion of Mr. Whitney's skull to relieve pressure, and we are keeping him in a drug-induced coma until the swelling on his brain has reduced."

"A coma?"

"It's precautionary. Mr. Whitney coded during surgery, but we managed to bring him back. He lost a lot of blood. We were able to stabilize him, but the next twenty-four hours will be the most critical period."

Abby heard the words but struggled to process them. *Coma . . . Fractured skull . . .* "Will he—is he—" she stammered.

"We're cautiously optimistic. Again, the next twenty-four hours will be crucial."

Abby felt the small room shrink even smaller as the lump in her throat grew larger. She lifted a shaky hand to her mouth and blinked. *This can't be happening.* She looked up at the doctor. "Can I see him?"

The doctor hesitated, then nodded. "We'll have you meet with someone from patient services to collect any information you might have about his insurance and healthcare directives after you see him."

Abby forced herself to focus. "Wait. A healthcare directive? I thought you said you were optimistic?"

He lifted his hands in a calming gesture. "It's standard

procedure to have any healthcare directives on file. Do you know if he has one?"

"Y-yes, he does—we do," she said. "I don't have it, but I can contact our attorney."

When they'd had their estate plan done, it had just seemed like a formality. She had never considered that she'd actually need to use any of the documents, at least not at this point in her life. Michael had always handled all the banking and insurance matters. She didn't even know where to find their insurance cards. Her ears grew hot. What must the doctor think of her?

The doctor nodded. "That would be great. I'll have the nurse bring you a fax number. We'll need a hard copy here."

Abby nodded slowly as a chill spread over her, permeating her bones and leaving her numb. The doctor said something else, but the words jumbled in her mind. She rubbed her temple and tried to clear the fog. "I'm sorry, could you please repeat that?"

"About his wife," he repeated. "She wasn't as lucky. Her injuries were so extensive, there was nothing we could do. She died before we could get her into surgery. I'm sorry."

Wait? What? She had to have heard that wrong. "His wife? What are you talking about?"

CHAPTER 4

The doctor stared back at her, his confused expression mirroring her own. "Mrs. Whitney, the woman he was with. She didn't make it," he said. "I'm terribly sorry. I'll have the nurse come and take you to see Mr. Whitney."

Abby nodded as though she were in a trance. The doctor stepped out of the room before she could think of asking anything else. *His wife was in the vehicle with him.* The words played over and over in her mind.

His wife.

What did that mean? Surely there was some misunderstanding. The doctor had to be mistaken. Perhaps he got his cases mixed up and was talking about another patient. Yes, that had to be it. She tried to shake it off. It didn't matter right now. What mattered right now was seeing Michael.

The door to the small room opened, and a nurse stepped in. "Would you like to see Mr. Whitney?"

Abby stood on shaking legs and grabbed the handle of her bag. "Yes," she said without hesitation. She'd get to the bottom of things after she saw Michael. She followed the woman through the swinging doors back into the ICU. The beeping of machines echoed in the hallway, and the powerful scent of antiseptics filled her nose as they walked through the unit. They stopped at a room near the end of the hallway.

The nurse turned to her. "Before we go in, I just want to prepare you a little for what you're about to see. Mr. Whitney is stable, but as the doctor told you, he's in a medically induced coma to help his brain heal. He's breathing with the help of a breathing tube, and there's a monitor for just about everything. His head is bandaged where part of his skull was removed to relieve pressure. He also has a broken leg, which is in traction, and there are some stitches along his cheek. It can be a lot to take in, but he's in good hands, and we'll be right outside if you need anything."

Abby blinked at her, trying to process what she was saying. The nurse touched her arm. Her gaze held Abby's for a moment, warm with encouragement, but also shadowed with sympathy. Then she pulled the door open. Abby took a step forward and stood just inside the room, her fingers tightening around the handle of her bag like it was the only thing keeping her upright.

The room was dim and quiet, except for the steady hum of machines and the soft beeping of monitors. Michael lay in the center of it all—still, pale, and almost unrecognizable beneath the tubes and wires. His head was heavily bandaged, and the slight swelling on the exposed side of his face gave his features a lopsided look. A thin line of stitches ran from his temple down to his cheekbone. His leg was suspended in traction, held in place by metal rods and padded slings.

The soft, rhythmic *whiz-bang* of the ventilator filled the space with each breath it delivered for him. Abby's heart twisted at the sight of it. She'd imagined him broken, but nothing had prepared her for this—the unnatural stillness, the utter vulnerability of it all. For a heartbeat, everything tilted.

The air in her lungs turned thin and the walls began to close in. She closed her eyes and forced herself to take a deep, slow breath.

"I'll leave you with him," the nurse said, her words grounding Abby somehow. "You can talk to him," she added with a gentle voice. "People in comas sometimes hear more than we think. I'll come back in fifteen minutes to check in.

Abby didn't even notice her leave. She rushed to the side of the bed and searched for Michael's hand. She gingerly wrapped her fingers gently around his.

"Hey," she whispered, voice catching. "It's me. Abby." She glanced behind her and eased the chair next to the bed a little closer, careful not to bump anything, then perched on the edge of the seat and stared at her husband.

He looked so helpless lying there, his chest rising and falling with the rhythm of the ventilator. *Whiz-bang. Whiz-bang.* The same awful sound that had only minutes before meant goodbye, now kept him alive. Kept him with her. Michael had always been the strong one. So commanding and confident. It was difficult to see him so . . . broken. A feeling of helplessness came over her. She bit her lip and swallowed back a sob. She might not be able to do anything to help him, but she would be there for him.

"Michael," she said again, remembering what the nurse had said about patients being able to hear when they're in a coma. She wasn't sure if he could actually hear her, but she decided that if there was any chance at all that he could, she would talk to him.

"Michael, it's Abby. I'm here." She lightly squeezed his arm and felt a slight twitch beneath her fingers. She glanced at the monitors beside his bed, their steady blips and soft pulses forming a rhythm she didn't understand—but it looked consistent. Unhurried. Calm. Michael's face, though pale and stitched, looked strangely peaceful. Not tense or agitated like she'd feared. Just still, as if he were caught in the middle of a deep, dreamless sleep. She felt some of the tension ease out of her shoulders.

"You always said you were too stubborn to quit. Guess now's the perfect time to prove it." She let out a shaky laugh, brushing her thumb along his. "I'm so glad you're still here. I —I need you to stay, okay? Just . . . stay."

An alarm sounded, and Abby froze. Her gaze snapped back to the monitors. The blip that had been steady just a moment earlier was now erratic. The line on the heart monitor jolted across the screen in a chaotic pattern. What was happening? Abby's stomach dropped. She stood; her fingers fumbled along the side rail searching for the call button. Where was it —where was it? Another spike on the screen. Another alarm.

She spun toward the door, her voice breaking. "Help! We need help in here!"

Footsteps pounded down the hall.

A team of nurses burst into the room. A man in a white coat followed seconds later, barking orders before the door had even closed behind him.

"Code Blue, ICU bed six. Get respiratory in here. Now."

Abby backed into the corner, unable to look away. She pressed a hand to her mouth, her breath coming in shallow gasps as the team surrounded Michael's bed.

One of the nurses silenced the alarm, another pulled back the sheet to access his chest. Someone else was calling out numbers—heart rate, blood pressure, oxygen. A bag valve mask appeared. Wires were disconnected. Hands moved fast, precise and practiced.

"You need to step out, ma'am," one of the nurses said, her voice terse.

Abby heard the words, but her feet were glued to the floor. She watched in transfixed horror as the nurse injected something into one of the tubes that ran into Michael's hand.

Another alarm sounded, and the nurse grabbed Abby by the arm and pulled her toward the door. She resisted. There was so much she wanted to say—needed to say.

"Ma'am," the nurse insisted, tugging on her arm a little harder this time. "You need to go back to the waiting area."

"I can't," Abby protested and wrenched her arm away. Her breath came in quick gasps and sweat gathered on her forehead. "I need to stay."

Someone came up behind her and put an arm around her shoulder. She glanced over and met the kind gaze of the nurse who had brought her to the room. Tears blurred her eyes.

"They'll be able to do their jobs better if you're out of the way," she said in a calming voice as she led Abby out of the room.

"Code Blue, ICU, stat. Code Blue, ICU, stat," a woman's voice sounded over the hospital's intercom system.

Abby gave a desperate glance back at the chaos in Michael's room as the nurse gently led her down the corridor. Away from Michael. Back to the waiting room.

"They're doing everything they can for him," the nurse reassured her as she settled Abby into the same chair she'd been in earlier. "Someone will be back to update you as soon as we can," she said, then rushed back down the hallway.

Abby sat alone in the room. The man who had been snoozing there earlier was gone. The game show still played on the television, the studio audience erupting in cheers as the contestant won a brand-new car. Abby stared at it, her hands clenched in her lap. How could anyone be cheering right now? Confetti rained down on the screen while just a few doors down, Michael was fighting for his life. She looked down at her hands, twisting the rings on her fingers, then closed her eyes while her mind drifted to a memory from early in their marriage.

———

It was the annual fundraiser gala at The Frick. Michael looked so handsome in classic Armani, while she wore a pale blue Elie Saab gown that had taken three fittings to get just right. They'd wandered through the galleries, champagne flutes in hand, and paused in front of a particularly avant-garde painting.

"That looks like something our housekeeper's cat might create if it stepped in paint," Michael had whispered, his breath warm against her ear.

She'd stifled a laugh, scandalized but delighted by his irreverence. "Michael! That's a Kandinsky!"

"Well, I think Kandinsky's cat deserves equal credit," he'd replied, and they'd dissolved into hushed giggles, earning disapproving glances from the serious art patrons nearby.

It had been one of those rare, perfect moments—just the two of them sharing a private joke in a crowded room, connected against the world.

———

Abby blinked back to the present, the memory fading as quickly as it had appeared. She glanced at her watch. Thirty minutes had passed since they'd brought her to the waiting room, but it felt like days. Her stomach twisted with worry.

Please God, let him live. When he got better, she vowed to try harder. She would be the wife he wanted, the wife he needed. They didn't *need* to have children to be happy. They were happy once. They could be again.

The door opened and she stiffened, holding her breath. A harried-looking couple slipped into the room; the man's arm wrapped protectively around the woman's waist. Abby couldn't tell if he was comforting her or holding her up. Their gazes connected for a fleeting moment, sharing a look of despair laced with the kind of desperate hope that can only be found in waiting rooms like this. She watched as the man gently guided his wife to a seat, still murmuring reassurances. The intimacy of their shared worry made Abby feel isolated.

If only this had happened in New York. At least there she'd have someone, anyone, to sit beside her in this sterile room with its too-bright lights and recycled air. In Los Angeles, she was utterly alone.

She reached for her phone, scrolling through her contacts. Her mother? No, she had that spa appointment at the Bathhouse. She'd mentioned it three times during brunch. Elaine, perhaps? Abby's thumb hovered over her friend's name. What would she even say? *"Hello, Elaine, Michael's been in an accident, and I'm falling apart in a hospital three thousand miles from home"?*

Before she could decide, the doors swung open, and Dr. Thomas walked toward her. His expression grim as he approached.

Abby jumped to her feet. "Dr. Thomas," she said, her voice catching. "How is he? Can I see him now?"

The doctor hesitated. "Ms. Whitney, why don't we step into the family conference room? We can talk privately there."

Her heart plummeted at his tone. "Just tell me if he's okay," she pleaded.

"Please," he said, gesturing toward the door.

She followed him on unsteady legs, each step feeling like she was wading through quicksand. The small conference room seemed to close in around her as she sat across from him and held her breath, waiting for him to tell her that Michael would be fine. That they were able to fix him. That she could go back and see him again.

Instead, he brought his hand up and squeezed the bridge of his nose, closing his eyes for a moment before taking a deep breath and meeting her desperate gaze. "I'm sorry, Ms. Whitney," he said in a low voice. "We tried everything, but there was nothing we could do. The injuries from the accident were just too severe."

Abby blinked. Her hands went numb, and it felt as though her stomach had relocated to her feet. She opened her mouth, but no sound came out. *There was nothing we could do.* The words echoed in her head.

"B-but he was stable. You said you were optimistic," she said, the words tumbling out in a choked rush.

Dr. Thomas's expression didn't change, but something in his eyes flickered—regret, maybe, or helplessness. "I know. And at the time, we were. But there was a sudden change. His brain pressure spiked, and even with intervention, it was too much."

Abby stared at him, willing the words to change. Willing herself to be anywhere but here. How could this be possible?

The doctor stood and placed a hand gently on her shoulder. "I'm so sorry for your loss. Take all the time you need. I'll send a nurse in with some water for you."

She nodded numbly, though she couldn't have said what she'd agreed to. The door closed behind him with a soft click, and the silence left in his wake roared in her ears. Her loss. Abby pulled her cell phone out of her purse and stared at it. She should have called her mother, but she couldn't bring herself to do it now. Instead, she simply held the phone in her lap and stared at it. He was gone. Michael was gone.

CHAPTER 5

Abby was still staring at the phone in her lap, her muscles frozen, when the door opened and a woman wearing navy dress pants and a light blue blouse came into the room followed by the nurse in the purple scrubs. The nurse placed a cup of water on the table in front of Abby along with a box of tissues. Was she crying? She didn't think so, though her cheeks felt wet. She thought back to the strangely hollow way her mother had carried herself after her father's sudden death and now understood it with brutal clarity.

The woman in the blue blouse carried a sheaf of papers and a plastic bag with a handle—Michael's belongings, Abby realized with a stab of pain. She blinked, disoriented. She had no idea how much time had passed since the doctor had left with those impossible words. *We did everything we could.* The clock on the wall seemed to move in slow motion. None of it mattered anyway.

Michael was gone. What was she going to do?

"Abigail Whitney?" the woman in blue asked, taking a seat in the chair on the other side of the desk.

Abby felt herself nod, but couldn't make her mouth move. Her throat felt like sandpaper, raw and dry. She reached out with trembling hands for the paper cup the nurse had left on the table and took a small, shaky sip of water.

She glanced up, realizing the nurse was gone—she'd quietly slipped out without a word. Her gaze drifted across to the table where the woman in blue sat stiffly, her expression tight but composed. She was an older woman, with cold blue eyes and straight gray hair that just brushed the tops of her shoulders.

"I'm Iris Benson from the business office," she said. "I'm sorry for your loss."

There it was again, *your loss*. Abby had said it countless times before in the course of her life, and she vaguely recalled the same sentiment being given when her father had passed, but hearing it now, it somehow sounded, well, ridiculous. Inadequate.

"I'll be going over the next steps with you," Ms. Benson continued.

"Does this have to be done now?" Abby managed to say as she met the woman's gaze. The last thing she wanted to deal with right now was paperwork. She couldn't think straight. Her mind was numb. Michael handled all their important paperwork, not her. But he was gone. How could they expect her to fill out forms so soon after . . .? Her lower lip trembled at the thought, and she raised a shaky hand to press against her mouth, as if to steady herself. Abby dropped her gaze to the phone in her lap, praying the screen would light up with some sort of escape from the nightmare she was in.

"I'm required to go through these papers with you," Ms. Benson said, her voice softer.

Abby looked up and nodded dully. There was no waking up, no escape. This was real. Hot tears trickled down her cheeks. Ms. Benson pulled a tissue from the box and handed it to her.

"It won't take long," she said, pausing while Abby wiped her face. "Here are Mr. Whitney's things." She placed the plastic bag on the desk.

Abby stared at the bag but couldn't bring herself to take it, and Ms. Benson slid it to the side, where it rested against the wall. Out of the way. Michael's existence reduced to the contents of a plastic bag. Ms. Benson said something else, but the words muddled in her brain.

"What did you say?" she asked, straining to focus. She couldn't have heard her correctly.

Ms. Benson repeated the same words Abby had heard the first time. "Mrs. Whitney's things can be picked up at the funeral home."

Abby shook her head. She'd convinced herself that the doctor had just mixed up his patients when he'd told her Michael's wife had also passed. It hadn't mattered then; all that had mattered then was seeing Michael. But there was no mistake here. "What are you talking about? *I* am Mrs. Whitney."

Ms. Benson furrowed her brow and shuffled through the stack of papers. "You're Abigail Nicole Whitney, correct?"

"Yes," Abby replied, unable to hide the irritation in her voice. As if losing her husband wasn't hard enough, being grilled by incompetent hospital staff was making things ten times worse.

The woman across the table looked at the paper in her hand and frowned. "I don't understand," she said. She pointed to a spot on the paper and looked up. "You are listed as one of Mr. Whitney's emergency contacts."

Abby nodded impatiently. "Yes, I am his wife. I *would* be his emergency contact."

Ms. Benson's face flushed a deep crimson as she moved her

finger to the previous line on the page. "And Lucia Whitney is listed as the other. It says *she* is his wife. Did you know Lucia?"

Abby blinked. *Lucia Whitney—his wife?* She felt the blood drain from her face, and she slumped back in the chair. There had to be some mistake, didn't there? She leaned forward and pulled the offensive piece of paper from Ms. Benson's hand. The woman said something, but Abby heard nothing as she read each line.

It was a patient information form and had been filled out the year before. Abby vaguely remembered Michael coming home from a business trip about that same time with stitches in his finger. He'd told her he cut it with a box cutter at the office and joked about making his assistant open packages from then on. Her eyes moved down the page to the emergency contacts section. There it was. In Michael's handwriting. *Name: Lucia Whitney. Relationship: Wife.* Followed by an unfamiliar phone number. Underneath, in the same scrawling print, was her name, and next to *Relationship* it simply said *family*.

Abby's heart pounded, and the remainder of the words swam on the page as she struggled to piece everything together. Why would he have listed another woman's name as his wife? Surely it had to be a mistake. Maybe Lucia was the name of one of his assistants. He'd been injured when he'd filled out the form and wasn't thinking clearly. That had to be it.

"It—it says you're family," Ms. Benson said as she took the sheet of paper back and placed it in front of her. "What relation are you to Mr. Whitney?"

Abby stiffened and yanked a tissue out of the box, swiping the moisture from her eyes. She made a concentrated effort to keep her tone level as she replied, "I am Michael's *wife*," she said, carefully enunciating each word. "I have no idea who this Lucia person is. There has clearly been some kind of mistake.

My husband must have been confused when he filled this out. Must we deal with this right now?" She would call someone at the Los Angeles office and get this straightened out. She just wanted to get out of this room. This hospital.

Ms. Benson frowned and pulled out a different piece of paper from the stack next to her and slid it across the desk. Abby stared at it. It was an account snapshot from the hospital's billing office. It had Michael's full name on it, along with Lucia Whitney, and an address in Glendale. *Glendale?* The corporate apartment was in Los Angeles proper, not Glendale. Abby rubbed her temples. It was all so confusing. She returned her gaze to Ms. Benson, who looked as confused as Abby felt.

Abby's shoulders slumped. "I don't understand," she said, her voice barely above a whisper. This had to be one big mistake. She closed her eyes, willing it to disappear. Her husband had just died; this could *not* be happening to her.

"I don't either," Ms. Benson said, giving Abby a sympathetic glance as she returned the paper to its stack and pushed two more in front of Abby. "Can you verify the phone number we have for you is current? And do you know if this is your—uh, Mr. Whitney's current insurance?"

Abby skimmed the papers in front of her. One was the same patient information form she'd just looked at, and the other was a photocopy of an insurance card. Her eyes tried to focus on the phone number next to her name, but all she could see was *Lucia Whitney, Relationship: Wife.* She pressed her hand on her chest, as though by doing so she might somehow hold the pieces of her heart together. After a moment, she forced herself to look at the copy of the insurance card. She had no idea if it was current. She swallowed hard and tried to find her voice.

"I—I believe so, yes." Her voice cracked with emotion. It was bad enough to sit there while a stranger told you your husband had listed another woman as his wife. Abby wasn't about to add insult to injury by admitting she had no idea what their current insurance was.

Ms. Benson nodded and pulled more papers from the stack. Abby watched her lips move as she explained each one, but she wasn't listening to the words. All she could hear was the sound of the alarms going off in Michael's room. Couldn't they have tried harder? Done more?

A hand touched hers, jolting her to the present. "Ms. Whitney," Ms. Benson said, waving a pen at her. "You need to sign this."

Abby blinked and returned Ms. Benson's concerned look with a blank stare.

The woman pointed at a line near the bottom of the page. "You need to sign this release so we can send Mr. Whitney's body to the funeral home," she said.

Without taking the time to read anything, Abby took the pen and scrawled her name at the bottom of the page. Ms. Benson took it, then slid a few papers and a business card in front of Abby. She stacked the rest of the papers together, then looked at Abby.

"The contact information for the funeral home is there," she said, pointing to the business card, "along with some resources you might find helpful. Do you have any questions before I go?" she asked.

Questions? Abby's mind swirled with questions. *Who was Lucia? Why was she listed as his wife? Why did Michael have a Glendale address? What was he doing driving a car?* Nothing this woman could possibly answer. The only one who could was Michael, and he was . . .he was gone. A fresh river of tears streamed down her cheeks, and she shook her head, averting her gaze.

Ms. Benson stood and stepped around the table, then

paused in the doorway. "I'm sorry, Ms. Whitney. Please feel free to stay in here as long as you need to."

Abby gave a slight nod, and the woman slipped out of the room leaving her there alone, staring at the brochure for the funeral home. What was she supposed to do now? She glanced at the bag on the side of the table that contained Michael's things, but couldn't bring herself to look through it.

She was pretty sure none of the resources in the paperwork in front of her would explain how to handle learning that your husband had another wife and died in a car accident with her. She pressed her fist to her lips as she stifled a sob. She needed help.

CHAPTER 6

The hours had dragged, stretching thin until she wasn't sure if it was still night or already morning. Her coffee sat abandoned on the table, stone cold and bitter, and her phone weighed heavy in her hand. She'd forced herself to wait, telling herself over and over that there was nothing she could do until the world outside these walls woke up.

Abby glanced at the clock on the wall: 6:15 a.m. With the time change, it would be 9:15 a.m. in New York. She unlocked her phone and scrolled through her contact list until she found the name she was looking for and pressed the phone icon. She took a deep, shaky breath and wiped her nose with a fresh tissue.

A woman answered on the second ring. "Rubinski Law."

"This is Abigail Whitney. I need to speak with Bernard. It's urgent."

"One moment." The woman put her on hold, and a few seconds later, she heard the familiar voice of her attorney.

"Abby, what an unexpected surprise. How can I help you?"

"Benny, I—Michael—" Abby's voice broke. How was she supposed to explain this? Saying it out loud would make it real, and she still wanted to believe it was all just a really bad dream. But at the same time, she needed help. She brought her hand up and pinched the bridge of her nose. The back of her throat burned, and she burst into tears.

"Abby, what's going on?" The tone of Benny's voice had changed from casual to concerned.

A tingling swept up the back of her neck and across her face. She pulled another tissue from the box on the corner of the desk and dabbed at her eyes. *A lady always holds herself together.* Her mother's words echoed in her mind again, crisp and unyielding. But how was she supposed to hold herself together when her entire world had just fallen apart?

"B-Benny, Michael's dead," she sputtered.

"What?" Benny exclaimed, a note of disbelief in his voice. "He's . . . dead? Abby, are you all right? Where are you?"

"Los Angeles. I'm at Cedars-Sinai Medical Center right now," Abby said, her breath hitching in her throat.

"What happened?"

"He was in a car accident. He lost a lot of blood. There was a liver laceration, and brain swelling—they had to take off part of his skull, and his leg was in traction. He looked so . . . broken. But they said he was stable. They said they were optimistic. And then—" Her voice trembled as another sob tore through her. "And then all the alarms went off and they made me leave and then he—he—" She stopped, unable to continue.

"Abby . . . I—I'm so sorry." Benny's voice faltered. "We were supposed to golf when he came back." He let out a shaky breath. "I can't even imagine what you're going through. Is anyone there with you?"

Abby pressed her fingers to her forehead. "No. I'm here by myself. But Benny, that's not all." She paused. How was she supposed to tell him the rest? It was still so surreal, she couldn't wrap her mind around it, let alone explain it to someone else.

"Abby? What do you mean?"

"They said he . . . The paperwork—" She choked out, her breath coming out in ragged gasps.

"Slow down, Abby," Benny said, his voice low and calm. "Take a deep breath and let it out slowly."

Abby did as he said.

"Now tell me what you mean. What paperwork?"

"There was a woman in the car with him." Abby sniffed. "She died too. They said she's his wife, Benny. She's on the papers."

"What do you mean, his wife? What papers?"

"The hospital has papers that Michael filled out—"

"He filled out paperwork before he died? I thought he was seriously injured."

"Yes—I mean no." Abby struggled to keep her thoughts from racing. "Do you remember when he cut himself at the office last year and had to get stitches?"

"Yes," Benny said.

"I think it's from then. He filled the paperwork out and listed—" She swallowed hard. "He listed someone else as his wife. And the hospital has an—an address for them in Glendale. Glendale. What was he doing in Glendale, Benny?"

"Wait," Benny said. "Back up a second. He listed someone else as his wife? That's impossible. I was at your wedding."

"So was I." She gave a short, stunned laugh that caught on a sob. "You toasted us." She pressed a hand to her mouth, breathing through the rising panic. "Her name is Lucia. I—I don't even know who she is . . . was."

"Try to stay calm," Benny said. "I'll help you figure this out."

Abby released a long breath, some of the tension easing in

her shoulders. Knowing she didn't have to navigate this alone was a small comfort.

"Thank you, Benny," she whispered. "I don't even know where to start."

"Let's start with the paperwork," Benny said gently. "What did they give you?"

Abby thumbed through the small stack of papers Ms. Benson had left. "There's a list of things to do from the funeral home and phone numbers for several area pastors."

"Did they give you his things yet?"

"Yes." She glanced at the white plastic bag that was still sitting on the desk. "I haven't looked through them yet."

"Look."

She opened the bag and pulled out a cell phone, key chain, wallet, and ring. None of them looked familiar. She opened the wallet and saw Michael's driver's license from New York, several credit cards, an auto insurance card, and a couple hundred dollars in cash. Abby knit her brows together and pulled out the insurance card.

The card trembled in her hand as she stared at the names printed side by side—Michael Whitney and Lucia Whitney. Beneath them, in bold type, the vehicle: 2019 Cadillac Escalade. She knew nothing about an Escalade. Like many Manhattan residents, they didn't own a vehicle. It didn't make sense to. There was no place to park in the city, and the company had a car on call for them at all hours of the day and night. It was one of the perks of Michael's job.

She reached for the ring next—small, unadorned. A simple silver band that looked as if it had never left his finger. It was a far cry from the gold one she'd slid onto his hand years ago, the one they'd chosen together at Tiffany's. She remembered how he'd smiled when he slipped it on, how he'd whispered that he'd never take it off.

But this—this band wasn't hers. This wasn't her Michael.

A wave of nausea pitched in her stomach, and she gripped the edge of the desk to steady herself. Everything inside her rebelled. Her husband—her Michael—was meticulous, traditional, loyal to a fault. At least, that's what she'd thought. He hated surprises. He double-checked restaurant reservations. He sent handwritten thank-you notes. How could that same man have lived an entirely different life in another city?

She closed her eyes, willing it all away. But when she opened them again, the proof was still right there in front of her. That insurance card. That ring. That name.

How could someone be your whole world—and still be a stranger?

"Abby?" Benny prompted. "What's in the bag?"

"A ring, but I don't understand," she whispered into the phone. "Benny . . . this isn't his ring. You remember the one he wore? Gold, with the diamonds around the edge?"

She heard Benny exhale on the other end. "Yeah. I remember."

"This one's plain." Her voice cracked. "Silver."

"Are you sure it's the right bag?"

"Yes, his—well, there's a wallet with his driver's license."

"Is there anything else?"

"There was an insurance card in the wallet for an Escalade."

"An Escalade?"

Abby nodded, then remembered he couldn't see her. "Yes, it's got her name on it too." Silence hung between them for a long beat. "I don't recognize any of this, Benny," she whispered. "The Michael I knew didn't keep secrets. He didn't . . . buy cars behind my back." Her voice caught. "Didn't marry someone else. How could he . . .? How could I not know? How could we . . .? I feel like I didn't know him at all."

"I don't know," Benny said quietly.

She straightened abruptly. "Benny, did you know? You were one of his closest friends," she said, her voice rising as the thought gained traction and swept through her like wildfire.

"No, Abby. I had no idea." He paused, then added, "If I had, if there'd been even a hint of something, I would've told you. You know that."

She stayed quiet, breathing hard.

"I know this is a nightmare," Benny went on, his voice gentle and soothing. "But you aren't alone here. I'm going to help you figure this out."

"Thanks," she said softly, the word catching in her throat. She wanted to believe him—needed to believe him—but doubt still clung to the edges of her thoughts like fog that refused to lift. Benny had been one of Michael's closest friends. If he didn't know . . . maybe no one did, and right now he was the only one she trusted to help her.

"All right," Benny said, his voice steady on the other end of the line. "Was there anything else?"

"A phone and a key ring." She picked up the unfamiliar cell phone. It had a much larger screen than the one she was familiar with.

"Can you get into it?"

Abby pressed the button to turn on the phone and the screen lit up, revealing a photograph of a pretty, young girl with dark, almost black hair. She was sitting on top of a dark brown horse, grinning at the camera. She looked to be about seven or eight years old. Abby's mouth went dry. She didn't recognize the girl, but her eyes were familiar.

"The phone is on. There's a-a-a girl," she stammered.

"What do you mean?"

"A girl, a picture of a girl. I don't know who it is."

"Can you unlock the phone?"

Abby pressed Michael's birth month and year into the phone. It was the same code he used for everything. Except for this phone, apparently. She tried her birthdate and got the same result.

"No, the code he usually uses doesn't work, and I don't want to lock myself out."

A beat of silence passed before Benny spoke. "You said there were keys, right?"

"Yes." Abby placed the ring back in the bag and pulled out the unfamiliar key chain.

"Do any of them look like house keys?"

Abby sifted through the keys. There weren't very many. One was clearly a key for the Escalade, as evidenced by the Cadillac logo on the fob. Another resembled Michael's office key in New York, and there were two others that looked as though they could be keys to a house. "Yes, I think so," she said. "There are two that are similar to the key for our apartment."

"Take a cab to the address in Glendale, then call me back. I have a client waiting, but I'll be done by the time you get there"

"What?" She had to have heard him wrong.

"Do *not* go into the building or try the key until you call me back," he said.

"You're serious, aren't you? I can't possibly—"

"Yes. You can do this, Abby. You need to. Glendale is a pleasant community; you'll be safe. I've got to go. Call me when you get there," he said and disconnected the call.

Abby stared at the phone, Benny's request still echoing in her ears. It felt absurd. Intrusive, even. She shifted her gaze to the unfamiliar items scattered on the desk. Nothing made sense anymore. She had so many questions. Maybe Benny was right. If there were answers to be found, they wouldn't be here. They'd be wherever Michael had been living his double life.

CHAPTER 7

As the cab wound its way through the maze of East Hollywood and Los Feliz on the way to Glendale, Abby's mind reeled, and she fought to keep control of her emotions. Michael was dead. He had somehow created an entire new life without her knowledge, and now she was about to confront it head-on. What had she missed? Yes, it was true that he was gone a lot, but a lot of husbands were gone a lot for work, and they didn't have secret wives. There had to have been signs. Things she'd overlooked. But what? Aside from his trips to Los Angeles, everything seemed normal—at least as normal as they had been. She frowned. Maybe his trips were becoming longer, and maybe they didn't spend as much time together as they used to. She couldn't even remember the last time they were intimate. She choked on a sob. How could she not have seen it?

The cab rolled to a stop in front of a four-story brick complex. Abby pressed the button to lower the window and leaned closer, taking in the modest, L-shaped building. A large playground sat tucked into the courtyard, the joyful laughter of children filled her ears.

This can't be right.

She glanced down at the address on the hospital form, then back at the building. It looked like the kind of place that housed young families or retirees on a budget—not high-level executives. Not Michael. Not the man who insisted on penthouse suites and concierge service.

The plain, unassuming exterior bore no resemblance to the sleek corporate apartment she remembered from the last time she'd traveled with him to Los Angeles—five years ago, maybe more. A quick overnight trip, little more than a formality. She hadn't been back with him since. He'd said her commitments in New York made things complicated. That her mother needed her. Now she knew better. She blinked at the building again, willing it to transform into something familiar. Something that made sense. But it didn't. Nothing did.

The driver turned in his seat and gave her a questioning glance. "This is where you wanted to go, right?"

No! Abby wanted to shout. She wanted to be back in New York with Michael. Not here. Anywhere but here. She chewed her bottom lip as she contemplated having the driver just take her to the airport. But then she'd always wonder. No, the answers, if there were any, would be here.

"Yes, thank you." Abby paid the driver, stepped onto the street, and waited while he unloaded her luggage.

The air was dry and faintly cool, typical for mid-May in Los Angeles. The slight breeze carried the distant scent of jacaranda and car exhaust. She stared at the building again. This wasn't just a different address—it was a different life. She waited until the cab pulled away from the curb, then pulled her cell phone out of her purse and tapped Benny's name from her contact list. It rang once before he picked up.

"Abby, good, you made it there. Does the key work?"

"I don't know." She swallowed; her clammy hands

gripped the handle of her luggage so hard her fingers hurt. "You told me to call you first," she hedged, her gaze darting down the street searching for a glimpse of the cab. "I don't know about this, Benny. Maybe I should just go back to New York."

"You're already there. Just take a quick look; you'll regret it if you don't," he said, echoing her thoughts from earlier. "Is it a house or an apartment?"

"It's an apartment building. But—it's a family building. There's a playground. This can't be right. Michael didn't want kids." Their conversation from the week before echoed in her mind. It was the last time she'd seen him.

"Is there a security door?"

Benny's voice pulled her back to the present. "I'm not sure, let me check." Abby glanced around to see if anyone was watching before she made her way to the glass entrance doors. She pulled the handle, but the door didn't budge. "It's locked."

Next to the door was a call box. Abby ran her finger down the list, her pulse thudding in her ears. She stopped at 1015. Sliding her finger over, her eyes landed on the name "Whitney, M. & L." She blinked hard, hoping she'd read it wrong. That her eyes had blurred or the print was smudged. But the letters stared back at her, stark and undeniable.

She'd hoped, foolishly maybe, that it wasn't true. That somehow, she'd get there and there'd be nothing to find. That it was all some enormous mistake the hospital had made. A paperwork mix-up. A cruel twist of coincidence. But this . . . this was proof. The name she'd shared with Michael for over a decade now appeared beside someone else's. *L.—Lucia.*

The weight of it pressed down on her chest, sharp and suffocating. Her hand shook as she pulled it back from the call box, fingers curling into a fist.

"Abby?" Benny's voice came through the phone, quieter now. "Talk to me. What do you see?"

Her voice was a rasp. "It's true," she whispered. "He lived here—with her."

There was a brief pause at the other end of the phone, then Benny said, "Try one of the keys."

Abby's gaze darted over her shoulder. The street was empty. Her chest felt as if it would burst as she pulled Michael's keys from her handbag. She slid one that looked like a house key into the lock. Nothing. She tried the second. A click.

"It worked!" She pushed the door open and stepped into a large, echoing entryway. The foyer was clean and impersonal, lined with polished silver mailboxes on one side and a pair of elevator doors on the other. A wall-mounted directory hung near the elevator doors. Apartment 1015 was on the main level.

"Okay," Benny said, "go to the apartment and knock on the door. If no one answers, see if the key will open the door to the apartment."

"Isn't that breaking and entering?" Abby whispered. The last thing she needed was to get arrested.

"You have a key, so it's a little bit of a gray area, but you *are* his wife," Benny replied. "You have legal standing. Want me to stay on the line?"

"You better stay on the line. This whole thing was your harebrained idea."

"Do you have a better one?"

"No."

"Then go find the apartment."

"Fine." She went through another set of doors and turned down a wide hallway. The clacking of her shoes on the tile floor seemed to ricochet off the walls as she dragged her luggage behind her.

"I don't feel right about this, Benny," she muttered.

"You need to find answers. This is the fastest way to do that."

She sighed and stopped in front of the door marked "1015." "Okay, I'm here."

"Knock on the door."

Abby let out a frustrated breath. She stood motionless in the hallway, one hand still clutching the handle of her suitcase, the other hovered in the air in front of the door. Her chest felt tight, like the silence behind the door might crush her. "What am I supposed to say if someone answers?" she whispered.

There was a pause on Benny's end before he finally said, "Just tell them you're Michael's wife. See what happens."

"What's going to happen is they're going to call the police, and I'm going to end up in jail."

"I know a brilliant lawyer." He gave a half-hearted chuckle.

"Somehow that doesn't make me feel any better." Shaking her head, Abby drew in a deep breath and knocked. Her knuckles hit the wood like a question she didn't want answered. Her heart pounded so hard it made her lightheaded. *Please don't let anyone be home. Please let this be a mistake. Please let it be anything but what it looks like.*

"Knock again," Benny said gently, his voice grounding her.

She knocked again, a little louder this time. No movement. No footsteps. No voices. Just the low hum of the building and the ringing in her ears. She turned, the wheels on her suitcase squeaking as she started back toward the entrance. "No one's home. I'm going to take a cab back to the hospital and get this figured out." She was annoyed now. "This was a bad idea. I never should have come here." The only person who could explain any of this was Michael. And he wasn't there. Not really. Not anymore.

But who else could she turn to? No one else had been at

the hospital asking about him, no one claiming him but her. What was she supposed to do—go back and ask to speak with someone? Who? Ms. Benson? She didn't have answers, only questions. Abby hadn't even called her mother.

The thought settled over her like a heavy shroud. Her mother didn't know Michael was dead. Abby couldn't face that call yet. Couldn't handle the confusion in her voice, the judgment. Her mother would ask questions—relentless, bewildered questions—and Abby had no answers to give. She didn't understand what was happening. So how could she explain it to her mother?

"Wait!" Benny all but shouted into the phone. "Go in. Go back and go inside."

"Bernard Rubinski, you've gone off the deep end."

"No, I'm serious," he insisted. "Let yourself in. You have the key."

Abby stopped in the hall, her hand tightening on the handle of her bag again. She was already in the building, already compromised. No one had answered the door, so it was safe to assume that no one was home. She could go inside, look around for just a few minutes, and leave right away. No one would have to know.

"Ugh." She turned and marched back to the door marked "1015." "You better be right about this."

The key turned smoothly in the lock, and Abby cautiously pushed the door open and stepped inside. To her right was a large kitchen with brightly colored canisters and brilliant white appliances. Everything looked cheerful. Domestic. Normal. Her throat tightened.

She took a few more steps inside, jumping slightly when the door clicked shut behind her. A soft beige carpet muffled her footsteps as she moved down the short hallway into the living room and positioned her carry-on under the breakfast counter.

"Hello?" she called into what she hoped was an empty space. "Is anyone here?"

"What do you see?" Benny asked.

She couldn't think clearly with him talking in her ear. "There's no one here. Let me call you back. I'm just going to look for a minute, and then I'm leaving." She ended the call before he could protest.

The living room was a decent size, with overstuffed brown leather furniture and a large flat-screen television mounted on the wall. A gaming system was spread on the floor in front of the sofa, and several game cases lay next to it. On the wall were photographs of the same girl Abby had seen on the lock screen of Michael's cell phone. There were photos of her as a baby wrapped in a pink blanket, as a toddler with a favorite doll, and what Abby assumed were yearly school photos. Three of them. That would make her what? Eight years old? Abby's breath caught as she stared. Michael's eyes. There was no mistaking them.

She stepped closer, hand trembling as she reached for one of the frames. The baby photo. Chubby cheeks, a hint of dark hair. It was almost identical to one of Michael's baby pictures. The truth hit her like a punch to the chest, and her phone slipped from her fingers, thudding on the carpet at her feet. This wasn't a maybe. This wasn't a misunderstanding. There was no doubt in her mind. This girl—this stranger—was Michael's daughter.

CHAPTER 8

Abby felt the blood drain from her face, and she backed away from the photos until the edge of the sofa brushed against the backs of her legs. She let herself drop onto the soft cushions, her body numb. Michael had a child. A daughter. How could she not have known? How many times had they argued about having children? Especially after her miscarriage. She'd all but begged him. But he'd been firm. *Not now, not ever*, he'd said, while he'd had a daughter the whole time.

Tears streamed down her cheeks as she brought a hand to her abdomen. She had carried their child—however briefly. He'd thrown himself into his work after that, while she'd been left to grieve alone. All the while he'd been . . . What? Changing diapers? Painting a nursery? The math worked. The girl in the photos—Abby guessed her to be about eight. That would make it the same year.

She tried to breathe, but the thoughts came fast and loud, impossible to silence. He'd looked her in the eye and said he didn't want children—while loving another child. Her gaze returned to the wall, taking in the rest of the display. Images of

Michael smiling with a pretty, dark-haired, tanned woman and the girl, at various ages, were artfully arranged in groupings that covered most of the wall.

She paused at a photo of the three of them at Disneyland. *Disneyland?* Michael always said he hated theme parks. Too crowded. Too hot. Too expensive. He used to mock the matching-shirt family vacation photos he'd see on social media. Yet, there he was—wearing mouse ears and a grin that split his face wide open. A real smile.

Abby fought off a wave of nausea. A knife-like pain twisted in her belly. *Who was I married to?* The question hit her hard. *Was I even married to him?* Her mouth went dry, and a million thoughts swirled around inside her head. Had she been so in love with the version of Michael she wanted to see that she'd never questioned the cracks in his story?

He used to kiss her on the forehead before leaving for "work trips." Ever increasing work trips. Always with the same cologne. The same travel bag. She'd watched him pack it. Watched him lie. And she never saw it. Never saw the lies. But deep down, part of her wasn't sure that was true. Maybe she'd chosen not to know. Chosen not to push. Because pushing might have broken the fragile thing they had. And now it was broken anyway.

How could he do this to *her*? She had been a faithful wife, always doing what he asked. She'd even quit school for him because he wanted her to stay home. She'd been in her final year at college, and he'd told her that he wanted her to have a happy, relaxing life, with him as her supporter and protector. He'd said it was important to him that she was active in their social circle, that it would help him get more business connections. And she'd believed him. Back then, it had made sense. Her mother hadn't worked. Staying home had felt . . . safe. Right. But now? Now it felt like the first layer in a carefully constructed scheme.

Her gaze shifted to the photo collage again, to the girl with Michael's eyes and the woman with her arms wrapped tightly around both of them. A family. He'd said he didn't want children. But maybe it wasn't about children at all. Maybe he just hadn't wanted children with her. The thought hit so hard she gasped.

Abby swiped the tears from her face with the back of her hand, but the hurt was already hardening into something sharper. Anger churned inside her. She'd buried so many doubts, ignored so many red flags, so many odd little moments she'd written off—times he was unreachable, weekends when his explanations didn't quite line up. She'd told herself everything was fine. That he was just tired, just busy, just a man who needed his space. But what if none of it had been fine? What if she'd been deliberately blind?

She stood, heat rising in her cheeks, and walked past the sofa toward the hallway. The photographs continued there too —more of the girl, of Michael holding her up on his shoulders, grinning in front of a Christmas tree, ice-skating on a frozen pond. The woman was always close, her hand curled naturally around Michael's arm like it belonged there. Abby's fists clenched at her sides. She wanted to tear the frames down. Smash them into smithereens.

Instead, she forced herself to move on. There were four doors in the hall. The first opened into a bathroom. Neutral colors, toothpaste smudges in the sink, a soft green towel crumpled on the counter. The second room was clearly the little girl's.

The room smelled faintly of strawberry shampoo and crayons. Lavender walls were splashed with posters of horses galloping through fields, a shimmering unicorn, and a smiling cartoon Barbie in a glittery gown. A pink and purple comforter hung askew on the unmade bed, one corner nearly dragging on the floor. A stuffed gray rabbit sat next to a pillow, one ear flopped sideways, the other standing tall like it was keeping watch. A pink heart was stitched into its chest, and the fur along its side looked rubbed thin from years of being held—loved. Abby's chest tightened. Whoever the little girl was, she clearly wasn't ready for the kind of grief waiting for her.

Books were stacked in uneven piles on the nightstand and floor—titles about horses, mermaids, and magical adventures. A tablet with a sparkly teal case was plugged in beside the lamp, its screen dark. Across the room, a desk cluttered with notebooks, markers, and half-finished drawings sat beneath a bulletin board pinned with ribbons—blue, red, yellow— neatly arranged beside snapshots of a grinning girl holding trophies nearly as tall as her.

On a shelf next to the bed, a row of shiny gold plastic horses stood at attention, manes frozen mid-prance, atop trophies for what she assumed were equestrian events. A few Barbies lounged at odd angles in a clear storage bin, their hair tangled, tiny shoes scattered around them.

Abby continued down the hall and opened the third door, revealing a linen closet. Stacks of neatly folded, colorful, plush towels filled one shelf, and a variety of pill bottles, antacids, a heating pad, and a thermometer filled a basket on another shelf. The top shelf held an assortment of what appeared to be office supplies. Abby closed the door and let out a deep breath. The last room had to be Michael's bedroom, *their* bedroom.

She paused at the door and squeezed her eyes shut. It was like her life had been split in two—the one she thought she had, and the one that had always existed just out of sight. Behind doors she'd never thought to open. And now . . . she couldn't not look.

With trembling fingers, Abby turned the knob and pushed the door open. A king-size bed dominated the center of the spacious room, adorned with a bright floral duvet that clashed with everything she knew about Michael's taste. Across from the bed, two mirrored sliding doors revealed a half-open closet. Brightly colored shirts and dresses hung on one side. The other side, presumably, contained Michael's clothes.

To the right, another door led—she guessed—to a bathroom, and along the far wall, large glass doors opened onto a small private patio. She crossed the room and peeked outside. Beyond the glass stretched a beautifully landscaped courtyard, with a sparkling blue swimming pool at its center. Chaise lounges lined the edges, shaded by colorful umbrellas. Children shrieked and splashed in the water while a teenage lifeguard sat slouched on a tall chair, twirling a whistle between her fingers, a bored expression on her tanned face. Palm trees and flowering shrubs were tastefully arranged into an inviting space. A space that was perfect for families.

Abby stepped back, the sound of laughter echoing in her ears. She turned and walked slowly to the long dresser. A delicate jewelry box sat in the middle, flanked by porcelain figurines—those wide-eyed, tear-shaped children in soft pastel colors. Michael used to scoff at things like that, saying they were tacky, sentimental junk. She stared at the display in disbelief.

Their Manhattan apartment was sleek, minimal—cold, almost. A black leather sofa, steel fixtures, and a single framed photo on the wall. He'd said clutter was stressful. That their home should reflect focus and ambition. He'd controlled the decor, the routines, the guest list. Everything. But here? Here was warmth. Color. Life.

Her gaze traveled slowly across the room, taking in every carefully curated detail. They didn't match the man she'd married. Not at all. Her stomach twisted, a fresh wave of nausea rolling through her. Which version of Michael was real? The charming, driven man who'd insisted she quit school to support his career—who'd kept their lives polished and private, who'd claimed he wanted simplicity and order? Or the man who lived here . . . among toys and trophies and ceramic figurines?

She wrapped her arms around herself and took a shaky breath. Maybe neither version had been real. Maybe she'd only ever known the parts he'd wanted her to see. And standing in the middle of their bedroom, Abby realized with icy clarity that she hadn't just lost her husband, she'd lost the illusion of knowing him at all.

The thought left a hollow ache in her chest. But underneath ran a current of something else. Maybe determination? If her marriage had been built on lies, she deserved to know the truth. She looked at the drawers and contemplated whether she should search through them. She wasn't sure what she was looking for, but she was done pretending this wasn't happening. *I've already come this far. I might as well go all the way.* She pulled open the first drawer.

It contained women's underwear and pantyhose. They were all neatly folded and stacked. The room began to spin, and Abby slammed the drawer and squeezed her eyes shut. No. She couldn't do this. She braced herself on the dresser and took several deep breaths before she opened her eyes again. She had to do this. She didn't have time to have the meltdown she deserved. She needed to find answers before someone came home. Who though? Who was there to come home? Michael and his . . . wife were both dead. *The girl.* Abby shuddered and straightened. She needed to hurry.

The second drawer held Michael's boxer briefs and socks. She rooted through the drawer, and when her fingers brushed something solid at the back of it, a rush of adrenaline surged through her. She reached in a little farther and pulled out a wallet. It was the one she had given him for his birthday the year before. She put her hand back in the drawer and found the cell phone she recognized as his and, tucked in the back corner, her fingers touched something small and cold. She pulled it out, and her shoulders sagged.

It was a wedding band. The gold, diamond-studded band she'd picked out for him at Tiffany's. The one she'd placed on his finger at the church so many years ago, in front of their friends and family, while they'd promised to love each other through good times and bad. For as long as they both shall live. Had he ever loved her?

Abby's throat and chest tightened, and her face grew hot. Her breath came in ragged gasps. She didn't know if she should cry or scream. She wanted to do both. *How could he? How could he do this to her? How long had she—they been living this lie?* A sudden thought ran through her, and she felt the blood drain from her face. *If he was supposedly married to this other woman, who did he marry first?* She might not even be his wife.

Putting a hand to her neck, Abby tried to slow her breathing. The room tilted, and once again she placed her hands on the dresser and closed her eyes until it passed. She realized she had eaten nothing since brunch with her mother the day before. Food was the last thing she wanted, but maybe some water would help.

In the kitchen, she stared at the row of white cupboards, trying to guess which one held the glasses. She opened the cabinet to the right of the sink and found neatly stacked bowls and plates in bright primary colors. The one on the left held glasses in several sizes on one shelf, while an assortment of mismatched coffee mugs lined the shelf above. She reached for a tumbler ringed with colorful stripes and filled it from the tap, taking a long drink, the cool water calming her dry throat.

The sound of a key jiggling in the lock startled her, and she nearly dropped the glass. Someone was coming in.

CHAPTER 9

Abby froze. Her gaze darted frantically around the kitchen, looking for what she didn't know. There was certainly no place to hide, and she couldn't go into the rest of the apartment without walking past the front door. Her stomach clenched, and she gripped the glass so hard she feared it might break in her hand as the door swung open.

A dark-haired girl—the same one from the photos—burst into the house and raced past the kitchen without even glancing in Abby's direction.

"Mom, I'm home!" the girl called cheerfully.

Abby grimaced. *She doesn't know.* A wave of nausea washed over her as she was hit with the realization that this girl's life was about to be shattered too. Whatever truths were coming, they would upend this little girl's life, just as much as her own. She swallowed down the bile just as the door opened again.

A second girl, about the same size but with blonde hair, skipped past the kitchen doorway. Abby pressed her back against the counter, barely daring to breathe. She reached for her phone, then remembered it was still on the living room floor. Her carry-on and handbag were in there too. All sitting out in plain sight. It was only a matter of time before the girls noticed her. Then what? They'd call the police for sure. She thought of Benny's somewhat flippant remark about being able to get her out of jail and hoped he'd been right.

The door swung open again, and a petite blonde woman stepped into the apartment. Her eyes met Abby's and widened in shock and fear. She opened her mouth, but before she could scream, Abby put her hands up, spilling some water from the glass onto the floor.

"Wait, please don't scream," she said, trying to defuse the situation. This was exactly what she'd wanted to avoid. Now her worst-case scenario was playing out in real time and she had no idea how to stop it.

"Girls! Girls, get back here right now!" the woman yelled. Both girls came running and stopped short when they noticed Abby. The dark-haired girl was holding Abby's phone. The woman pulled the girls behind her like a momma bear protecting its cubs. "Go back to our apartment," she ordered, "and dial 9-1-1."

"You can do it with this phone." The dark-haired girl handed Abby's phone to the woman.

If there was ever a time in her life that Abby wished she could snap her fingers and disappear, this was it. "Wait, please," she tried again, her voice shaking. "I have a key."

The woman paused, phone frozen in mid-air, and narrowed her eyes as she glared at Abby. "Who are you, and what are you doing in this apartment?" she demanded.

"I—I—" Abby faltered. Her gaze flicked to the dark-haired girl, now staring up at her with quiet curiosity. In person, she looked even more like Michael—and the resemblance made Abby's stomach heave. She gave a panicked glance around the kitchen, turned, and bolted to the sink, vomiting up the water she'd just drunk.

"Eww, gross," one of the girls said. "That's disgusting. What is she doing here?"

"I can't believe she's barfing in our sink," said the other.

Neither can I, Abby thought, gripping the counter as another wave overtook her.

"Are you going to call the police?" the first girl asked.

"I don't know yet," the woman replied. "Stay behind me."

Abby's body shook as she heaved one last time. Her ribs ached. She turned on the faucet, rinsed her mouth, and wiped her face with a paper towel before facing them again. Three pairs of wary eyes stared back at her.

"I'm so sorry," Abby said, her voice raw. She gave the dark-haired girl an apologetic glance before turning to the woman glaring at her, the cell phone still poised in her hand. Abby couldn't tell if she was planning to call the cops or throw it at her. Puking in the sink didn't help the situation. "Please don't call the police. I didn't break in. I have a key. I can explain."

"You'd better start," the woman snapped. Her eyes narrowed and her lips pressed into a thin, grim line.

"I'm Abigail Whitney," Abby said, forcing the words out. How was she going to explain this?

"Abigail?" the woman and the dark-haired girl said in unison.

The woman lowered the phone, and her expression softened. "Mike and Lucy never mentioned you were coming for a visit. They'll be thrilled to see you."

Abby blinked. *Mike?* Michael hated being called that. She closed her eyes and gave her head a small shake. *This can't be happening.* This was worse than a bad dream. No, it was a bona fide waking nightmare. She opened her eyes, disappointed but not surprised to find herself still standing in the kitchen.

"You know who I am?" she asked, trying to make sense of the surreal conversation.

"Of course," the woman said with a gentle smile. "We've heard all about you. You're Mike's sister." She held the phone out to Abby. "I'm Julie Herrera, their neighbor."

If Abby had still been holding the water glass, it would have shattered on the floor. She stood frozen, jaw slack. She knew she must have looked like an idiot standing there with her mouth open, but she felt like she was in an episode of *The Twilight Zone*. His sister? He'd told them she was his sister? If he weren't already dead, she might have had to kill him. She glanced at the dark-haired girl, and a wave of guilt washed over her.

"You're my Aunt Abby?" The dark-haired girl looked at Abby quizzically, her hazel eyes narrowing under wrinkled eyebrows. "Why haven't I met you before?"

Abby glanced from her to Julie and back, not sure what to say. It was obvious that no one in the room had heard about the car accident. She tucked her hair behind her ear and took a step backward. She wasn't about to be the one to tell this girl that she was now an orphan. Not like this. What could she say, though? All eyes were on her, and she wrapped her arms around her stomach. She hated the idea of lying, especially now—adding lies to lies, but what choice did she have?

"I . . . uh—that is, I have a busy job, and it's hard for me to get away." The words tasted foul coming out of her mouth. She needed to talk to Julie, alone.

"Is there any chance we can talk privately for a minute?" she asked, taking the phone and giving Julie a pointed glance. Waves of guilt washed over her, even though deep down she knew that none of this was her fault.

"What's going on?" Julie's smile was replaced by the same guarded look she'd had when she first came in, and she put her hands on her hips in a decidedly annoyed gesture.

"I can explain everything," Abby said. "It would be better

if it were just you and me." She gave Julie a meaningful stare. "Trust me."

Julie hesitated for only a few seconds, but it seemed like hours to Abby. She just wanted this nightmare to be over so she could go back to New York. What a mess Michael had made.

"Girls, why don't you go back to our apartment and see if Grandma can help you stick some pizza rolls in the toaster oven. I'm going to talk to Cami's Aunt Abigail for a few minutes, and I'll be right back."

"M-o-o-m-m-m," the blonde girl whined. "Cami said we could play her new video game."

Cami. That must be Michael's daughter's name. Abby looked at the girl again, who blinked at her over eyebrows that squished together in confusion. Abby inexplicably felt sorry for her. If she had an aunt that she'd never met, who'd shown up out of the blue, and then was asked to leave her own home, she'd be confused too. Plus, who knew what had been said about her. *Michael told them I was his sister.* Abby couldn't even begin to wrap her head around that.

"You can come back and play it when we're done talking," Julie said firmly. "Now scoot."

The girls turned and walked toward the door, Cami slowing to glance curiously at Abby on her way out.

"She's really tall," Abby heard the blonde girl say.

"She looks like a giraffe," Cami said as the door clicked shut.

A giraffe? She'd been called a fair number of things in her life, but she'd never been called a giraffe.

"Pay no mind to them," Julie said, offering a sympathetic smile. "You know how eight-year-olds can be."

Actually, she didn't. But she would have. The ache behind the words caught her off guard. She squeezed her eyes shut and forced the thought away. *Not now.*

"Let's sit in the living room," Julie said.

Abby opened her eyes and followed Julie into the living room, heart pounding. They settled on opposite ends of the sofa, the silence stretching just long enough to make Abby second-guess everything. Julie stared at her expectantly, her expression cautious, yet kind. Where should she even start? It all sounded so surreal that she scarcely believed it herself, and she was living it. She took a deep, shaky breath.

"There's been an accident."

Julie froze. "What do you mean? What kind of accident?"

Abby rubbed her palms on her chinos, trying to steady herself. "Yesterday morning, I got a call from the hospital. I flew in from New York as soon as I could."

Julie leaned forward, eyes wide. "From which hospital?"

"Cedars. They said Michael was in a car accident. He—he's gone."

Julie froze, and the color drained from her face. "What? What do you mean gone? What about Lucy? Where's Lucy?"

Abby swallowed hard, searching for the right words. Only there were no right words. "When I got to the hospital, Michael was in the ICU. The machines started going crazy almost as soon as I walked in." Her voice caught. "They tried, but it was too late."

Julie lifted her hand to her mouth as the realization of what had happened dawned on her, her eyes filling with tears. "What about Lucy?" she managed in a strangled voice.

Abby's shoulders slumped. She'd never had to be the one to tell someone their friend or loved one had died. That would have been hard enough, but how could she explain this when she didn't understand it herself? She shook her head. "They said she didn't even make it into surgery."

Julie didn't say anything at first. She just sat there, stunned, her eyes brimming with tears.

"I'm so sorry," Abby whispered.

Julie finally blinked, wiping at her eyes. "I can't believe it. Mike and Lucy . . ." She shook her head slowly, her voice trembling with sobs. Almost as if she did it for long enough, this wouldn't be true. Abby sat and helplessly watched her for a few minutes, hot tears streaming down her face. She didn't know what to do. She didn't know this woman. Didn't know Lucy. But clearly they had been close friends. Her grief was almost palpable.

Abby pulled a couple of tissues from the box on the coffee table and slid closer to Julie, pressing one of the tissues into the palm of Julie's hand. She brought the other up to her own face and tried to wipe some of the sorrow away.

"What about Cami? Oh, that poor girl," Julie sobbed. "She's going to be devastated. Is that why you're here?"

Abby paused. How was she going to explain why she was there?

"Is that why you came here, to the apartment?" Julie repeated her question. "I know Mike and Lucy named you as guardian, in case something were to happen to them."

"W-what?" Abby breathed. "How do you . . . What?"

"I was a witness when they had their wills made. Mike was insistent about it being you, being his only family, even though Lucy and Cami had never met you." Her eyes narrowed as she dabbed at her eyes with the tissue. "Why had they never met you? Mike said you had some demanding, international job and were gone all the time." She looked Abby up and down. "But to never visit?"

His only family? It was true that Michael's parents were both gone, had been since before they'd been married, but he had a brother. Granted, they hadn't spoken in years, but still —a brother. The lies just kept coming. Abby returned her gaze to Julie and lifted her hands in a helpless shrug before letting them fall into her lap. "This is where it gets really hard to explain," she said quietly.

Julie crossed her arms. "How hard can it be?"

"You'd be surprised." Abby let out a slow breath. "I'm not Michael's jet-setting sister," she said, making air quotes with her fingers. "I'm not his sister at all."

Julie's eyes narrowed. She shifted a few inches farther down the couch. "Then who exactly are you?"

Abby cringed. "I'm his wife."

Chapter 10

J ulie burst into laughter. The sound was sharp, jarring. "Come on. Be serious," she said. "I've known Lucy and Mike since they moved into this building five years ago. Lucy is his wife."

"It's true." Abby's throat burned. She swallowed hard against the rising sob. "I didn't know about Lucy—or Cami." Her voice cracked. "He never told me. He—he was living some sort of double life." The words sounded ridiculous to her own ears, she couldn't imagine what Julie must be thinking.

Silence settled between them like a fog. Heavy. Suffocating.

Julie stared at her; disbelief etched across her face. "Why should I believe you?"

"Why would I make this up?" Abby let out a frustrated breath. "Who would make up such a grandiose tale?"

"Exactly," Julie countered, her voice flat.

Abby stood and ran her hands down the front of her pants. "Come with me," she said and stepped around the sofa and paused. "I can prove it."

Julie didn't move. "How do I know I can trust you? That you aren't some . . ." Julie trailed off.

"Burglar?" Abby gave a mirthless chuckle. "Be serious. Why would I tell you I had a key and then get sick from nerves if I were a burglar? I'd be the worst thief in world. I can prove who I am. Just—come on."

Julie rose slowly, wariness in every step as she followed Abby down the hall. They entered the master bedroom where Michael's wallet, ring, and cell phone were still lying on the dresser. Abby picked up his wallet and opened it.

"What are you doing?" Julie reached for the wallet, but Abby pulled it back.

"Just wait." Abby's tone sharpened. She *had* to prove this, to prove who she was. Maybe then she'd get some answers. "Just give me one second. Please. You've got to trust me."

Julie sniffed and rested her hands at her sides.

Abby slid her fingers into the slot across from where Michael's driver's license should have been and pulled out a photo. She glanced at it before handing it to Julie. It was a wallet-sized photo from their wedding.

Julie took the photo and studied it, glancing at Abby and back to the photo again. "This doesn't mean anything," she said in a weak voice. "You could be a crazy ex-wife of his."

"That's true," she conceded. "But I'm not. We got married almost fifteen years ago."

"That doesn't mean anything."

"Then why would he say I'm his sister?" Abby countered.

The two women stared at each other for a long moment before Julie handed back the photo. She took several steps backward and collapsed on the bed. "I don't understand," she said. "I've known them for years. There was never any . . ." Julie twirled her hand.

"Sign?" The word caught in Abby's throat. She set the wallet and photo back on the dresser before collapsing next to

Julie on the bed. She slouched forward and let her hands fall into her lap, palms up. She could almost hear her mother scolding her for not sitting up straight, but right now she couldn't care less. Her entire world had been flipped off its axis. "I've been asking myself that all day."

Julie glanced at her, a look of sympathy on her tear-stained face. "I'm sorry. This must be incredibly hard for you too," she said. "I can't imagine. I mean, Lucy and Mike were my friends, but you—" She stopped, her eyes searching as she studied Abby's face. "You really didn't know about them, did you?"

Abby swallowed hard and shook her head as tears coursed down her cheeks. Julie hesitated, then reached across the space between them and wrapped her arms around Abby in a tentative embrace. Abby didn't resist. She leaned in, letting herself be held for just a moment.

Julie abruptly pulled back and looked at Abby, fresh tears forming in her eyes. "Oh my goodness," she said. "What are we going to tell Cami?"

Abby grimaced. "I have no idea." She thought about herself at that age and wondered how she would have handled that kind of catastrophic news.

Cami was an only child, just as Abby had been. What would she have done? Who would have taken her in? Who would take Cami in? Abby knew Michael had a brother, Jack, but they'd been estranged for years. She didn't know if he was married or had a family of his own, let alone whether he'd take in a child. She had no idea if Lucy had family or not. Then something Julie said earlier slammed into her thoughts with the force of an anvil.

"Did you say they named me as guardian of *their* child?"

"Yes," Julie nodded, then froze as the realization of that implication hit her. "Oh . . ."

"But—why?" Abby's mind reeled. As if having a secret child—a secret life—wasn't bad enough, why would Michael do something as cruel as naming her that child's guardian when he *knew* how badly she wanted a child of her own? It was diabolical.

"I—I don't know," Julie said. "Maybe he thought nothing would happen. This is such a mess."

Mess was an understatement. Her chest tightened, her thoughts spinning. Was it even legal—being married to two women at the same time? How could he have done this? Would that affect the validity of the will too? Could they force her to take Cami? There had to be another option. She turned and studied the woman sitting next to her, desperate for a clue, for some answer.

"You're good friends with them," Abby said, her voice trembling. "Couldn't you take her? She already knows you, and she and your daughter seem like good friends."

The color drained from Julie's face and tears welled up in her eyes. Her chin quivered and she wrung her hands. "I can't take her," she said in a barely audible voice.

Abby sat back, momentarily rebuffed, her mind trying to register the significance of those four words. She frowned. "Why?"

Julie blotted her damp lashes with the sleeve of her shirt and sniffed. Her shoulders hunched and she folded her hands in her lap, staring at them. "Lucy and Mike moved into this building about five years ago. I had just finished a chemo treatment, and Ava wanted to play. We were in the courtyard, and I was trying so hard not to get sick."

"Cancer?"

Julie lifted her eyes and nodded. "Breast cancer. It was hard on Ava. Hard on all of us. My husband, her dad, had just left me." She released a sharp breath of air. "So much for 'in sickness and in health.' Anyway, I was sitting on one of the benches and suddenly, there she was."

"Lucy?"

"Yes. I don't know what I would have done without her. Our daughters were the same age, and she helped me out so much with Ava until I went into remission. My mom came and helped too, of course, but Lucy was a lifesaver. I was so grateful to have a neighbor like her. And then Cami was the same age as Ava, which was a blessing. Mike traveled often"— she grimaced—"as you know, and we just sort of leaned on each other. She was quiet but kind." She sniffed, dabbing her eyes with the soggy tissue. "I'm really going to miss her."

Abby nodded. She hadn't wanted to hear how wonderful Lucy was. What a great neighbor and friend she was. It was easier to imagine that she'd been standoffish and difficult. But the image of the smiling woman in the photos didn't look like someone who was difficult and standoffish. She looked like someone Abby could see being a good neighbor and friend. She thought about her own friends in New York. How would they describe her?

"She sounds like she was a great friend, but I don't understand what this has to do with why you can't take Cami."

Julie shot her an annoyed glance. "I'm getting there." She brought her hands up and ran her fingers under her eyes and then through her hair. "I'm sorry. This is just so hard to process. I know snapping at you isn't going to make things easier."

"It's okay. Believe me, I understand."

Julie's shoulders dropped, and she drew in a shaky breath. "The cancer is back, Abby."

Abby closed her eyes, her heart aching for this woman she barely knew. "I'm so sorry, Julie. Did Lucy know?"

"Yes. It came back right around the same time Mike had the wills done. That's how I heard about you."

"When was that?"

"Not that long ago, maybe five or six months."

Abby's mind raced back in time. Five or six months ago

would have been last fall, close to Thanksgiving. Had Michael acted any differently then? She didn't think so. Nothing that immediately came to mind, anyway. He'd spent Thanksgiving in Los Angeles . . . *Here*, she realized. But that wasn't unusual; he'd worked most holidays. He'd always told her that he worked the holidays so the families with children could be together and someone would still be at the office. She'd always thought it was generous of him, but now . . . She forced her attention back to Julie.

"The cancer, is it . . . Are you going to be okay?"

"The doctors are optimistic, but it's much more aggressive this time. My mother's moved in with me and Ava to help out. As much as I love Cami, I just can't—" A sob choked off the sentence.

The doctors are optimistic. That's what they'd told her about Michael too. This woman was a single parent with a child. It just wasn't fair. This time it was Abby who wrapped her arms around Julie, pulling her in. Trying to soothe the ache.

"I'm so sorry, Julie," she said. "You're absolutely right, you need to focus on your treatment and your daughter."

Julie sniffed and nodded as she pulled away and reached for a fresh tissue. "Thank you for understanding. I feel just awful about it."

"Don't. Please. I'm just glad your mother is here to help you. I can't imagine trying to go through that alone." Abby thought about her own mother. Would she have moved in with Abby in the same situation? The fact that she was wondering spoke volumes about their relationship. Maybe that needed work too. Would she ever be able to look at a relationship, a friendship, the same after this?

"Me too, she's been—well, I don't know if I could do this without her. But that still leaves Cami . . ." Julie trailed off, her fingers running back and forth across the tissue in her lap.

"What about Lucy's family? Surely there must be someone else?"

Julie shook her head. "Lucy moved here from Mexico. Her parents passed years ago, and I don't think she has any family left. None that she ever mentioned. Mike and Cami were everything to her."

A lump formed in Abby's throat. Michael had been everything to her too. *Hadn't he?* She looked around the room again. A framed photo of Michael and Lucy hung on the wall next to the closet door. She rose from her spot next to Julie and walked over to it. It was taken on a beach near sunset. The vibrant orange and pink in the sky reflected off the water while waves crashed on the shore. Abby could almost hear the ocean.

Lucy wore a pretty white sundress. She had long, dark hair too, but where Abby's hair was a mess of curls, Lucy's was straight and shiny. She wasn't a tall woman, or particularly thin, but she had a natural beauty that outshone anything makeup could do. And she looked happy. Michael wore beige cotton pants that were rolled up to mid-calf, and he was barefoot. He had on a garish, bright Hawaiian-print short-sleeved shirt, and he held Lucy in an embrace. They weren't smiling at the camera but staring into each other's eyes. A simple snapshot capturing a spontaneous display of affection.

Had he ever looked at her like that? She thought of the photos of her and Michael back at their home in New York. Each one perfectly staged and posed. Nothing unplanned or in-the-moment. She felt Julie's presence behind her.

"That was their wedding day," she said. "They got married in St. Thomas."

St. Thomas? When had Michael gone to St. Thomas? How had she not known? She felt like such a fool. For years she had stayed in New York because her mother and Michael didn't want her in Los Angeles, and Michael had a secret life there all the while. With another wife and a child. No wonder he didn't want her there.

She stared at the smiling woman in the photo, trying to assess her age. She looked like she might be older than Abby, closer to Michael's age. Her father had introduced her to Michael when she was just nineteen years old. What if he . . . No. No, that was impossible. He couldn't possibly have married Lucy first. He wouldn't. He couldn't. Could he? "Do you know when they were married?" Abby asked, not sure she wanted to know the answer.

"I can't remember what year she told me it was. It was before Cami was born, though, I'm sure," Julie said. "Before I met them."

Abby's stomach fell. *What if I'm the second wife? And what about Cami?* Abby's heart felt for the girl, a child she didn't even know. She still couldn't fathom why she'd been listed as Cami's guardian, but that was another thing she would need to discuss with Benny. Right now, she and Julie needed to figure out how to tell the poor girl that life as she knew it would never be the same again.

"I take it Cami and your daughter are good friends?" she asked Julie.

Julie nodded. "They're best friends. They were—" She choked on a sob. "They were having a sleepover last night so Mike and Lucy could get away for a couple of days. You know, some alone time." She flushed, then grimaced. "I was just bringing her home. We live on the second floor," she explained. "Right above . . ." She trailed off, pointing her finger at the ceiling before letting her hand fall limply to her side.

She stared at Abby. The pain and anguish on Julie's face caused tears to well up in Abby's eyes.

"I don't know how to do this," Julie said through her

tears. "How do you tell a child she'll never see her parents again?"

"I don't know," Abby replied. She let herself plop down on the bed and fall back. She didn't know anything right now. She needed to call Benny.

Julie took a deep breath and exhaled slowly through puckered lips. "You can't tell her who you are—that you and Mike . . . She'll never understand. It's too much."

Abby furrowed her brows as she considered Julie's request. There had already been so many lies. The very idea of adding another, to a child no less, turned her stomach. Yet there was something in what Julie said that made sense to her too. Finding out that your parents were dead was going to be more than any child should have to deal with. Finding out that your father had a secret wife in another part of the country on top of that? Abby wasn't sure there was a therapist around that could undo that kind of damage. But it was still another lie.

"I don't know . . ." It was an impossible decision, and she wasn't used to having to make many decisions, let alone life-altering ones. It was too much. The whole day was too much. Abby tented her hands over her mouth and tried to rein in her emotions. "I don't want to lie to her."

Julie put a reassuring hand on Abby's arm. "I get it," she said. "I don't condone lying either under normal circumstances. But this . . . this isn't normal."

Abby gave a reluctant nod of agreement.

"We need to tell her." Julie pulled her phone out of her pocket and tapped the screen a couple times before holding it up to her head. "Ava," she said into the phone.

Abby sat up and folded her hands in her lap.

"I need you to send Cami back over here." Julie paused. "No, just Cami. You stay there. Have her come right away, and tell her I'm in her parents' room." Another pause. "No, you can play the game later." Julie went silent while she listened, and she pressed her lips into a thin line. "Ava, I'll explain later, just do as I asked." She pressed the screen again, and the phone went dark. She sat next to Abby on the bed, and they waited.

"I'll contact my attorney and try to figure out what to do with the . . ." Abby waved her hand in the air. She was about to say funeral, but the word wouldn't come out of her mouth. Surely, she wasn't responsible for making arrangements for Lucy too? The thought completely overwhelmed her.

The sound of the front door opening prevented the conversation from going any further, and Abby swiped her face with her fingers. Cami's footfalls on the carpet as she walked down the hall toward the bedroom were almost ominous. Abby's heart beat erratically, and she struggled to breathe. She glanced at Julie, who had turned pasty white.

The girl stopped short when she saw both women sitting together on the bed. She looked back and forth between them. "What's going on?" she asked, a confused expression on her young face. "Why are you in Mom and Dad's room?"

"Honey, come over here," Julie said, beckoning for Cami to come closer.

Cami's eyes grew wide, and she took a step backward. "What's going on?" she asked again. This time, panic laced her voice.

Abby had always heard that kids had a sixth sense when it came to things like this, and it seemed as though that was the case here. Her throat tightened as she watched the realization forming on the girl's face.

"Where's my mom and dad? Why aren't they home yet? And why is she here?" She looked pointedly at Abby. A bright sheen of tears formed in the girl's eyes, and she took another step backward. She stood in the doorway, a scared little rabbit ready to bolt.

"Cami, honey, there's been an accident," Julie said, her voice wavering slightly.

"No! No! No!" Cami cupped her hands over her ears and turned before running out of the room. A second later, the sound of Cami's bedroom door slamming shut echoed through the otherwise quiet apartment.

Abby sat in stunned silence while she stared at the empty doorway. She'd come here looking for answers, but this? How did she get herself into this?

CHAPTER 11

"I don't really know what to do," Abby said at last, her voice cutting through the heavy silence. "Should I try to talk to her? I—I'm not very experienced with children."

Julie lifted her head and looked at Abby. Her red-rimmed eyes welled with tears as she shook her head. "No, she doesn't know you," she said. "Give her a few minutes, then I'll try to talk to her. It might be better if it's just her and me."

Abby nodded in agreement, somehow feeling both slighted and relieved at the same time. They sat together in silence for several minutes, but the awkwardness between them had disappeared.

"I suppose I should go talk to Cami," Julie said at last, her eyes reflecting sadness and regret.

Abby nodded. She was grateful she wasn't going to be part of that conversation. It would give her a chance to call Benny. A dull pressure started to build behind her eyes. She had no idea what to do first, and Benny would be able to help. She needed to make a list. That always helped her clear her mind when she was overwhelmed.

"Do you know if there is a pen and some paper I can use?" she asked Julie.

Julie stared at her blankly for a moment, as if she were trying to process what Abby had asked for. "Paper?" She frowned. Then her eyebrows raised, and she nodded. "I'm sorry," she said. "I'm not sure what I thought you said. There are notebooks and pens in a bin in the hallway closet. On the top shelf."

"Thanks, I need to make some phone calls," she said.

The two women stared at each other for a moment before Julie rose and rubbed her hands on her arms. It wasn't cold in the apartment, but Abby understood the feeling.

"I wish I knew what to say," she said. "Good luck doesn't seem right, but neither does anything else, really."

Julie gave her a grateful glance and took a deep breath. "It's okay. Nothing seems right anymore. We'll talk about the next steps when I've finished speaking with Cami. I'd like to help as much as I can."

Abby let out a sigh of relief, grateful she didn't need to navigate this alone. "Thank you. I appreciate that more than you know."

She watched Julie walk into the hallway. A few seconds later, she heard a soft knock on Cami's door and the sound of the door sliding open on the carpet, followed by a click as it closed once again.

She took another glance around the room before grabbing Michael's wallet. She found the notebooks and a small box of pens in the hall closet exactly where Julie had said they would be. It struck her that Julie knew such intimate details of this family's daily life and their home. Abby thought about her own group of friends. Was she that close to any of them? Did any of them know where to find a notebook or a pen in her house? She didn't think so—most of them didn't even know what kind of cocktail she liked. She couldn't recall the last time any of them had even been *in* her house. They either met for lunch or saw each other at some committee meeting or event. Her life suddenly felt vastly shallow. What would it be like to have friends like Julie?

Pushing that line of thought from her mind, Abby grabbed a pen and notebook and went into the living room. She pulled out her phone and glanced at the screen. She'd missed five calls. Three of them were from Benny, and two of them were from the same number that had called to tell her Michael had been in an accident. The voicemail icon was also lit, but she couldn't bring herself to listen to her messages right now.

Abby grabbed her purse, sat on a stool at the breakfast counter, and opened the notebook. She wrote the word "Notify" across the top of the page and started to make a list of the people she needed to call. What would she tell them? Shame and embarrassment washed over her in a wave that made her nearly drown. She couldn't tell them about any of this. She already dreaded the looks of sympathy and pity she knew were coming when she returned to New York. If her friends found out about this . . . She couldn't imagine how her friends would react—the Manhattan gossip mill would have a field day with this. No, she would simply tell everyone that Michael had died in a car accident. Keep it simple.

The pressure behind her eyes sharpened into a full-blown headache. Reaching into her purse, she fished around until she felt a bottle of aspirin at the bottom. She pulled it out and dumped two of them into the palm of her hand before dry-swallowing them. Then she picked up her phone and dialed Benny. He answered on the first ring, sounding more than a little agitated.

"Where have you been? I was starting to get worried," he said. "What's going on? Are you all right?"

"Yes, I'm—well, I'm still here at the apartment," she

answered, her tone flat. She barely registered the sound of her own voice. "Benny," she said, quietly, "the girl? It's his. Michael had a child with Lucia"

Silence.

Abby pulled the phone away to check the screen, half expecting the call had dropped. Still connected. She brought it back to her ear. "Benny, are you there?"

"I'm here," he said. Abby could hear the shock in his voice. "Did I hear you right?"

"He has a child, Benny," Abby repeated, slower this time. "An eight-year-old child." Her throat tightened, and the tip of her nose tingled as she tried to blink away the burn behind her eyes.

"Are you sure?" Benny asked.

"I've met her," Abby said. "She looks just like him."

Benny let out a low whistle on the other end of the phone.

"He was married to Lucia, Benny," she continued. "To Lucy. How could that be? Oh, and that's not all. Apparently, he's named me as the girl's guardian. Michael told them I was his sister. His *sister*!"

"You can't be serious."

"I couldn't make this up," she cried out. "Benny, what am I going to do? Am I responsible? Apparently, Lucy doesn't have any family here. Who is supposed to arrange the funerals?"

"Funerals?"

"Yes, funerals," she said, emphasizing the "s" at the end. "Lucy died too, remember? If she has no family here, who is responsible for making the arrangements?"

"Slow down, Abby," Benny said softly. "You're getting ahead of yourself."

Abby took a deep breath and tried to calm herself. It was all too much for her to deal with. Michael had always taken care of everything. He paid all the bills, took care of the bank and investment accounts, everything. Yes, she managed their social calendars, but that certainly wouldn't benefit her now. Before she and Michael got married, her parents had taken care of everything. It's just the way it was. She'd never thought to question it before, but now . . . now she was left feeling helpless and unprepared. Foolish.

"Do you have a safe at home?" Benny asked. "Or do you use a safe deposit box?"

"We have a safe in the wall in our bedroom, but no safe deposit box," she said, then hesitated. "At least not that I *know* of."

"If Michael preferred using a safe in New York, there may be one there too. Have you seen one? Or maybe a computer?"

Abby rubbed her temple. "No, I don't remember seeing a safe, but I wasn't really looking for one either. I saw a tablet in the girl's room."

"I don't think there'd be anything on the tablet, but see if you can find another one. And look for a safe," Benny said. "If there is one, see if you can get it open. What was Lucia's last name again?"

Abby plucked the sheet of paper from the hospital out of her bag and set it on the counter, then skimmed it with her eyes. "It just says Lucia C. Whitney. Why?"

"I'm going to make some phone calls, and see what I can find," he said. "Call me back as soon as you find something, anything." He clicked off the call.

Abby stared at the notebook for a moment before walking back to Michael and Lucy's bedroom. If there was a safe, it would most likely be in this room. Their safe in New York was hidden behind a Salvador Dali oil painting. Abby's gaze slid from one wall hanging to another. All of them appeared to be too small to cover up a wall safe. She looked around the room again. *The closet!*

She stood in front of the closet where Michael's clothes

hung and slid them from one side to the other. There was nothing on the wall behind them. Several pairs of shoes were lined up neatly on the floor, but nothing else. She stepped over to the mirrored glass door on the other side of the closet and slid it across, revealing Lucy's wardrobe. Brightly colored dresses, skirts, and shirts hung neatly on their hangers. Abby hesitated for a moment, then slid them from one side to the other, but the wall behind them was empty as well. Her gaze shifted to the floor. There, tucked in the corner, was a small safe with a combination lock on the door.

Abby's breath hitched as she sank to her knees and tried to pull it out of the closet. It wouldn't budge. She stared at the combination lock. The combination for their safe at home was Michael's birthday, so she carefully turned the dial on the lock and pulled the handle. Nothing. Next, she tried their anniversary. Nothing. She didn't know what Cami's or Lucy's birth date was, and she made a mental note to ask Julie for them when she was done talking with Cami.

Abby backed out of the closet and returned to her feet, her eyes scanning the room for anything else that looked like it might contain some information, any information, but she saw nothing. She walked back into the hallway and paused at Cami's door. She could hear Julie's voice but wasn't able to understand what she was saying. Cami's sobs wrenched Abby's heart, and she pressed on the center of her chest with the heel of her hand. *That poor girl.*

She didn't owe Michael anything—certainly not after everything he'd done, and she wasn't sure she even knew the half of it at this point. She had no reason to step in and take on the responsibility of caring for his daughter—but Abby couldn't help wondering where Cami would go. What if the courts stepped in and Cami was tossed into a system that couldn't possibly nurture a child who had experienced the depth of loss she'd endured? Abby squeezed her eyes shut.

She could feel the tightness returning to the back of her throat and forced herself to shake it off. She needed to concentrate on finding a laptop and a combination for the safe. Doing her best to shut out the sounds coming from behind the bedroom door, Abby turned and stepped toward the hallway closet. She pulled open the door and looked closer, paying particular attention to the shelf where she'd gotten the notebook and pen, but she didn't see anything of interest.

There had to be another computer. Michael was on theirs at home frequently, and she made another mental note to scour it when she got home. She used it periodically, but not nearly as often as Michael did. Unless he'd had it with him, there should be one here somewhere.

Abby made her way back into the living room, checking to see if she'd missed it when she was in there earlier, but she didn't see anything. She turned and padded back to the bedroom. She pulled open each drawer on the dresser but found nothing but clothes.

Next, she went to the taller chest of drawers and pulled on the top handle. To her surprise, it flipped down, revealing a hidden desk compartment comprised of storage slots and numerous petite horizontal drawers with small knob pulls. A butler's desk! On top of a sheaf of papers rested a small black laptop. Abby's breath caught in her throat as she lifted it from the compartment and brought it to the bed.

She sat and placed it across her legs, flipped open the lid, and pressed the power button. The screen went through the standard opening sequence and turned black for just a moment before a photo of a smiling Michael and Lucy on the beach popped up in the background. The sky behind them was a brilliant blue, and they stood in front of crashing waves, arms around each other, smiling like neither had a care in the world. Abby wanted to punch him.

"What are you looking for?" a voice from the doorway startled her, causing her to fumble with the laptop.

She glanced up and met Julie's curious gaze. "Hey. How's Cami?"

Julie's eyes clouded with sadness. "She cried herself to sleep," she said, her voice thick with grief. "She's worried about what will happen to her. I can't blame her." She glanced down the hall toward Cami's room for a second before turning back to Abby. "I am too." She padded across the room and sat next to Abby on the bed. "What are you looking for?"

"I'm trying to find . . ." She paused, looking down at the laptop as if she were waiting for it to finish her sentence. What exactly was it that she was trying to find? Evidence of Michael's unfaithfulness? She'd already found plenty of that. A reason why she wasn't enough for him? Tears pooled in her eyes. Deep down, she knew there would be no answers to any of those questions, and she honestly wasn't sure how much more of the truth she could handle. She brought her gaze back up to Julie's, emotion flushing her face. "I—I don't know," she sobbed.

CHAPTER 12

Julie gave her hand a reassuring squeeze, then leaned over to take a closer look at the screen. "Have you found anything?"

"No, I don't know the passcode," Abby said, sliding the laptop over to Julie.

Julie took it and stared blankly at the screen for several minutes before snapping it shut. "I don't think there'd be anything useful on this one anyway," she said, shrugging her shoulders. "Lucy used it for making Cami's school lessons, but I'm pretty sure Mike didn't use it at all." Her eyes widened, and she straightened. "Oh my goodness," she said. "I completely forgot! I need to run to my apartment. I'll be right back." She shoved the laptop back onto Abby's lap, leaving Abby to watch in quiet amazement as she ran out of the room. Seconds later, Abby heard the sound of the front door closing.

Abby placed the computer on the bed next to her. She'd try to get into it later. Stretching, she stood and wandered to the butler's desk again. She rifled through the papers in the various cubbies, but all she found were a few bills and lesson plans for school. She found it interesting that Lucy homeschooled Cami. She couldn't imagine her own mother home-schooling. She was lucky she had gone to a prep school for girls instead of being sent to a boarding school.

A small framed photo of Lucy and Cami stood in one of the cubbies. Abby imagined Lucy pulling it out and setting it on the desk as she worked to plan Cami's lessons. The resemblance between the two of them was strong, and Abby found herself wondering what it would be like to have a daughter of her own. Would they look alike, like Cami and Lucy did? *Would I have wanted to homeschool her?* She was overcome by a profound sense of emptiness and rested her forehead against the cool laminated edge of the dresser while she tried to regain her composure.

The sound of the door opening snapped Abby out of her thoughts, and she placed the photo back in the cubby before Julie burst into the room, waving an envelope in front of her.

"Lucy said if there was ever an emergency, all the information would be here. I can't believe I didn't think of it right away," she blurted. She hesitated for a minute before handing it to Abby.

Abby stared at the unfamiliar, loopy handwriting on the front of the envelope. *Mike and Lucy Whitney—Emergency Only.* Well, this was certainly an emergency. She put her fingers on the closure and pried open the clasp. She lifted the flap and exposed a single sheet of paper. Grasping it between her fingers, she pulled it out and unfolded it. Three numbers were written on it:

1-24-17

She handed it to Julie.

"The combination for the safe," they said in unison.

Abby raced to the closet and dropped to her knees,

praying they were right. She carefully turned the dial again and this time heard the satisfying click of the tumblers releasing as the door unlocked. She looked triumphantly over her shoulder at Julie. "It worked!"

Julie made her way to the closet and knelt beside her. Together they pulled the contents out of the safe. It was mostly papers, several thick envelopes, and a couple of velvet bags. They brought it all out and spread it across the bed.

Abby reached for the envelope marked "Wills." She opened it with shaky fingers and pulled out several documents. There were two powers of attorney, and two thicker documents entitled Last Will and Testament. Abby glanced at the power of attorney documents and was shocked to see her name listed on both as an agent. She frowned and glanced at Julie, who averted her eyes.

"He said you were his sister," Julie said, shaking her head in disbelief. She reached over and gave Abby's hand another small squeeze. "I'm so sorry, Abby."

Abby gave her a small, grateful smile. "Thank you for being here," she said. She couldn't imagine going through these documents alone. Going through this—as alone as she felt, having Julie here was a godsend. She was someone Abby would have liked to have as a friend. She almost envied Lucy. The side of Michael she saw here was so different. More relaxed. Then there was Cami, and—no—she had to focus on getting through this so she could be done with it and put it behind her. If that would ever be possible.

Abby placed the power of attorney documents on the bed next to her and handed Lucy's will to Julie before paging through Michael's. It appeared to be standard boilerplate language from what she could tell. It named her the executor and left everything to Cami. She ran her finger down the page until she found the words she was looking for.

IN THE EVENT MY WIFE DOES NOT SURVIVE ME, AND IT IS NECESSARY TO APPOINT A GUARDIAN, I APPOINT ABIGAIL NICOLE WHITNEY GUARDIAN OF MY CHILD(REN).

There it was, written in black and white. Abby let the paper fall from her fingers and onto her lap as the air left her lungs. She struggled to catch her breath, and Julie looked up at her with concern.

"Are you all right?"

Abby shook her head, her breath coming in short gasps. Seeing it written on the page made everything too real. Her heart raced inside her chest, and she could feel her throat closing. Was she having a heart attack? She looked at Julie in a panic, unable to form any words. Julie sprinted out of the room and returned a few seconds later with a small brown paper bag. She handed it to Abby.

"Breathe into this," she instructed. "You're having a panic attack."

A panic attack? Abby had never had a panic attack in her life. She did as Julie said, however, and lifted the bag to her mouth.

"Take long, slow breaths, in through your nose and out through your mouth," Julie directed.

Abby closed her eyes, and while she felt quite foolish with a bag over her mouth, she followed Julie's instructions. Her breathing began to feel more regular, and her heart stopped pounding. Once she was able to breathe normally, she removed the bag from her mouth and gave Julie a grateful look. "Thank you," she whispered.

Julie shrugged. "Happened to Lucy all the time," she said. "That's why she kept a stack of paper bags in the kitchen."

Abby blinked at her. "Really?"

Julie nodded. "Yeah. She never made a big deal of it, but I saw her use them more than once."

Abby fell silent, the bag crinkling slightly in her fingers. Maybe this wasn't the first time something like this had happened to her either. She could remember moments—years back—when her chest had tightened out of nowhere, when her vision had blurred at the edges, and when she'd felt trapped in her own body. But she'd always brushed it off as stress, dehydration, skipped meals. Never once had she considered that it might be something more.

She glanced at the bag in her hands again, her grip tightening. Was that what Lucy had dealt with all the time? Her gaze drifted toward the closed bedroom door again, her thoughts spiraling. If Lucy had struggled like that, did she know about her? Her stomach churned at the thought.

But what if she didn't know? What if Michael had lied to both of them? That thought brought a new ache, sharp and cold. Abby bit her lip, blinking fast. She didn't know which was worse—Lucy knowing and being part of the deception, or Lucy being just as naive as she had been. Either way, Michael had betrayed them both.

"I think the wills are identical," Julie said, placing them in a neat stack with the other paperwork, pulling Abby back to the moment.

Abby turned her attention to the rest of the contents of the safe. She pulled out several envelopes containing information for different bank accounts and life insurance policies. She placed them on the same stack as the wills. Another envelope contained five thousand dollars in cash, but that was no surprise to Abby. Michael had insisted they keep that exact amount of cash in their safe at home, in case of an emergency. Julie raised her eyebrows at the stack of bills but didn't say anything.

The next envelope contained Cami's birth certificate.

Camila Rose Whitney. Rose was Michael's mother's name. Her heart wrenched as she touched the line where Michael's name was listed as Cami's father. *Don't go there.* Abby tried to clear the thought and set the certificate to the side, then picked up the next envelope. Inside was Michael and Lucy's marriage certificate. Her hands shook as her eyes scanned the document, desperately searching for a date. There it was: January 24, 2017. Abby handed the certificate to Julie, as a wave of relief washed over her. He had married her first. What that would mean going forward, she wasn't sure. She just knew it was important.

"When did you get married to him?" Julie asked, looking up from the certificate in her hands.

"We were wed in 2010," Abby said.

Julie nodded and placed the certificate on top of Cami's birth certificate. She hesitated, then asked, "Was their marriage even legal?"

"I honestly don't know," Abby said. "My attorney will figure it out."

"What a mess." Julie frowned. "I can't believe he lied about all of this. Lucy would have been devastated," she said, then looked at Abby, guilt washing over her fine features. "Oh my goodness. I'm so sorry. I can't imagine what you must be feeling."

Abby shook her head and put her hand up. "It's okay, I know what you meant," she said. Somehow it seemed as though she and Julie had become a sort of strange team, and Abby was glad she was there. "Let's go through the rest of this so we can figure out what to do next."

The remaining envelopes contained some information about stocks and another bank account that had Cami's name on it. The two velvet bags held a ring and a necklace that Abby recognized as having belonged to Michael's mother. She had thought they were in the safe in New York, but Michael must have brought them here.

"I'm going to run back to my place and check on Ava. I'm sure she's wondering what's going on," Julie said. "That will give you time to call your attorney. Cami should be fine; she was sound asleep."

"Sounds good," Abby replied, and gathered up the papers.

They walked into the living room together. Julie stopped at the breakfast counter and wrote something in the notebook Abby had out, then turned and offered her a sad smile. "That's my number. Give me a call if Cami wakes up before I come back."

"Thank you," Abby said. "I appreciate it."

"Good luck," Julie said and left the apartment.

With a sigh, Abby climbed back onto the stool at the breakfast counter and dialed Benny.

"Abby," he said, sounding relieved to hear from her. "Were you able to find anything?"

Abby filled him in on the contents of the safe. "What does it all mean?" she asked.

"Well, being that your marriage was first," he explained, "Michael's marriage to Lucy wasn't legal."

"How can something like that even happen?"

"There isn't a national marriage registry," Benny said. "You said the certificate was from St. Thomas?"

"Yes."

"I'll bet he never had it registered in the United States," he said.

Abby let that information sink in, her mind reeling. "Who's responsible for overseeing the funeral arrangements?" she asked, remembering the missed call she'd seen from the hospital.

"That's a good question," Benny said. "Have you contacted Jack yet?"

"No, he was next on my list of people to call."

"Ask him if he'd be willing to handle Michael's funeral, and then see if that friend of Lucy's will take care of her arrangements," he suggested.

"That's a good idea. What about Cami?" Abby asked, glancing down the hall at the girl's bedroom door.

"Cami?"

"Michael's daughter. They named me as her guardian, remember?" she said with more than a hint of exasperation. "What am I supposed to do with her?"

"You don't have to do anything with her," Benny said.

"But I was named her guardian."

"You aren't legally obligated to accept that appointment. If there's no other family to take her in, child services will put her in a foster home until she's either adopted or turns eighteen."

Abby was silent as she tried to process the hard-to-swallow information. Ten years in foster care? The thought twisted her gut. Basically, the fate of an eight-year-old child rested on her decision.

"You could ask Jack," Benny said.

Abby had never met Michael's brother, Jack. She thought it odd that he hadn't been invited to their wedding, but Michael had explained that they'd had a falling out after their father died. Now she wondered if that was true. If anything Michael had ever told her was true. The more she found out, the more it seemed her entire marriage had been a lie. How could her whole world fall apart in less than forty-eight hours?

"Abby?"

"Yes, I'm sorry," she said. "I'll ask him, but is there a way to find out if Lucy had other family?"

Benny sighed. "I can hire a private investigator," he said. "But it won't be cheap."

"Do it," Abby said without hesitation. If Lucy did have

family that could take Cami in, then maybe she wouldn't have the rest of her life uprooted.

"All right, I'll be in touch. Call me if anything else comes up before you come back to New York. Once you get here, I'll help you sort through the financial and estate stuff. Bring all the paperwork you found and anything else you think might be useful."

"Okay. Thank you, Benny," Abby said and clicked off the call.

She needed to call Jack but didn't have his number. As she tried to remember where Michael had said he lived, she noticed Michael's phones sitting on the counter next to the notebook, where she'd left them earlier. Picking up the familiar one he used in New York, she unlocked it and scrolled through his contacts, stopping when she found Jack's name. She pressed the screen to initiate the call and held her breath while it rang.

"I told you not to call me again," an irritated male voice answered.

"Uh, is this Jack Whitney?" Abby asked.

"Who is this?" the surly voice demanded.

"This is Abby Whitney, Michael's . . . wife."

"Abby? Why are you calling me? Michael can't do his own dirty work anymore?"

Abby pulled the phone from her ear and blinked at it a couple of times before replacing it. To say that they didn't get along was apparently an understatement. "Jack, Michael is dead. He was killed in a car accident."

"What am I supposed to do about it?" he snapped.

Abby frowned. "Did you hear me, Jack? He's dead. Michael is dead." The other end of the phone went silent, and Abby was just about to check if the call was still connected when Jack spoke.

"What do you want me to do about it?"

"Well, it's sort of complicated," Abby said.

"If it involves Michael, it's bound to be. Not my problem. You let me know, you've done your duty."

"Wait!" Abby cried, sensing he was about to hang up. While Michael had told her they were estranged, his reaction was not at all what she'd expected. "He has a daughter," she blurted out.

"I don't recall hearing you had any children." Jack sniffed. "Not that I'm surprised he didn't tell me. What does that have to do with me?"

"She's . . . not mine." Abby waited a beat, then continued in a rush. "I got a call from the hospital and flew here to LA. Michael died at the hospital, and they told me he had a wife. Lucia. She died in the accident too. Then I discovered they had a daughter. Cami. She's eight."

Jack's silence on the other end of the phone lingered.

"Jack?" she finally said.

"What do you want, Abby? This has nothing to do with me."

"Yes, it does. You're Michael's only family," she said. "She needs a home."

"Not my problem."

Abby sat in stunned silence.

"Michael ever tell you the reason why we don't talk?" Jack asked, taking Abby by surprise.

"He—he said it was because you were jealous of his success."

Jack gave a harsh laugh. "Yeah, that sounds just like Michael," he said, his voice hard and controlled. "He borrowed an enormous amount of money from our parents. He told our dad it was for an investment in a new company. Michael was always in on the latest get rich quick schemes and had blown all his own money. He'd said this was a sure thing and guaranteed he'd double their investment in six months."

Abby's stomach formed a knot as she listened.

"Dad cleaned out their life savings and gave it all to Michael," Jack continued. "Of course, he lost his shirt. Every penny of my parents' retirement money was gone. They lost everything."

More lies. "I'm so sorry," she murmured.

"They were humiliated. By the time I found out, it was too late to save their house. Dad had a heart attack and died the day they were served the foreclosure papers. Mom had Michael written out of the will after that, and of course, he blamed me for it. Said I turned her against him. That's about the same time he started working for your father. He bragged that he'd found himself a rich little daddy's girl to marry."

Abby's jaw went slack. Her mouth went dry, and she was unable to speak. Had their life together been part of some sick plan? Had he ever loved her, or was she just the bankroll? The name?

"I'm guessing that was you," Jack said. "I can't help you, Abby. I washed my hands of Michael a long time ago."

"B-but, what about his daughter?" she sputtered.

"I can't help you," he said and disconnected the call.

Abby dropped the phone onto the counter, the thud echoing in her brain. She turned and looked down the hallway as her hand dropped limply to her side. First Julie, now Jack. What was going to happen to that poor little girl?

CHAPTER 13

Abby heard the doorknob turn and quickly swiped the residual tears off her face with her palms. Julie entered the room and perched on the stool next to Abby.

"You look tired," she said.

"Tired doesn't begin to describe what I feel." Abby sighed. She hadn't realized how exhausted she felt until that moment. Every bone in her body ached. A sudden wave of guilt washed over her as she looked at Julie. For the first time, she noticed the dark circles under the other woman's eyes and the pale, almost gray tint of her skin. Julie had been caught off guard as much as Abby had, plus she was dealing with cancer on top of it. Abby straightened and tried to put on a brave face.

"What did your attorney say?" Julie asked.

Abby filled her in on her call with Benny. Julie sat quietly for a moment, then looked at Abby, her face clouded with uneasiness. "What are you going to do about Cami?"

That's the million-dollar question. She lifted her shoulders. "I'm honestly not sure."

"What about funeral arrangements? I can take care of that if you want."

Abby sagged back in the chair, relieved to finally hear some good news. "Really?"

"They were my friends," Julie said. "And as much as I'd love to throttle Mike right now, I know you're in way over your head with everything else, and my guess is that the last thing you want to do right now is plan a memorial service for . . ." She trailed off, lifting her hand and making a rolling gesture with it.

"Thank you, Julie," Abby said.

"I talked to my mother about it, and she said it's the least we can do. Unless you'd rather have his service in New York?"

"No," she answered without hesitation. She was sure her mother wouldn't approve of the decision, but it solved a huge social issue for Abby and, quite frankly, she didn't think she was up to planning a service for Michael under the circumstances.

"We can also keep Cami with us for a few days until you figure out what you're going to do."

Abby's eyes filled with fresh tears. She didn't ever remember crying so much in her life, but she had also never met anyone as unselfishly generous in her life either. Julie had absolutely nothing to gain by helping her or by taking Cami in, yet she was willing to help anyway.

"I—I don't know what to say," she choked out. "Thank you."

Julie gave her a sympathetic smile. "You need to get some rest. I hate to say it, but you look just awful."

Abby laughed through her tears. "I feel just awful."

"Why don't I get Cami and take her upstairs, and you can rest and get something to eat. We can meet up tomorrow morning and . . ." She looked around the room. "Start going through this stuff."

Abby considered her suggestion for a moment. "That sounds good. I don't feel comfortable staying here though," she said. "I'll get a cab and a hotel room."

"Are you sure? It would be fine if you stayed."

"I don't feel right about it," Abby said. It was one thing to be in the house Michael shared with another woman, but there was no way she would be able to stay in their bed. It was too much. "I think I need some space and time to decompress. This has been—well . . ."

Julie nodded. "I understand," she said. "I'll get Cami. You have my number. Call me if anything comes up."

Abby grabbed the pen and wrote her number down on a blank page in the notebook, then tore it out and handed it to Julie. "That's mine if you need me. What time should I come back?"

"Is eight o'clock too early?"

"No, that's perfect," Abby said. "Thanks again, Julie."

Julie nodded. "Talk to you then. Get some rest if you can," she said, and slid off the stool. She went down the hall and disappeared into Cami's room.

Abby called a cab. Next, she did a quick search on her phone and made a reservation at the nearby Glenmark Hotel. She made sure she had Michael's keys, grabbed her luggage, and hurried out of the apartment, grateful she was able to leave before Julie came out of the bedroom with Cami.

———

The first thing Abby did after she checked into the hotel was kick off her shoes and order Thai food. The second was to take a hot shower. She stood under the soothing water as long as she dared, getting out and wrapping herself in one of the hotel's plush robes and encasing her wet tresses in a towel just as her food arrived.

She unpacked the pad thai and sat in the middle of the bed, tucking her feet beneath her, and ate. Michael hated Thai food. Or at least that was what he'd told her. It was a luxury she enjoyed when he was out of town. Was that a lie too? A lump formed in her throat, and she put her fork down, the food now tasting like cardboard in her mouth. She swallowed, then slid off the bed and made her way to the window. The palm trees along the boulevard swayed in the wind like dancers on stage, their fronds waving like hula skirts.

Michael was gone. It was so surreal to her. Regardless of what she'd discovered about his secret life in California, she would miss their routine. It was comforting to know when he'd be home, at least with some level of consistency. Michael always decided what events and dinner parties they would attend when he was in Manhattan. While he was gone, she did her ladies' luncheons and obligatory brunches with her mother, but she preferred to spend as much time as possible at home by herself, reading books or working on puzzles. Now there would be no one coming home. She'd be alone for the first time in her life.

Abby packed up the rest of her food, stuck it in the mini fridge in her room, and pulled the towel off her head. She ran a comb through her unruly curls before plopping on the bed and stretching her long legs. Her hand wandered over to the pillow next to her. While she was used to sleeping alone because Michael was gone more than he was home, it was odd to think about never lying next to him again.

An image of the photo of Michael standing on the beach with Lucy floated into Abby's mind. Her chest tightened and her lips thinned with irritation. He'd told her that he loved her, made her believe in him all these years. Yet he'd had a lover—a *wife*—and a child in Los Angeles all the while. Her entire marriage had been one enormous lie after another. Her hands coiled into tight balls.

How dare he! She punched the pillow. The gesture was simple, maybe even foolish, but it somehow released something that had been building and building. Her eyes burned. She choked out a sob and smashed her fist into the pillow again and again. Tears flowed freely down her face as she kept punching the pillow, using both hands.

"How could you?" She punched again. "I trusted you!" *Punch, punch.* "You lied to me." *Punch, punch.* "You had a child," she sobbed. *Punch, punch, punch.* The sobs turned to wails, and she grabbed the pillow and hugged it to her chest, burying her face in it. She clung to it like it was the only thing she had left in the world. Maybe it was. "She should have been *our* child," she wept. "She should have been mine."

Abby cried for a long time. She cried for all the lies and all the secrets. She cried for her father. She missed him terribly. He would have told her what she should do. She cried for the relationship she'd never had with her mother. And she cried for the child she'd almost had, but lost, with Michael. She cried until there were no more tears. Then she lay on the bed and stared blankly at the ceiling.

She glanced at the clock and did the mental math for the time change. It was getting late in New York, but her mother would still be awake. Abby dreaded making the call but knew it had to be done.

"Abigail?" The tone in her mother's voice immediately made Abby wish she'd waited to call. "I thought you'd have checked in by now, but I'm sure you must have been busy." The implication of her being a neglectful daughter was clear. "How's Michael?"

"Michael is dead," Abby replied, too tired to try to explain herself.

Marilyn gasped on the other end of the line. "Dead? You said he was in an accident, dear, not that he was on the verge of dying."

"I didn't know how serious it was until I arrived."

"When did he die?"

"Late last night."

"And you waited, what, more than twelve hours to call me?"

Abby gritted her teeth and tried to control her voice. She was far too tired to get into an argument with her mother. She braced herself and continued. "I called as soon as I was able. I've been dealing with some . . . well, it's complicated."

"What do you mean complicated? How complicated can one's death be?"

"He—uh, that is—Michael had a child."

"Abigail, please speak clearly. I can't understand you when you are stammering like that," her mother chided. "I thought you said he had a child. Please repeat yourself."

"That's what I said. He had a child and a wife."

"Of course he had a wife. I'm not sure I understand."

"He had another wife, Mother. Another wife *and* a child here in Los Angeles," Abby said slowly and clearly.

"What?" her mother gasped.

Abby explained in the shortest version possible what she had found after Michael's death at the hospital. For once, her mother listened without interruption.

"What will people think?" her mother asked when Abby was done. "We'll be the laughingstock of Manhattan."

Abby blinked and looked up at the tiled ceiling in disbelief. Of course, she would be more worried about what people would think than about how her own daughter was handling the situation.

"What am I supposed to do, Mother?"

"What do you mean?"

"Funeral arrangements need to be made, and I am not sure where or how—" She stopped, suddenly feeling completely overwhelmed and exhausted. "Then there's Cami, Michael's daughter. Benny said that child protective services would put her in a foster home until other arrangements can be made, but—"

"But what? That girl is not your concern," her mother snapped. "Benny is right. Let child services deal with her. This is going to be a huge scandal as it is. I don't know how we'll keep it out of the press. You'll have enough to deal with without being saddled with a child you don't want."

Something in the way her mother said that last bit gave Abby pause. "Are you speaking from experience?" The words tumbled from her mouth before she realized what she was saying, but Abby didn't regret them. It was something she'd felt her entire life.

"Abigail," her mother hissed. "Do not speak to me in that tone."

"Why not?" Abby shot back. The door had been opened, and she was going all the way through it. "It's a simple question. You never really wanted me, did you?"

Her mother's silence on the other end of the line confirmed what Abby had always known. Her eyes burned, and she closed them, hot tears escaping through her eyelashes before rolling down her cheeks. Something inside her changed at that moment. She felt stronger and more in control of her life than she ever had before.

"I'll let you know when the funeral arrangements have been made. Goodbye, Mother." She pressed the screen to end the call without waiting for a reply.

She was exhausted, but sleep only came in fits and starts. Instead, she kept seeing the words over and over again that named her as Cami's guardian. Why would he do something like that? It was a question she knew she'd never get an answer to.

Abby's thoughts wandered to Cami and how she was doing. She nearly texted Julie to ask, but decided it really wasn't her business. The girl didn't know her at all, and she wasn't *really* Abby's responsibility. Benny and her mother had been very clear that she should let child services step in and deal with Cami. Maybe they were right. She would be a daily reminder of Michael's infidelity.

Abby thought about the charity work she'd done in New York at the Children's Aid Society. They had a number of programs for youth in the foster care program. The women from the country club chose a charity to help every year, and the Children's Aid Society had been a regular on the rotation. They would host a fundraising gala to collect money for the charity, then they'd make a big to-do about presenting the check. They never actually did any "volunteer" work.

Abby had spent a lot of time reading about the work the Children's Aid Society did. She'd seen the photos of the children who waited for a forever home. The blend of hope and despair in their eyes haunted her. It was the same look she'd seen in Cami's eyes. That would be Cami if someone—if she —didn't do something. She'd be shuffled from house to house, her belongings stuffed into old suitcases or—even worse—trash bags, wondering if anyone would ever want her again.

Abby closed her eyes and tried to force the image from her mind, to think of something, anything, else. But one thought refused to leave. Abby sat up and swung her legs over the side of the bed. Pacing to the window, she looked out at the unfamiliar skyline. Could she do this? It wouldn't be easy. Her mother definitely wouldn't approve. But the idea of that poor child, who was the most innocent victim in all of this, going into the system—she couldn't, wouldn't let that happen. She felt more certain about this than any decision she'd ever made. And she'd made it on her own. She would give Cami a home, at least until Benny found her other family.

CHAPTER 14

"Have you lost your mind?" Benny roared when Abby called him early the next morning.

"I told you," Abby said firmly. "I don't want her to end up in a foster home. I've read about how bad some of those places can be."

"It's not your problem, Abby. What will people say?"

That seemed to be the measuring stick for everything lately. Since Abby had made the decision to take Cami in, she'd never felt so . . . so charged, so empowered. She knew it was the right thing to do, felt it in her soul, regardless of what everyone else said.

"Abby? Are you still there?" Benny's voice brought her out of her reverie.

"Yes," she replied. "You know, maybe if people stopped worrying so much about what other people thought and more about doing the right thing, the world would be a better place."

"So you're going to save the world now?"

"That's enough, Benny," she said. "I'm doing this, and

neither you nor anyone else is going to change my mind. It will be a lot easier for me if you'd help me, though."

"All right, all right," he conceded. "I just don't want to see you get in over your head, Abby. This is a lot of responsibility, and when you're in a fragile emotional state, it's really not the best time to make major life decisions. What about the friend? The one that's helping you. Can't she take her?"

"She's a single mom with cancer, Benny."

"Oh, I'm sorry. You're right, child services would never place the girl with her."

Abby sighed. "Cami didn't choose for this to happen. And what else am I supposed to do? Wait until she's been run through the system so my 'fragile emotional state' can heal? This is the right thing to do. I just know it is."

"It's just temporary, right?"

"Yes, as soon as your private investigator finds Lucy's family, we'll place her with them, with family."

"What if we don't find any family? Have you considered that?"

She had. She'd spent hours going over the possibilities. In the end, she'd determined it was this one thing, this one gesture, that could right all of Michael's wrongs. But she didn't want to try to explain that to Benny, so she simply said, "We'll deal with that if we end up there. I need to do this."

"All right," he said, his voice quiet. "There's a lot at stake here, and I don't want to see you get hurt, that's all."

"I know, Benny, and I appreciate it. You're a good friend. I'm hoping to have things wrapped up here in the next couple of days. I trust you'll have all the paperwork taken care of by then?"

"Yes, of course. Have a safe trip."

"Thank you. I'll be in touch as soon as we arrive in New York." She clicked off the phone and called a cab to take her back to Michael's apartment. On the way there, she prayed for guidance on how to break the news about all of this to Cami.

When Abby got to the apartment, she found Julie in the kitchen. The aroma of freshly brewed coffee filled the room. She turned and greeted Abby with a smile, her eyes tired.

"You came back," she said softly.

"Did you think I wouldn't?"

Julie lifted a shoulder. "Honestly? I wasn't sure. I'm glad you did."

"Thanks," Abby said.

Julie gave a small nod and pulled a coffee cup out of the cabinet. She held it up and lifted her eyebrows at Abby.

Abby nodded. Coffee sounded amazing right now. "I just . . . needed time to think."

Julie filled the cup with the rich, dark liquid and handed it to Abby. "Did it help?"

Abby dropped her bag by the door and walked over to the counter. She looked down at the mug of coffee in her hands for a moment, then raised her eyes. "Yes. It did." She drew in a slow breath, then blurted out, "I'm going to take her."

Julie blinked. "I didn't see that coming. You're sure?"

"I'm sure," Abby said. "Our—my attorney is going to hire an investigator to see if Lucy had any other family. I can keep her until then."

"What if they don't find anyone?"

"I've thought about that too, and I guess I'll deal with it when, or if I need to. If this . . ." She made a spinning motion with her hand. "Has shown me anything, it's how quickly things can change. I know it won't be easy. My life, the apartment—none of it's kid-friendly. But I'll figure it out." She paused to sip her coffee. "Cami needs someone. And I can't . . . I can't just let her go into a system where who knows what will end up happening to her. Not after everything she's been through."

Julie's shoulders sagged. "You have no idea how much I was praying you'd say that."

"I think I was praying too," Abby said quietly, her voice catching just a little. "Even if I didn't realize it."

Julie crossed the kitchen and pulled her into a tight hug. "You're amazing," she said as she stepped away.

The corners of Abby's mouth turned down. Amazing was the furthest thing from how she felt.

Julie glanced down at her mug. "Listen, about what we tell her . . . I think it might be best if you continue to let her think you're her Aunt Abby."

"You think so?"

"I do," Julie said. "She doesn't need more upheaval, more confusion. The truth . . . it's too much right now. Let her feel like there's still some family left. Someone who loves her."

Abby hesitated, then gave a slow nod. "Okay. We'll let her keep believing I'm her aunt. At least until—" She shrugged. "Until it makes sense to say otherwise."

Julie's eyes met hers across the kitchen. "You good with that?"

"No," Abby said honestly. "But I think it's the right thing."

Julie's eyes filled with tears. "I wish I could take her. God knows I love that little girl like she's my own. But with the cancer treatments . . ."

"I know," Abby said, reaching out to squeeze Julie's hand. "You don't have to explain again. I promise I'll take care of her."

Abby released Julie's hand, and they stood in silence for a few minutes, both lost in their own thoughts. Abby finally broke the silence. "How should we approach this? I mean, I'm a stranger to her."

"But you're family—at least, that's what she believes. We

can build on that." Julie took a deep breath. "She's playing *Mario Kart* in the living room with Ava."

"Is it better there, or should we have her come in here?"

"The living room is fine. I'll send Ava upstairs." Julie reached out and squeezed Abby's arm. "Ready?"

Abby's stomach churned. The conversation they were about to have would change two lives forever. This was no small thing. She nodded and followed Julie into the living room on shaking legs.

The girls were sitting cross-legged on the floor. Ava was fully engaged in the game, but Cami wasn't playing, just watching with vacant eyes. A stuffed rabbit, the same one Abby had noticed in her room the day before, was clutched tightly against her chest.

"Ava, honey," Julie said gently. "Would you mind going back to our apartment for a little while? Maybe you could get your room ready for a movie night later?"

Ava looked reluctant but nodded, setting down her controller. She gave Cami a small pat on the shoulder before quietly leaving the room.

"Cami, sweetie," Julie continued once Ava had gone. "Aunt Abby and I need to talk to you about something important."

Cami looked up, her eyes immediately filling with tears. "I want my mom and dad," she whispered.

Abby's heart twisted as she struggled to blink back her own tears, and she and Julie shared a pained glance.

Julie sat on the couch and patted the space beside her. Cami climbed up, her movements mechanical, still holding her stuffed rabbit tightly. Abby took the armchair across from them, leaning forward with her hands clasped.

"Honey," Julie began, "we need to talk about what happens next. About where you're going to stay."

Cami's eyes widened slightly through her tears. "I can't stay here?"

Julie tucked a strand of hair behind Cami's ear, her own eyes misty. "Oh, sweetheart . . . I know this is really, really hard. But your mom and dad had talked about what they'd want if something ever happened. They wanted your Aunt Abby to take care of you."

"But I don't know her," Cami cried. "I don't want to live somewhere else."

"I know," Abby acknowledged. "But I'd like the chance to get to know you."

Cami's face crumpled. "I want my mommy!" she cried, her small body shaking with sobs. "I want my mommy and daddy!"

Julie pulled her close, rocking her gently. "I know, sweetie. I know."

Abby moved to the couch, sitting on Cami's other side. She wanted to help, to comfort her, but she didn't know what to say or do. How was she going to do this without Julie?

Julie glanced at her and gave her a small, reassuring nod.

"It's okay to cry, Cami," Abby said. "It's okay to be sad and angry and scared."

"I w-want them to come b-b-back," Cami cried, her words muffled against Julie's shoulder. "Why can't they j-just c-come back?"

"I wish they could," Abby said softly, fighting her own tears. "I would do anything to make that happen for you."

After several minutes, Cami's sobs turned into quiet hiccups. She looked up at Abby with red-rimmed eyes. "Where do you live?"

"I live in New York City," Abby said.

"Can I bring Lola?" She squeezed the stuffed rabbit she was holding.

"Of course you can," Abby said. "And we'll bring anything else that's important to you."

"What about my toys? And my books? And Mommy's picture by my bed?"

"We'll pack everything you need," Julie assured her. "And you can call me whenever you want. We can even video chat so you and Ava can see each other."

Cami looked back and forth between the two women, her face a storm of confusion and grief. "When do I have to go?"

"In a few days," Abby said. "That gives us time to pack your things and say goodbye to Julie and Ava."

"I'm scared," she whispered.

"I know, sweetheart," Julie said, as tears streamed down her cheeks. "But you're so brave. And Aunt Abby is going to take really good care of you."

Abby reached out hesitantly, placing her hand lightly on Cami's back as the child clung to Julie. Was she making the right choice? She barely knew how to take care of herself right now, let alone a grieving child. But looking at Cami's small, shaking shoulders, she knew there was no other option she could live with.

———

Abby and Julie spent the better part of the next couple of days going through the apartment room by room and deciding what Cami might like to keep, what should be donated, and what they should throw away. Abby had taken a cab to the closest department store to get enough clothes to get her through the week and continued to stay at the hotel. Cami was quiet and withdrawn to the point that Abby was beginning to question if this was the best option for her. But, with Julie's assurance things would work themselves out, they continued as planned.

Abby couldn't bring herself to sort through Michael and Lucy's room, so Julie did most of it herself, selecting a few items for Cami to keep, while Abby focused on the kitchen. She selected several cookbooks, as well as a few things that looked like they might be family heirlooms, for Cami to have as she got older, and boxed them up.

During their brief time together, Cami made it clear she didn't want anything to do with Abby. She rejected every attempt Abby made to connect, spending most of her time with Ava, and when she wasn't with her, she sat quietly whispering to her stuffed rabbit. She went to Julie for comfort, and Abby felt very much like an outsider. She kept telling herself that it would take time, but couldn't help but wonder if she and Cami would ever have that same level of closeness.

Julie and her mother took Cami to her parents' funeral. Abby opted to stay back at the apartment and continue packing. She was tired of being in California and wanted to go home. She couldn't bring herself to go to Michael's funeral and try to explain who she was to strangers who knew him as "Mike—Lucy's husband." Their New York friends weren't attending. Neither was her mother nor Jack, not that this was a surprise.

What Abby did find surprising, however, was that not one of her "friends" from New York had called her to see how she was handling his death. She'd called Elaine, who she considered her closest friend back home. Elaine, who had been shocked at the news of Michael's death and betrayal, had offered her sympathies over the phone, but hadn't called Abby since. The more time she spent with Julie, the more she realized that her friends weren't the same kind of friends that Lucy had. She'd begun to wonder if her friends were more concerned about who was with them for lunch, a who's who they could use to boost their image, than who truly cared about each other. She would miss Julie and was glad that keeping Cami in contact with Ava would also give her a reason to stay in touch with her.

CHAPTER 15

The apartment was finally empty and clean, and all the things that were to be kept had been shipped to New York. Cami and Ava were crying as if they'd never see each other again, despite assurances from both Julie and Abby that a trip to visit would be planned soon. Because Cami was homeschooled, and a good student, Julie assured Abby that she'd be fine until fall. What Abby would do then, she had no idea. She'd have to start looking at schools near the apartment—assuming Cami was still with her then. Abby stood in the empty living room with Julie and thought about how much her life had changed in little more than a week. She would never be the same again.

"You can call me anytime," Julie said, sticking her hands into the back pockets of her jeans. "I mean, if you have questions about Cami or anything."

Abby smiled. "Thank you, Julie. For everything. I couldn't have gotten through this without you. Lucy was incredibly lucky to have a friend like you."

Julie met her gaze, her eyes brimming with tears. "She was

an amazing friend." She sniffed. "I'm really going to miss her, and Cami, of course."

Tears stung Abby's eyes as she looked at Julie. In the short time they'd spent together, she'd really grown to enjoy not only the other woman's company, but her perspective. It was such a refreshing change from what she was used to. She would miss that, miss her. A heaviness settled in her chest. "I promise we'll keep in touch," she finally said.

They stood across from each other, neither sure what to do next. Abby's phone buzzed. The cab had arrived to take them to the airport. Julie stepped forward and pulled Abby into an embrace. Julie's affectionate nature still caught Abby a bit off guard since Abby's friends didn't give hugs, and neither did her mother. Even Michael had frowned upon physical displays of affection, at least with her anyway. Abby admired how freely Julie expressed her affection, frequently giving the girls hugs and affectionate touches, and she vowed to be more like that as she wrapped her arms around her new friend and hugged her back, tears spilling down her face.

"I'm sorry we had to meet this way," Julie said when they pulled away from each other. "But I'm glad we met. Mike was such a fool," she whispered, so Cami wouldn't hear.

Abby nodded. "I'm glad we met too," she said, feeling a new sense of loss. "I—I'll miss you."

Julie squeezed her hand. "I'll miss you too." She turned to Cami, who stood with red-rimmed eyes and a forlorn expression, clinging tightly to her rabbit. "I'm going to miss you too, Cami. Are you ready for your big adventure with your Aunt Abby?"

Cami sniffed. "Lola is scared to fly," she said in a quiet voice.

Julie crouched down in front of her. "Tell Lola that everything will be just fine. Your Aunt Abby will make sure she's safe." She pulled Cami into a quick hug and planted a kiss on the top of her head before standing.

Abby swiped tears off her cheeks and tried to smile. "We'll call Julie and Ava as soon as we land and you can tell them all about the airplane ride," she said, trying to emulate Julie's confidence. She was met with silence. "Remember, they promised to come to New York to visit just as soon as we get you settled. Then you can show Ava your new room, and we can take them to Central Park. It will be a lot of fun. Maybe we can even go to see a musical on Broadway."

"That sounds like a lot of fun! We'll see you again in no time," Julie said.

Cami clamped her lips together, her chin quivering as she nodded. "Okay," she whispered.

Ava, who had been standing quietly behind Julie as they said their goodbyes, stepped forward and gave Cami a small pink gift bag. "It's so you don't forget me," she said, her breath hitching as she hugged Cami. The girls clung to each other tightly for a long moment until Abby's phone pinged again.

"We'd better go before the cab takes off without us," Abby said, feeling both reluctant to separate the girls, yet anxious to be on their way.

Cami didn't say a word as she grabbed the handle of her carry-on with one hand and wiped her face with the other. She followed Abby out of the apartment and into the waiting cab. They both waved out the window as the cab sped away until Julie and Ava were no longer in sight.

Cami sat beside Abby, small and quiet, the pink gift bag on her lap, its handle clutched in one hand, and Lola, the rabbit, tucked securely under her other arm.

"What did Ava give you?" Abby asked, nodding toward the pink bag.

Cami glanced at the bag, then at Abby, but didn't move to open it.

Abby noticed the slight hesitation. She wasn't sure what she'd expected—conversation, maybe—but the quiet between them felt heavy. It hit her then that Cami was probably just as unsure of her as she was of Cami. They barely knew each other. And now they were flying across the country together.

"Can I see?" Abby asked, keeping her voice even.

Cami gave a tiny nod, then pulled back the tissue paper. Inside was a child-sized beaded bracelet, strung with pink and purple plastic hearts. The beads were mismatched, and a few lettered beads had been added to spell something out—BFF—crooked but clear. Next, she pulled out a folded scrap of paper. Cami unfolded the note and read silently. Abby watched her chest rise and fall, saw the way her chin quivered as she blinked hard. Without a word, Cami slipped the bracelet onto her wrist and clutched it to her chest.

Abby's heart twisted. She reached over slowly, resting her hand lightly on Cami's. The girl didn't look up, but after a long pause, she didn't pull away either. They rode the rest of the way in silence, the city moving past the windows. Abby glanced at her several times, but she stared out the window the entire way, and Abby wasn't sure what to say to her. It was different without Julie there as a buffer.

They arrived at the airport without incident. Abby held out her hand, and Cami stared at it for a moment before slipping her small fingers between Abby's. A small win.

As they made their way through the airport, Abby glanced at the little girl beside her. Cami's face was pale, drawn, her eyes flicking nervously from gate signs to security lines. Her fingers were small in Abby's hand, her grip a little hesitant, like she wasn't sure if she wanted to hold on or let go. Abby understood the feeling.

A week ago, she hadn't known this child existed. Now, she was walking her through a crowded airport like she was supposed to know how to do this—how to comfort her, how to parent her, how to help her survive the worst thing that had ever happened to her. She'd barely made sense of Michael's double life. And now here she was, stepping into the fallout, holding the hand of a little girl who probably wished she was holding someone else's hand.

At the ticket counter, Abby upgraded them to first class since Cami had never flown before. She figured a little extra comfort, and privacy, might be good for them. It might be a little more fun for Cami too. Cami hadn't said a word since they'd gotten out of the cab, but Abby could see the interest as she watched everything with wide, wary eyes, Lola clutched tightly to her side.

"It's not scary," Abby assured her, though her stomach was knotted with anxiety. Not about the flight—she'd flown countless times—but about what awaited them at their destination. "Takeoff feels a little like a roller coaster, but then it's smooth."

"I've never been on a roller coaster either," Cami mumbled.

Abby blinked in surprise. "Never? Well, there's a huge amusement park on Coney Island. Maybe we could go sometime."

Cami shrugged, but Abby caught a flicker of interest in her eyes.

At the security checkpoint, Abby helped Cami place her backpack and shoes in the plastic bin. "Lola has to go through the scanner too," she explained gently.

Cami's face paled. "But what if they take her?"

"They won't," Abby promised, and pointed to the security line next to them. "See that little girl over there? Her teddy bear just went through and came right back to her."

Cami hesitated, then reluctantly placed Lola in the bin. She watched anxiously as the stuffed bunny disappeared into the machine, Cami's small body tense until it emerged safely on the other side.

Once through security, they found their gate with time to spare. Cami's initial nervousness about flying had given way to curiosity as she pressed her face against the window, watching planes take off and land.

Finally, it was time to board. Once they were settled in their seats, Cami offered Abby a curious glance. "Are you rich?" she asked.

The question caught Abby off guard. She had never been asked that before. By some standards, she supposed she'd be considered rich, but she didn't really think of herself that way. "I'm comfortable," she decided to say.

Cami nodded, like she was filing the information away for later. As the flight attendants went through their safety speech, Abby noticed the way Cami sat up straighter, her little hands gripping the armrests. Her legs didn't quite reach the floor, and her sneakers swung just above the carpet.

"You okay?" Abby asked softly.

"I guess," Cami mumbled, eyes still forward.

"There's nothing to be afraid of," she tried to assure her. "Your dad flew all the time." It was so strange to have that word roll off her tongue.

"He drove all the time too, and it didn't help him."

Touché. Abby swallowed hard and sat back in her seat. Therapy. First thing on the list when they landed.

The airplane taxied down the runway, and as it picked up speed and went airborne, Cami grabbed Abby's arm and held on tightly, her grip surprisingly strong. Abby didn't move, just let her hang on. As the plane leveled out, Cami's grip relaxed, and she turned toward the window, pressing her forehead against the plexiglass. The airline attendant came around and offered them a snack and beverage.

Cami asked for a soda, and sipped it slowly, and leaned

close to the window. "Oh my gosh," she said. "Are we really in the clouds?"

Abby leaned forward to get an unobstructed view of the small window. Puffy white clouds floated past the window like giant cotton balls against a backdrop of brilliant blue sky. "Yep. Doesn't it seem like you could reach out and touch them?"

Cami looked over her shoulder at Abby, her hazel eyes wide. "Do you think you really could? Like, if you stuck your hand out?"

Abby thought for a second. "I don't know," she said. "Maybe? I'd like to think so."

Cami was quiet for a moment, her brow furrowed. Tears welled in her eyes as she turned to Abby. "Do you think that's what heaven is like?" she asked in a small voice, and a tear rolled down her cheek.

Abby's heart clenched. "Maybe," she said, carefully.

Cami's bottom lip trembled. "Do you think that's where my mom and dad are?"

Abby didn't answer right away. She didn't want to lie, but she also didn't want to burden this little girl with more uncertainty than she already carried.

"I hope so," she said gently. "I really do."

Cami scrunched her nose. "Don't you know?"

"I really don't know much about heaven," Abby admitted.

"Don't you go to church?"

The question landed like a quiet accusation. Abby tried to remember the last time she'd been at church. Christmas, a few years ago. One of her mother's friends was in a choir, and her mother had cajoled Abby into going with her to listen. It had ended up being a pleasant evening. Other than that, the only time she remembered going to church was for funerals, and her wedding, of course. Her parents never talked about church or faith, and neither had Michael. Still, she believed in God, and even prayed . . . sometimes. She shook her head as a wave of guilt and shame washed over her. Maybe once she and Cami were settled, church could be part of their new routine.

Cami's expression turned stony. She reached for the headphones the attendant had given her earlier and put them on, slipping into a kids' movie without another word. The rest of the flight passed in silence.

———

Abby hailed a cab to take them to the apartment. It was good to be back in familiar territory. She tried to point out a few major landmarks as they made their way from LaGuardia to the Upper East Side—Central Park, the Met, even a bakery with pink-striped awnings—but Cami didn't respond. She stared out the window, shoulders hunched, Lola clutched in her arms.

Abby decided to take her on a "proper" tour of New York after they were settled. When Cami wasn't so overwhelmed.

The cab dropped them off in front of the building, and the doorman greeted them and helped with their luggage. In the elevator, Cami stayed quiet as they rode up to Abby's floor.

Abby was eager to be in her own space and was looking forward to showing Cami her new bedroom, which was much larger than the one she'd had at the apartment. She unlocked the door and ushered the little girl inside.

Cami stopped just past the threshold and looked around, her eyes wide. The floor-to-ceiling windows caught her attention first. "You live here?" she asked.

"I do," Abby said with a smile. "What do you think?" Abby waited while Cami surveyed the room. She'd always been proud of the pristine, elegant apartment. But now, this . . . child's opinion suddenly mattered to her more than any decorator's could.

Cami wrinkled her nose. "It looks like one of those houses in the magazines. The ones with no toys or crayons or shoes anywhere. It doesn't look like real people live here."

Abby glanced around the room. It did feel cold, especially compared to the apartment where Cami had lived. "Well, maybe you can help me fix that."

Cami shrugged. She walked up to the wall of windows, standing on her toes to look down. "That's a long way down. Don't you worry about falling out?" she asked, glancing back at Abby.

"The windows don't open."

Cami rolled her eyes and turned back to the window. "What's the point of having them if they don't open?"

"The view."

"That's weird. Where's my room?"

"Upstairs. I'll show you." Abby turned and walked toward the stairs. It all seemed much easier when watching Julie interact with the girl. Right now, she felt totally out of her element.

Cami followed her upstairs and into the guest room. The room was large, with a queen-size bed in the center and a long dresser against one wall. Floor-to-ceiling windows overlooked Central Park on the other wall.

"It's got its own bathroom," Abby said, pointing to a door on the other side of the room.

"Where's the TV?"

"There's one down in the living room."

Cami looked around and narrowed her eyes. "What about my stuff? Where's my stuff?"

"It's scheduled to arrive tomorrow." Abby tried to smile. She hadn't thought about what it would be like for her to arrive and not have anything except what was in her backpack. "I will check the tracking on it to make sure."

Cami stomped to the far side of the room. "What am I supposed to do? There's nothing to do here. It's boring." Her voice rose. "I hate it. I don't want to be here. Why couldn't I stay with Ava and Julie?"

Abby swallowed and tried to keep her tone steady. "We talked about that in California, remember?"

"I hate it here!" She balled her small hands into small fists at her side and glared at Abby. "I want you to leave. Get out!"

Julie had warned her that there might be some emotional outbursts, but Abby hadn't expected this. She didn't know what to do . . . to say. "Cami . . ."

"I said I want you to leave!" Cami shouted. "I wish you were the one who died instead of my mom!"

Abby froze, her breath catching. The words cut deep, leaving her shaken and unsure what to do. For a long moment she stood still, then, heart pounding, she slowly backed toward the doorway, giving Cami space. Cami's face crumpled. "I hate you," she burst out, her voice cracking. With a sob, she ran forward to slam the door. A sharp click echoed as the lock slid into place.

Abby leaned against the wall, closing her eyes for a heartbeat. Her chest heaved as she drew in a shaky breath, the echo of the slam still ringing in her ears. The hallway seemed to stretch in front of her, silent and empty. How was she going to navigate this without Julie there to help her? To help them? What had she gotten herself into?

CHAPTER 16

Abby stood in the doorway of what was now Cami's bedroom, watching as the eight-year-old girl frantically rummaged through another cardboard box. Stuffed animals, books, and clothes were scattered across the pristine hardwood floor—a chaotic island in the otherwise meticulous Upper East Side apartment.

"Do you want me to help you find a spot for your books?" Abby asked hesitantly as she maneuvered around a pile of mismatched socks.

Cami didn't look up. "They don't go anywhere. There's no bookshelf." Her voice was flat, accusatory.

Abby glanced around the room. Adult furniture, neutral colors, and not a single thing that suggested a child had ever set foot in it before yesterday. The queen-size bed, with its crisp Egyptian cotton sheets, looked absurdly large with Cami's small purple backpack tossed onto it.

"We could get a bookshelf," Abby suggested. "Maybe tomorrow we could go shopping for—"

"I already had a bookshelf," Cami interrupted, hugging

her stuffed rabbit to her chest. "It was white with flowers on it. My mom painted them."

The word "mom" hung in the air between them. Not Abby. The other woman. The real mom.

Abby twisted her wedding ring and tried again. "I know this isn't like your old room, but maybe we could make it better? Different, but still nice?"

Cami turned away, carefully placing her rabbit on the pillow. "Lola doesn't like it here. She says it smells funny."

"What does it smell like?" Abby asked, genuinely curious.

"Like a hotel." Cami wrinkled her nose. "Not like home."

Abby sank down onto the floor beside an open box, not caring that her linen pants would wrinkle. "I know. I'm sorry, Cami." She reached into the box and pulled out a framed photo of Lucy with Cami at what looked like a beach. "Where would you like to put this?"

Cami snatched it from her hands. "It goes on my nightstand, but everything is wrong here." Her voice rose. "This bed is too big and too high, and these sheets are scratchy, and there's no place for my books, and my lamp doesn't match and —" She stopped abruptly, tears streaming down her cheeks.

"Hey," Abby said softly, fighting the urge to reach out. She'd learned that lesson already. "What if we move some things around? We could push the bed against the wall, like you had it before."

Cami clutched the picture in her hands tighter. "You don't know how I had it before."

"You're right, I don't." Abby took a deep breath. "But you could show me. We could draw it out, like a map."

For the first time since they'd arrived in New York, Cami looked directly at her. "You'd change everything?"

"If that's what you want." Abby nodded at the crates stacked by the door. "There are still more boxes to go through. Maybe your bookshelf is in one of them."

Cami's eyes widened. "My bookshelf came too?"

"I don't know," Abby admitted. "But we could look."

They spent the next fifteen minutes opening boxes; With each one that didn't contain the bookshelf, Cami grew more frantic, and Abby's unease deepened. She was almost certain it had been packed, but everything about those last days had been such a whirlwind that she'd have to confirm with Julie later. Cami hesitated, then held Lola out toward Abby. "She wants to help look."

Abby felt something tighten in her chest as she accepted the stuffed rabbit. "Thank you, Lola. I could use the help."

After rifling through the last box, Cami's shoulders slumped, worry creasing her small face. "It's not here," she said. "They didn't send it."

"We'll figure it out," Abby said softly. "If it really is missing, maybe we can find another one."

Cami's face crumpled. "But what if it's gone? My mom painted the flowers on it. She made each one different," she cried. "You can't just buy that."

"How about we take a break?" Abby suggested, setting Lola gently on the bed. "I thought maybe we could go out and see something cool in the city. Get some fresh air."

Cami shrugged, wiping her face with the back of her hand. "Whatever."

An hour later, they stood at the entrance to the American Museum of Natural History, surrounded by excited tourists and school groups. Abby had changed into a pair of tailored navy ankle pants and a soft linen-blend blouse, while Cami wore the same clothes she'd had on all morning—a faded T-shirt with a unicorn on it and mismatched leggings.

"They have dinosaurs here," Abby said, trying to sound

enthusiastic. "And the planetarium show is supposed to be amazing."

Cami stared at the massive banner hanging over the entrance without expression. "I've been to the one in Los Angeles."

"Oh." Abby's smile faltered. "Well, this one's different. It's . . . bigger."

Cami kicked at a discarded ticket stub on the sidewalk. "I don't care about dinosaurs."

"What about the butterfly conservatory?" Abby checked her phone. "It says here they have thousands of live butterflies you can walk among."

"Butterflies are okay, I guess." Cami's voice was barely audible over the noise of a passing bus.

Inside, the grand entrance hall bustled with activity. Abby purchased two tickets, wincing slightly at the price, and then handed Cami a map of the museum. "Where should we start?"

Cami folded the map and shoved it into her pocket without looking at it. "I need to use the bathroom."

"Of course. It's right over there." Abby pointed toward a sign. "Should I come with you?"

"I'm not a baby," Cami muttered, already walking away.

"I'll wait right here," Abby called after her, earning a few curious glances from nearby visitors.

Five minutes passed. Then ten. Abby shifted her weight from one foot to the other, checking her watch. Maybe there was a line? She moved closer to the entrance of the bathroom, peering inside.

"Excuse me," she said to a woman who was exiting. "Is there a little girl with dark hair in there? Eight years old, wearing a unicorn shirt?"

The woman shook her head. "Sorry, no. Just me and my son."

Panic flared in Abby's chest. She pushed into the bathroom, checking under each stall door. Empty. Empty. Empty.

"Cami?" she called out, her voice echoing against the tile walls. No answer.

Abby rushed back into the hall, frantically scanning the crowds for any sign of her. How had she lost her? What kind of guardian loses a child within ten minutes?

Earlier that day, she'd attempted to make pancakes for breakfast—something simple to start the day on a positive note. But she'd burned the first batch, setting off the smoke detector, which sent Cami into a panic.

"My mom never burned pancakes," Cami had said flatly, picking at the second, slightly less charred attempt.

When Abby tried to help her brush her hair afterward, Cami had screamed that she was pulling too hard, then locked herself in the bathroom for almost an hour. By the time they'd left for the museum, Abby's hands were shaking so badly she could barely button her coat. She was in way over her head.

"Excuse me," she grabbed the arm of the first security guard she found. "My . . . my niece. I can't find her. She's eight, dark hair, unicorn shirt—"

"Ma'am, calm down. Children wander off in here all the time." The guard's radio crackled. "When did you last see her?"

"About fifteen minutes ago. She said she needed to use the bathroom, but when I checked, she wasn't in there."

The guard nodded, speaking into his radio. "Code Amber, main hall. Eight-year-old female, dark hair, unicorn shirt."

Abby's throat tightened. This was all her fault. She should have gone with her, should have been watching her more carefully. What would Michael say? What would Lucy think, knowing that Abby had lost their daughter in a crowded museum?

Their daughter. Not her daughter. A child she barely

knew, who was now missing in one of the largest museums in the world.

"Ma'am?" The guard's voice cut through her spiral. "Does your niece have a phone?"

Abby shook her head. "No, I . . . I don't think so. I don't know. I don't know what she has." The admission felt like a knife twisting in her stomach.

Twenty agonizing minutes later, another security guard approached with Cami in tow. The girl's eyes were red-rimmed, her expression defiant.

"Found her in the Hall of Ocean Life, underneath the blue whale," the other guard explained. "Said she was looking for the exit."

Relief flooded through Abby, quickly followed by anger, and then guilt for feeling angry. "Cami, you scared me to death! Why did you run off like that?"

Cami crossed her arms. "I want to go home."

"We will, but you can't just—"

"No, not here. Home. My *real* home. In California." Cami's voice rose, drawing stares from passersby. "I hate it here! I hate this stupid museum, and I hate that apartment, and I hate—" She stopped, but the unspoken word hung between them: You.

Abby knelt, ignoring the hard marble floor against her knees. "I know this is hard, Cami. I'm really trying, but I don't know what I'm doing either."

"Then why did he pick you?" Cami's voice cracked. "Why didn't he pick someone who knows how to be a mom?"

The question hit Abby like a physical blow. "I don't know," she admitted quietly. "I really don't know."

As they walked in silence toward the exit, Abby's phone buzzed with a text from her mother.

"Dinner at Le Bernardin tonight? The Prestons are in town."

Abby looked down at Cami, at the child who had just tried to run away from her, and texted back a single word:

No.

She had bitten off more than she could chew. But somehow, she had to find a way to make this work—for both their sakes.

CHAPTER 17

"Why haven't you returned my calls?" Abby's mother swept past her into the apartment, stopping short when she saw Cami sitting on the rug in front of the television, headphones on and a game controller in her hands.

Abby cringed. She hadn't spoken to her mother since she'd left California and hadn't quite figured out how to tell her that she'd brought Cami home with her. This was one way for her to find out. "What are you doing here, Mother? It's not like you to show up unannounced." She closed the door and took a deep breath before turning to face her mother.

"Who is that?" Marilyn pointed toward Cami, who was still oblivious to their guest. "Is that Michael's—" She stopped and turned to Abby. "What is *she* doing here?" Her eyes narrowed. "Abigail Nicole Whitney, what have you done?"

Abby had been asking herself that exact question for the last two days, but she wasn't about to let her mother know that. "I told you; I was named her guardian. She's going to stay with me until other arrangements can be made."

"Who else knows she's here?"

Abby blinked. "What difference does it make?"

"What difference? How am I going to explain"—she waved in Cami's direction—"this?"

"What's there to explain? It's no one's business but mine. I'm not going to argue with you about it. I made my choice." Abby had never stood up to her mother before, and she had to admit that it felt good.

"Don't be ridiculous, Abigail. You can't possibly care for a child. That's what child services is for."

Abby stiffened as anger built inside her with every word her mother said. "I am not going to let that child end up in foster care," she said through her teeth, thankful that Cami was wearing headphones and couldn't hear their conversation.

"Why should you care what happens to her?"

Abby gasped. "This is my choice, Mother, not yours."

"You don't know the first thing about being a parent, Abigail."

"I could say the same about you," Abby shot back. The two women glared at one another for several minutes before Abby said, "If you don't want to accept it, you can leave. Cami is staying."

"She's not yours," her mother spat. "She's nothing but a reminder of her father's disgrace."

"Shut up!" Cami shouted from the living room.

Both women turned in surprise.

Abby felt her face grow hot. How much had she heard? She watched as Cami untangled herself from the headphones and game controller and stood. She stomped across the room, stopped in front of Marilyn, and placed her hands on her hips. "You shut your mouth about my dad," she said.

Abby cringed as she took in the scene before her. Cami had refused to shower or change clothes since they'd arrived two days earlier. It had been a constant battle between the two of them. Her long, dark hair was greasy and full of tangles, and pizza sauce was smeared across her face and down the front of her shirt.

Marilyn recoiled in disgust, pressing her hand to her chest. "This child is a mess." She wrinkled her nose. "And she stinks. You can't even manage to keep her clean, let alone this apartment." Her gaze scanned the disarray in the room.

"Get out!" Cami shouted and gave Marilyn a shove toward the door.

Marilyn, moving faster than Abby had ever seen, grabbed Cami by the wrist and held her at arm's length. "Don't you dare touch me, you dirty little urchin."

"Mother!" Abby was horrified. She stepped between them and pried her mother's hand off Cami's wrist. "You need to leave." She stared into her mother's eyes and saw something in them she'd never seen before. Fear.

It was gone as quickly as it had appeared, and Marilyn ran both hands down the front of her suit as she regained her composure. Her face once again a mask of haughty indifference, she lifted her chin and walked calmly to the door. "You'll regret this, Abigail," she said over her shoulder as she walked out, letting the door slam shut behind her.

Abby took a deep breath and tried to calm her nerves before turning to face Cami. She had never spoken to her mother that way before and felt a twinge of guilt for having reacted so emotionally. She felt strangely protective of the girl, and quite frankly, she was tired of being judged by her mother for every little thing she did.

Cami had both arms wrapped around herself, and she stared wide-eyed at the door. Abby admired the girl's courage, however misguided, but she needed to address the violence. "No matter how angry you are," Abby said in as gentle a voice as she could muster, "you do not push, shove, or hit people. Do you understand?"

Cami's gaze shifted to meet Abby's. For a moment, Abby

saw understanding in them. But it was quickly replaced by something else entirely as she furrowed her eyebrows at Abby. "You aren't my mom! You can't tell me what to do!" She ran up the stairs and seconds later, Abby heard her bedroom door slam.

Abby was certain she'd heard that sound more in the last couple of days than she had in her entire life. She let out a shaky breath, the chaos of the past few days settling heavy around her as exhaustion crept in.

Abby's phone buzzed again as she locked the apartment door, a reminder she still hadn't read Clarissa's text. She sighed and opened her messenger app.

> You missed the third committee meeting in a row. The Botanical Garden fundraiser is in two weeks. Are you still co-chairing or should we replace you?

She couldn't deal with committee politics just yet.. She slipped the phone back into her pocket without responding. Last night, it should have been her and Michael hosting their table at the gala—an event she'd spent months planning for on the committee. Instead, she'd been home with Cami, attempting to make macaroni and cheese that wasn't "the wrong kind."

She'd texted her regrets to Clarissa yesterday, explaining the situation with as much dignity as she could muster. The response had been a terse, "Of course, we understand," followed by radio silence until now.

When she'd tried calling Elaine earlier that morning, she'd sounded uncomfortable and distracted. "Things are . . . complicated right now, Abby. People are talking. You know how it is." She'd paused. "They're saying that maybe if you'd traveled with Michael more often . . . well, you know what they're saying."

She did know. She was Manhattan's latest cautionary tale. The wife who was oblivious to that fact that her husband had started a second family. And now, instead of offering their help or support, her so-called friends were giving her the cold shoulder, as if scandal were contagious. She was seeing that her exclusive circle had no idea what life outside their bubble was like, and that their solution to every problem—throw money at it—wasn't working this time.

Abby glanced at the empty space on the shelf where the wedding photo of her and Michael had been displayed. Yesterday, she'd moved it to her bedroom closet after Cami had seen it and started asking uncomfortable questions about why "Aunt Abby" was wearing a white dress with her dad. Cami had already been upset about the bookshelf, and Abby couldn't bear to explain the truth yet.

Muriel had walked in just as Abby was trying to comfort the sobbing child, surveyed the chaos of unpacked boxes, scattered toys, and a kitchen full of dishes from their failed attempt at making cookies, and announced she was quitting. "Mrs. Whitney, I clean houses, not daycares," she'd said, setting down her cleaning supplies. "And I certainly didn't sign up for . . . this situation."

Abby's throat grew thick, and her eyes burned as she surveyed the once pristine room. *You'll regret this.* Her mother's parting words reverberated in her brain. No. Abby was determined to prove her wrong. Prove them all wrong. Cami was a child. Not a regret.

Abby dug her phone out of her purse and plopped herself down on the sofa in a decidedly unladylike manner. She tapped the screen until Julie's name appeared, then hesitated. Aside from letting her know they'd arrived safely, they hadn't spoken. *She said to call anytime,* Abby reminded herself. She took a deep breath and pressed the call button.

"Abby, I was just thinking about you," Julie answered on the other end of the line. "How are things going?"

Abby swallowed hard, and the corners of her mouth twitched as she tried to answer in a steady voice. "Everything is . . ." Her face crumpled, and she burst into tears. She'd been trying so hard to be strong. Be what Cami needed. But everything she did was wrong. "Awful."

"What's going on?"

"She hates me. She hates being here. She won't shower or even brush her hair." Abby leaned forward and rested her head on her hand. She was at her breaking point.

"I know it's hard, but this is exactly what I thought she'd do. It's nothing you're doing wrong," Julie said.

"It is? I'm not? I feel like I'm doing everything wrong."

Julie sighed. "I feel like that all the time, Abby."

"You do?" Her breath hitched. "But Ava doesn't hate you."

"Oh, sometimes she says she does, but I know she doesn't really mean it. Cami has been through an incredible ordeal. She's going to act out. You just need to be patient and consistent with her. I was doing some research yesterday about childhood trauma and found some books that you might find helpful. Would you like me to email you the links?"

"I would love that. Thank you." Abby was overcome by the kind gesture and another sob escaped before she could stop it.

"Has she started with the therapist yet?"

Abby rolled her eyes, even though Julie couldn't see her. "She refused to leave the apartment to go to the appointment, so I managed to set up a Zoom meeting, and she just sat there. Refused to even acknowledge the therapist. Maybe I'm the one who should be in therapy for agreeing to do this."

"It's all going to work out," Julie assured her. "It will just take some time. We knew it wasn't going to be easy."

"I know. I guess I just didn't think it was going to be this hard. I don't want to make things worse for her." She glanced around the room. "It's so much harder being here than I thought it would be too. Cami hates it. And it—it doesn't feel like home to me anymore either. Michael is everywhere. Nothing feels right."

"I can't imagine," Julie said and then paused. "What if you went somewhere else?"

Abby wiped the tears off her cheeks and sat up straighter. "What do you mean?"

"Do you have somewhere else you can go? Some place that Mike didn't go? Maybe somewhere you used to go before you met him, or some place you always wanted to go but never got around to?"

Abby thought about it for a minute, and a smile slowly formed on her lips. "Julie, you're brilliant! Thank you!"

"Anytime. Look, I need to go, but text me your email address and I'll send you the links to those books."

"I'm glad I called you. I really appreciate the advice."

"You can call anytime. I mean that."

"Thank you." Abby hung up and texted Julie her email address. For the first time in days, she actually felt hopeful.

CHAPTER 18

Abby opened her laptop and searched for summer rentals in Bluefin Bay. Nothing was available. Her heart sank. She made a quick call to the travel agent she and Michael always used, who promised she'd find something.

With each call she made, Abby felt more and more confident that this was the right decision. They certainly couldn't continue like this—locked doors, tantrums, and isolation. Cami needed boundaries, structure, and a fresh start. And Abby needed to find her footing if she was going to be any good to either of them.

With her plan taking shape, she went upstairs and knocked on Cami's door.

"What?" Cami shouted from the other side of the door. "Stay out."

"Cami, let me in," Abby said. "I need to talk to you."

"Well, I don't want to talk to you."

Abby tried the handle on the door, but it was locked. She took a deep breath, steeling her resolve. After the museum incident, she'd realized they needed clear boundaries. The locked door felt like another power struggle she couldn't afford to lose. "Cami, open the door. I want to talk to you about our trip."

"What trip?"

"I can't tell you about it through the door." She waited and heard a rustling on the other side. Within a few seconds, the doorknob turned, and the door creaked open just enough for Cami to peer at her through the crack. Abby felt a flash of irritation at being held to ransom like this, but she kept her expression neutral. She would figure out how to remove the door locks from the rental house if she had to.

"What trip?"

"Can I come in?"

Cami made an exaggerated huffing sound before pulling the door open wide. The room was even messier than before. Stuffed animals had joined the scattered clothes, and it looked like Cami had attempted to build some kind of fort using bedsheets draped over a chair. Lola the bunny sat propped against the pillows on the bed as if she were supervising the chaos.

Abby tried not to look at the mess and instead focused her attention on Cami. The little girl stood with her back against the dresser, arms folded across her chest, lower lip thrust out in a pout that was both defiant and childish. It was a look Abby was becoming all too familiar with. She hoped the trip she'd planned would change that.

After the incident at the museum, Abby worried about taking Cami out into the city again, but she knew that keeping her cooped up in the apartment all summer wasn't an option either. They needed a fresh start, somewhere new for both of them.

"I decided that you were right," Abby said, as she slowly entered the room.

Cami tilted her head to the side, her eyes narrowing suspiciously.

"This place *is* pretty boring."

"Well, yeah," Cami said, kicking at a stuffed animal on the floor. "What does that have to do with a trip?"

You need to be patient with her. Julie's words echoed in Abby's mind as she tried to focus on the message she wanted to relay to Cami rather than focusing on the girl's attitude. "I thought it might be fun if we spent the summer in Bluefin Bay."

Cami's nose wrinkled. "Bluefin Bay? Where's that?"

"It's in North Carolina," Abby confirmed. "On the Outer Banks."

Cami flopped dramatically onto the bed, making Lola bounce. "What's so great about that? It sounds boring. And it has a fish name."

Abby let out a slow, measured breath and tried not to let her frustration show. She'd been so sure that Cami would have been excited to leave the apartment—to leave New York. The little girl had refused every suggestion Abby had made, even turning down the ice cream at the fancy shop downstairs that Michael had raved about. She considered Cami's question for a moment before she answered.

"When I was about your age," Abby began as she made her way over to the bed, sitting down next to Cami. "I spent a couple summers at Bluefin Bay with my grandparents."

"Grown-up stuff is always so boring," Cami mumbled, rolling onto her stomach and making Lola hop across the bedspread.

Abby ignored the comment and continued. "I just remember that those summers were probably some of the best of my life," she said softly. "I made some friends there, and we had the best time riding our bicycles all over town. My grandfather would take us to the ice cream parlor, and Grandmother baked us treats. We spent hours on the beach, listening to waves and searching for shells."

She'd felt free there, in a way she hadn't since—well, since even before she had married Michael. It was one of the few times in her life that she could do what she wanted and make choices purely for herself. Before the whirlwind courtship with Michael and the wedding her mother had orchestrated, followed by the carefully curated life in this apartment, where everything matched and nothing was out of place. Even her charity work and social calendar had been selected to complement Michael's career and their social standing. Now, with Cami, the walls seemed to be closing in on them.

"That sounds boring. Do they have horses there?" Cami asked, peering up from behind Lola's floppy ears, a glimmer of interest breaking through her scowl.

"They actually have wild horses," Abby said, feeling a flutter of hope at Cami's first sign of interest in days. "On Corolla, which isn't far from Bluefin Bay. They're descendants of Spanish mustangs that swam ashore from shipwrecks hundreds of years ago. They roam free on the beaches."

Cami sat up a little straighter, still clutching Lola but no longer hiding behind her. "Real wild horses? Not in a zoo or anything?"

"Completely wild." Abby nodded. "They have tours where you can see them from a safe distance. The horses have lived there for generations without being tamed."

"Could we . . ." Cami hesitated, as if afraid to show too much enthusiasm. "Could we maybe see them? If we go there?"

Abby smiled, feeling a small spark of connection. "Absolutely. We can sign up for one of the tours as soon as we get there." She watched as Cami's eyes lit up for the first time since they'd arrived in New York. Bluefin Bay had always been magical for her as a child. She only hoped it would work the same magic on Cami. She was out of ideas—this had to work.

Chapter 19

Abby's travel agent wasn't optimistic about finding accommodations. It was peak season in the Outer Banks, but she finally secured a last-minute cancellation—not luxury, but it was beachfront. Abby didn't care. The only thing that mattered was getting her and Cami out of New York. With flights to Wilmington booked for the next day, Abby decided they'd pack one suitcase each and purchase whatever else they needed once there.

Surprisingly, Cami accepted Abby's help with sorting through her clothes. After a full day's work, Cami's bags were packed and her room organized. She'd even taken a shower. Bluefin Bay was already working its magic.

Abby, on the other hand, had a much more difficult time packing. Where Cami's wardrobe was already primarily beach-ready casual, Abby's was the exact opposite. She sat on the bed and stared at the clothes hanging in her enormous closet. Nearly everything was black or white. She recalled how bright and vibrant Lucy's wardrobe had been and frowned. Abby liked colors, but her mother had always insisted that white and black made her look elegant and refined. Michael had preferred her in those two colors as well. Now she knew why —it was easier to keep his dual lives straight when they were distinctly different.

Her gaze drifted to Michael's side of the closet. Anger flushed through her body as she walked to his office and retrieved a pair of scissors from his desk. Blinded by equal parts rage and tears, she pulled his clothes from their hangers and began cutting and ripping the fabric until she got halfway through the pile, when she stopped abruptly.

What was she doing? Her behavior was no better than Cami's. She dropped the scissors in the middle of the pile, defeated. The sunlight coming through the large windows reflected off the diamond in her wedding ring, creating a prism on the floor. Abby held out her hand and gazed at what was supposed to be a symbol of the love and unity between her and Michael. Now, it was a gaudy, mocking reminder of Michael's lies and infidelity. She twisted and pulled the ring until it slipped off her finger. She dropped the ring inside the mahogany jewelry box on her dresser, then shut the lid. She was no longer Michael's wife. She never really had been, despite the piece of paper that said otherwise. Not in the ways that mattered, anyway.

She returned her large suitcase to the back of her closet. She'd take what she could fit into her carry-on and purchase more appropriate clothing in Bluefin Bay. The clothes she'd worn in Glendale were still in a small laundry pile, waiting to be washed. She felt a certain lightness in her chest just thinking about it.

The chirping of her cellphone in the living room interrupted her thoughts, and Abby rushed downstairs to grab it. She glanced at the screen before answering.

"Benny," she said, trying to catch her breath.

"Abby, did I catch you at a bad time" he questioned. "I was just about to leave a message."

"No, sorry. I was, uh, sorting through some clothes in the bedroom and forgot my phone downstairs." Abby opted to leave out the part where she'd destroyed most of Michael's clothing. "What did you find out?"

The day she and Cami had returned from California, Abby had sent him all their insurance policies and anything from Michael's office that had looked important, as well as the paperwork she'd brought back with her from California.

"That's not why I'm calling," Benny said, his tone making the hair on the back of her neck stand up. "Who does your accounting, Abby?"

"Michael did," she answered, sinking onto the sofa. "He handled everything himself. Said he didn't trust accountants." Her chest tightened at the irony.

"There are some discrepancies. I'd like to examine your books and bank accounts to make sure everything's in order."

Michael had done their books and had managed all their accounts since the day they'd gotten married. It hadn't been a big deal for Abby because her mother's accountant had managed her accounts before that—at her mother's insistence, of course.

Abby didn't know the first thing about balancing a checkbook, let alone managing trust funds and all of Michael's business accounts. At thirty-four, she felt completely incompetent. When had she lost her independence? Her sense of control? Had she ever had it?

"I'll look in the office again," she promised. "I'll send whatever I can find before we leave."

She hung up and made her way back to Michael's office to look for the information Benny needed. She pulled out several files, looking for anything that might be useful. In one of the folders was a photo of Michael and Cami. She stared at it for few moments, studying the similarities between them.

"What are you doing?"

Abby spun around, startled to see Cami standing in the doorway. The little girl's eyes were fixed on the photo in Abby's hand.

"I was just looking for some papers that my attorney needs," Abby said, slipping the photo back into the folder. She forced a smile. "Boring grown-up stuff."

Cami stepped into the office, her gaze darting around at the stacks of journals and files. "That was my picture."

"Yes," Abby admitted. "I found it while looking through some files."

"My mom took that picture at the beach," Cami said, her voice small. "She said I looked just like my dad when I smiled."

Abby's throat tightened. "You do. You have his smile."

Cami stood there for several minutes, twisting the hem of her T-shirt between her fingers. "Are we really going to see wild horses?"

"Absolutely," Abby said, grateful for the change in subject. "Our flight leaves tomorrow morning. Are you excited?"

Cami nodded. "Lola's excited too. She's never been on an airplane before."

"Well, this will be her second time flying," Abby corrected gently. "She flew with us from California, remember?"

"That doesn't count," Cami said, her expression suddenly serious. "She was too sad to look out the window."

"I understand," Abby said, and she did. The flight from Los Angeles had been a blur of grief and confusion for both of them. "Tomorrow will be different," she promised.

Chapter 20

The taxi ride to JFK the next morning was quiet. Cami sat with her face pressed against the window, Lola clutched to her chest, watching the city buildings give way to the busy highway.

Abby had spent most of the night scanning documents for Benny and trying not to think about what the "discrepancies" might mean. Whatever Michael had been involved in, she hoped it wouldn't affect their getaway to Bluefin Bay.

At the airport, Abby guided Cami through security, relieved that she cooperated without complaint. The lines had thankfully been short, and they found their gate with time to spare.

"Are you hungry?" Abby asked, gesturing toward the food court. "We could get breakfast before we board."

Cami shook her head, her eyes fixed on the planes visible through the large windows. "Is our plane here yet?"

"Not yet," Abby said, checking the departure board. "It should be here soon."

"What if it crashes?" Cami asked suddenly, her voice barely audible.

Abby turned to look at her, understanding dawning. Of course—Michael had died in an accident. Cami's fear made perfect sense.

"That's very unlikely," Abby said, choosing her words carefully. "Flying is actually one of the safest ways to travel. It's even safer than cars."

Cami's grip on Lola tightened. "But it could happen."

Abby sat down beside her. "Yes, it could. But so could lots of things that we don't worry about every day. The pilots are very well trained, and the planes are checked carefully before each flight."

Cami didn't look convinced. "My mom didn't like flying."

"I used to be scared too," Abby admitted. "When I was about your age, my father took me on my first airplane ride. I was so nervous that I felt sick to my stomach."

"What happened?" Cami asked, looking up at her.

"He taught me a pretty cool trick. When the plane starts to take off, you slowly start to count. By the time you reach thirty, the scariest part is over." Abby smiled at the memory. "We can count together if you want."

Cami seemed to consider this. "Okay. But Lola might need to count to fifty. She's extra scared."

"We can help Lola count as high as she needs to," Abby assured her.

When their flight was called, Cami hesitated at the entrance to the Jetway.

Abby felt her stiffen, saw the panic rising in her eyes. "Remember," Abby said softly, "we're going to see wild horses. They're waiting for us."

Cami took a deep breath and nodded. Together, they boarded the plane.

As the aircraft accelerated down the runway, Abby heard Cami's whispered counting beside her. "One, two, three . . ."

Abby joined in, flashing her an encouraging smile.

By the time they reached twenty-seven, they were airborne, the city falling away beneath them.

"Twenty-eight, twenty-nine, thirty," they finished together.

Cami exhaled shakily. "We did it."

"We did," Abby agreed, feeling as though they'd crossed more than just a physical threshold. "Bluefin Bay, here we come."

As the plane climbed higher, Abby watched Cami's face relax. The little girl even held Lola up to the window so the stuffed bunny could see the clouds. For the first time since Michael's death, Abby felt a flicker of hope. Maybe, just maybe, they could find their way through this together.

———

Once in Wilmington, they picked up their rental car—a shiny red sedan—and began the three-hour drive along the coast to Bluefin Bay.

Cami was full of questions about the town. Abby hadn't been there since she was about Cami's age, so she wasn't very helpful in answering her questions. She just remembered it being the one place she could go and be . . . herself, where she didn't feel like she was under a microscope. Abby always found it interesting how her grandparents seemed so different from her parents. She had never met her mother's family and often wondered if her mother was responsible for the change in her father, although he had a softer side that showed through every now and then. Unfortunately, that generally only served to make her mother double down on her rules and expectations.

Thinking about her family made Abby realize she really didn't know much about Cami, and even though this was only supposed to be a temporary stay, she was determined to make the situation as pleasant as she could. Abby began asking Cami questions about herself, and to her surprise, Cami opened up a little. She revealed that while she was home-schooled, she really wanted to go to "regular" school like Ava. She loved video games and action movies, when her mother would let her watch them, and she loved chocolate and cheese puffs. Together.

"That sounds disgusting." Abby laughed. She was enjoying the scenic drive and the company.

Cami could be very charming when she wasn't throwing a fit or slamming doors. *Charming, like Michael.* Except Cami was a child, not a grown man who used that gift of charm to get away with lies and deception. She pushed those thoughts far into the back of her mind and returned her focus to chocolate and cheese puffs.

"Have you ever tried it?" Cami asked.

"Uh, no, and I don't intend to."

"You're weird." Cami giggled.

"I'm not the one who eats cheese puffs with chocolate. I think that makes you the weird one. Did you put the address into the GPS?"

Cami held up Abby's phone. "Yes, it says we're about fifteen minutes away. The GPS says we'll be crossing over a bridge to get there."

Abby nodded, remembering the bridge that led into the small coastal town. As they approached, the waterway came into view. The mid-afternoon sun sparkled on the water's surface, making it look like scattered diamonds.

"There's the bridge!" Cami exclaimed, holding up Lola so she could see.

Abby felt a rush of adrenaline surge through her as they slowly traversed the water. Cami was glued to the window, watching boats in the harbor and seabirds swooping overhead. Abby couldn't believe she had really done this all on her own. It was a wonderful feeling. Freeing.

"Oh, look!" Cami pointed out the window. "We're here."

They drove past a large wooden sign with colorful letters welcoming them to Bluefin Bay. Abby's pulse quickened as they drove down the quaint main street toward their rental. Colorful awnings shaded the storefronts, and pedestrians strolled along the sidewalks, stopping to talk to people they knew. They passed a charming bookstore with a display of beach reads in the window, and across the street stood an old-fashioned hardware store where an elderly man swept the sidewalk with methodical care. Farther down, they glimpsed the town square with its white gazebo surrounded by blooming hydrangeas. The businesses appeared to be well-tended, and the street was lined with old-fashioned light poles with hooks holding colorful flower baskets. It was exactly how Abby remembered it.

"It's kind of small," Cami observed, a note of reservation in her voice. "Is there going to be anything to do here?"

Abby glanced around. Compared to the constant hustle and bustle of New York and the enormity of Los Angeles, Bluefin Bay was slow and tiny. There were less than five thousand people in the entire town, but that was also part of its charm. She hoped the slower pace might help Cami adjust more easily—fewer people, less noise, more predictable routines.

"I'm sure we'll find plenty of things to do." Abby smiled. "Where do I need to turn?"

Cami guided her down beautiful tree-lined streets, past the docks, and toward a group of small bungalows. "There it is, right there!" she exclaimed. "It's so nice, and look, it's got a name."

Abby felt a rush of relief at Cami's enthusiasm. Since Michael's death, this was the first time she'd seen genuine excitement on the little girl's face—not anger or sadness or that careful blankness she often wore. Maybe this trip had been the right decision after all.

"Seahorse Villa," Abby read aloud. "Sounds fancy!"

Abby pulled the rental car to a stop in front of the small house. It was painted sea-foam green with peach trim, and a painted wooden sign attached next to the front door identified it as "Seahorse Villa." *Villa? More like a hut,* she thought and picked up her phone. *This has to be a mistake.* She scrolled through her emails until she found the one from the travel agent and checked the address. No, this was the right place.

She glanced at the house next door. It was exactly the same, only a reverse color scheme to the one she'd rented. All the houses on the street were identical. It was like someone had taken a cookie stamp and went up and down the block, stamping out houses. They were a far cry from the large, historic homes they'd passed going through town. Abby bit her lip and hoped Cami wouldn't be disappointed when they got inside. The last thing she wanted was for this moment of happiness to fizzle out.

"Let's go check it out." Cami flung her door open.

"I'll race you to the door!" Abby called, surprising herself as she jumped out of the car and they raced up the walkway to the small, covered porch. She couldn't remember the last time she'd run anywhere—certainly not in New York, where every outing was a carefully choreographed event. But something about Cami's excitement was infectious.

"I won!" Cami giggled as she tented her eyes with her hands and peered through the small window on the front door, then looked over her shoulder at Abby. "It's cute!"

The door had an electronic lock, and Abby looked at the

email to get the code, carefully punching in the numbers. The light on the lock turned green, and Cami pulled the door open and ran inside before Abby could tell her to take her shoes off. Aside from being somewhat disappointed with the rental so far, her idea of returning to Bluefin Bay was doing what she'd hoped it would.

The excitement and smile on Cami's face was a great change from the sullen, brooding child she'd brought to New York. Watching Cami bounce from room to room, pointing out every little detail with delight, Abby allowed herself to hope that this summer might heal them both in ways she hadn't thought possible.

Abby slipped off her shoes and looked around. The interior of the bungalow was furnished in maritime decor. The walls were painted light turquoise with white trim and white crown molding. The floors were a light hardwood, or at least Abby thought they were hardwood. The living room contained a pastel floral-print sofa and matching chair, along with several framed photographs of various lighthouses. White French doors led to a small kitchen and dining room. The cabinets were painted white, and the countertops were black marble, including a large breakfast counter with two black barstools. Four colorful fabric placemats adorned a square whitewashed table and chairs that stood in the center of the dining area. She glanced at the sliding glass door that led outside, but decided to look at the rest of the house before she checked out the backyard.

She made her way through the kitchen to a short hallway that ran along the back side of the house. There were three doors branching off the hall. One led to the bathroom, which was about the same size as her bedroom closet back home. The other two doors led to nearly identical bedrooms, each containing a queen-size bed, a dresser, and a small closet. The only difference being the color scheme of the decor. One was decorated in a seashell theme and the other in a lighthouse theme. Abby let out a disappointed sigh. *There's only one bathroom?*

It was then that she realized Cami was nowhere to be seen. Her stomach twisted into a knot. This was exactly what had happened at the museum in New York, when Cami had disappeared for nearly half an hour after saying she needed the bathroom. She spun on her heel and hurried into the kitchen, nearly running into Cami, who had just come through the sliding door. Abby caught her breath, then let out a sigh of relief.

"Where were you?" she asked, with a little more edge than she'd intended. Walking that fine line between establishing much-needed boundaries and not pushing Cami further away was like walking through a minefield.

Cami's smile fell. "I went to check out the backyard," she said, her eyes downcast as she kicked at the floor with the toe of her sneaker.

Abby grimaced at the abrupt change in her demeanor. "I'm sorry, Cami, you just startled me. Next time, can you let me know before you go outside? Just so I know where you are?"

The little girl's gaze shifted back up, and she studied Abby for a moment before her smile returned. Abby let out a sigh of relief. The last thing she wanted right now was for Cami to have a meltdown.

"Okay. There's a table with an umbrella back there and a barbecue!" Cami bounced on her toes, her excitement quickly returning.

"A barbecue?"

Cami gave her a strange look. "Yeah, you know, a grill? For hotdogs and stuff?"

"Oh, right." Abby shifted uncomfortably. She was pretty much useless in the kitchen, let alone with outdoor appliances.

"And the ocean is really close," Cami continued, not missing a beat. "Can we go look at it? Please, please, please?" She clasped her hands together dramatically.

"After we get unpacked."

"Can I have the seashell room?" Cami asked, already heading toward it.

"Sure." Abby nodded, rubbing the back of her neck. They were going to be on top of each other in this small house. She remembered what the travel agent had said—they were lucky to get anything at all.

Cami studied Abby for a moment, then frowned. "Don't you like it here?"

Abby caught herself before voicing her concerns. She didn't want to give Cami a reason to start complaining too. Instead, she forced a smile. "I'm just getting used to it. It's a lot different than my—our place in New York."

Cami raised her eyebrows. "There's only two of us," she said, stating the obvious. "How much room do we need?"

Abby blinked. She did have a point. She recalled the apartment where Cami had lived with Michael and Lucy. It wasn't any bigger than this house. "I guess I'm just used to having more space." She smiled wearily and shrugged.

"Well, I like it." Cami lifted her chin. "Your house is too fancy." She grinned. "Plus, we can hear the ocean from here!"

Abby felt her tension ease at Cami's enthusiasm. She had a point. What did they need with all that space? If Cami liked the small house, she'd make it work. It was just a couple of months, after all. Maybe the coziness would help them connect. Plus, she reluctantly admitted to herself, the girl wasn't entirely wrong about her New York apartment. It felt less and less like home every day. Maybe this change would be good for her too.

"Then let's get the car unloaded." This time, her smile came easily as she gestured toward the door.

Cami exited the house ahead of her. They'd just brought the last of the luggage inside when Abby's phone chirped. She pulled it out of her pocket and glanced at the screen. It was Benny.

"Just a second," Abby said to Cami, who was already dragging her suitcase toward the seashell room. "I need to take this." But as she watched Cami struggle with the luggage, then stop to readjust her grip on Lola before continuing her determined march down the hallway, Abby made a decision. Whatever Benny needed could wait. She declined the call and slipped the phone back into her pocket.

"Hey, Cami," she called, following the girl into the seashell room. "Let me help you unpack."

Cami looked up in surprise, then smiled. A real smile, the kind that reached her eyes. Abby's heart soared.

"Okay." She placed Lola carefully on the pillow, adjusting the stuffed bunny so she was sitting up. "Lola wants to supervise."

"That's a perfect spot for her," Abby agreed, kneeling beside the suitcase.

As they sorted through clothes, Cami seemed to relax more with each item they put away. "I like this dresser better than the one in New York," Cami said, running her hand along the painted wood. "It's not so fancy that I'm scared to touch it."

"This whole room feels more comfortable, doesn't it?"

Cami nodded, then peered out the large window at the swaying plants that grew in clumps beyond where the yard ended. "Is the beach behind those plants?"

Abby looked out the window, spotting the beach grass Cami referred to. "Yes, that's beach grass. It grows on the sand dunes. We can explore them later, if you want."

"That would be cool," Cami said.

They worked together, tucking away Cami's clothes and

arranging the books she'd wanted to bring on the dresser. Abby noticed that several of Cami's outfits were a bit snug. Maybe while they were here, she'd update Cami's wardrobe too. Abby smiled, feeling hope take hold for the first time in weeks.

CHAPTER 21

Abby unpacked the few items of clothing she'd brought, carefully hanging them in the closet, then padded out to the living room. Cami lay sprawled on the couch, completely absorbed in a game on her tablet. The soft pings and cheerful music from the device filled the otherwise quiet room.

"I was thinking we should head into town," Abby said. "What do you think? We could get some groceries and maybe check out the area a little."

Cami hesitated, then looked down and toed the floor in front of her with her bare foot, her hands twisting together at her waist.

"What's wrong, Cami?"

Cami's gaze slid from the floor to Abby and then back to the floor. "Umm . . ."

Abby frowned. "Cami, look at me," she said gently and waited until Cami's gaze shifted again, this time holding Abby's. "What is it?"

Cami chewed her bottom lip, her cheeks flushed bright

pink. "Do you think I could get a new coloring book? And maybe some markers or crayons?"

Abby smiled, relieved that it was such a simple request, and pleased that Cami was getting more comfortable with asking for things she wanted. "That sounds like a great idea."

"I miss having my art stuff," she went on, her words coming so fast Abby had to pay close attention to understand them. "I left all my good markers in New York."

"Let's see what they have in town. Maybe we can find an art store."

Cami's face lit up. "Thank you! Can we go now?"

"You bet."

"Cool! Let me get my sneakers." She turned, but then stopped and looked back at Abby. "Is that what you're wearing?"

Abby glanced down at her outfit—black slacks and an ivory cotton shirt. It was one of her most casual outfits. "Yes, why?"

"Do you always dress up? You always look like you're going to church; well, if you even went to church." Cami rolled her eyes, then continued, "Or like you're going to a fancy meeting or something."

Abby smiled at the girl's candid observation. "How about if you help me find some new clothes too?" She'd been planning to do that anyway. Maybe it would make Cami feel more comfortable with her, and maybe she'd figure out her own style. "I think I'm ready for something different."

"Okay, I love to shop. My mom—" Cami's hazel eyes clouded, and her bottom lip quivered for a moment. She blinked hard a couple of times, then wiped her nose with the back of her hand. "My mom didn't like shopping very much, though. She said it made her feet hurt."

The sadness coming off the girl was palpable. Hopefully,

their trip into town would help take her mind off things for a while.

———

They drove downtown and parked in front of the coffee shop. She'd die for some caffeine right now. The street was lined with old turn-style parking meters, and Abby dug through her purse for some change. She found enough to give them two hours, which was fine since it was already late afternoon.

Abby glanced up and down the street at the welcoming displays in the storefronts. They passed the bookstore she'd noticed when they first drove through town. Next door, a pet supply store had a colorful array of dog toys and leashes artfully arranged behind the glass. Across the street, a bakery with "Seaside Sweets" painted in swirling letters on the window was doing brisk business. Smiling customers emerged with white boxes tied with blue string, and Abby made a mental note to stop there another day. Pedestrians strolled along the sidewalk on both sides of the street, carrying shopping bags and pushing strollers. The door to the coffee shop opened with a jingle as a group of laughing women stepped out and walked past them. The enticing aroma of freshly ground coffee filled the air.

Abby inhaled deeply. She desperately needed coffee. "Let's make a stop here first, okay?"

"Can I have a strawberry smoothie?" Cami asked.

"Sure, we can see if they have that."

Ten minutes later, with Abby's iced coffee with caramel drizzle and Cami's strawberry smoothie in hand, they strolled down the sidewalk. A light breeze gently swayed hanging baskets that were filled with colorful flowers, and Abby caught a faint, briny whiff of the nearby ocean. Everyone they passed looked so relaxed and happy.

"Oh, there's an art store." Abby pointed at a shop across the street called Coastal Creations.

They crossed the street and within twenty minutes walked out of the store with a new sketchbook, a couple of coloring books, colored pencils, and a set of markers for Cami. Abby had also picked up a small watercolor set that Cami had been eyeing but was too shy to ask for. The girl's face had lit up when Abby added it to their purchases, and she happily hugged the bag with her new art supplies to her chest as they continued down the street.

Next door to the art store was a clothing boutique called Blue Magnolia. The items displayed in the window looked more like everyday clothing versus the touristy items sold in the gift shops they'd walked past. A striped blue and white awning extended over the entrance, and the window display featured flowy, bohemian-style dresses and artsy tops artfully arranged with beach hats and colorful scarves. Abby opened the door, and the jingle of a bell announced their entrance. Cami spotted a couple of chairs arranged near the changing room and made a beeline for them so she could open her new coloring book and colored pencils.

"Hi. May I help you?" a friendly voice behind her asked.

Abby turned. A woman about her age with short, dark brown hair smiled at her. She wore a blue-and-green sundress with tan espadrilles and stood nearly as tall as Abby. Abby returned the woman's warm smile and gestured at her clothes. "I'm looking for something a little more casual."

"You've come to the right place. I'm Beth Allen," the woman said as she extended her hand.

"Abby Whitney." She shook Beth's hand. "And that's Cami." She gestured toward where Cami sat coloring with her new pencils.

"Are you two visiting?"

"Yes, how did you know?"

"You look too stressed to be a local. Plus, I've never seen you here before. Small town and all that." Beth glanced at Cami and chuckled. "I have a daughter about the same age. I remember when I was that age, I'd be outside from sunrise to sunset. Now it takes an act of Congress to get my daughter away from her video games." She returned her attention to Abby. "Let's see what we can find you."

Abby loved the upscale bohemian style of the clothes in the shop. The racks held flowing maxi dresses, well-crafted cotton separates, and artisanal accessories that managed to be both elegant and casual at the same time. She'd wanted to major in fashion design in college, but her parents wouldn't have it. *You need to have a practical education*, they'd insisted and had steered her toward business instead, which she'd dutifully pursued before Michael had convinced her to drop out.

She ran her fingers down the gauzy sleeve of a teal blouse and briefly wondered where her path would have taken her if she'd been strong enough to stand her ground back then. Would she still have married Michael? Would she have acquiesced to a lifestyle that allowed him to live a double life? Since discovering Michael's secrets and lies, she'd often found herself wondering about the different turns her life could have taken. She gave herself a mental smack. The past was in the past. It needed to stay there. She was in control now, and that's all that mattered.

Focusing on the matter at hand, Abby deferred several times to Beth's opinion, and the two of them visited easily while Abby shopped. Beth had grown up in the small town and owned Blue Magnolia. There was something about her that reminded Abby a little of Julie, an openness and warmth that Abby immediately connected with. It was a refreshing change from the closed-up women she'd associated with in New York. She was the kind of person Abby would want for a friend if she lived here.

They took the stack of clothes Abby selected to the register, and Beth was ringing up Abby's purchases when a young girl with a dark brown ponytail bounded into the store.

"Mom, are you almost done?" She sighed dramatically, folding her arms across her chest. "We're going to be late!"

"Abby." Beth smiled, then turned and gave her daughter an exasperated glare. "This is my daughter, Piper."

"Hi, Piper," Abby said.

She was exuberant and carefree. *Was Cami like this before the accident? Will she ever be like this again?* It struck Abby how little she knew about the girl she was now responsible for. She didn't know what made Cami laugh, what scared her, what her normal temperament was like before tragedy struck. All she knew was this subdued, cautious version. She had no baseline, no way of knowing how much of Cami's current behavior was grief and how much was simply her personality.

"Piper, Abby has a daughter that's your age too," Beth said, and handed Abby her receipt, nodding her head toward Cami.

Cami stared back at them with wide eyes, a look of horror passing over her features. Abby's stomach dropped. *Oh no . . . no . . .*

"I'm not—" Abby began.

"*She* is not my mother," Cami interrupted, jumping to her feet. Her eyes pooled with tears. "My mother is dead," she choked out before she ran out of the store.

Beth's face turned a deep shade of crimson, and her mouth opened, then closed several times, while Piper stared slack-jawed at the door.

"I'm so sorry," Abby said as she grabbed her bags and headed toward the door. "She just lost both her parents. I'm her—guardian now," she said over her shoulder, not sure why she felt the need to explain. She knew the woman meant no harm, and it was an easy assumption to have made. Still, she couldn't bring herself to say that she was Cami's aunt.

"I'm so sorry, I didn't know. Please come back," Beth called. "I'd love to visit with you again."

Abby rushed through the door without replying, her gaze searching the area for Cami. She darted forward, not watching where she was going, and slammed straight into a wall of muscle.

"Whoa there," a deep voice said as strong hands steadied her to keep her from falling. "Might want to look where you're running."

Abby looked up into the stern face of a tall man with dark brown hair and a strong jaw. He wore a dusty button-down shirt with the sleeves rolled up, revealing tanned forearms. His eyes, a piercing blue under the brim of his worn cowboy hat, regarded her with irritation.

"I'm sorry," Abby stammered, flustered by both the collision and the urgent need to find Cami. "My . . . I need to find—"

"Just be more careful," he said curtly, releasing her and stepping aside. He tipped his hat slightly before continuing on his way.

Abby barely had time to register his retreating form when a quick movement caught her attention, and she spotted Cami running on the boardwalk toward the beach. The boardwalk ran perpendicular to the shopping area and was near where Abby's rental car was parked. She pressed the button on her key fob to open the trunk and tossed her bags inside. The encounter with the cowboy forgotten, she slammed the lid shut and ran as fast as her Tory Burch pumps would allow.

"Cami!" Abby called. "Cami, wait!" She ran to the point where the boardwalk met the sand. She'd lost sight of Cami but knew she had to be on the beach. There was nowhere else she could have gone in such a short time. Her eyes frantically scanned the horizon, and she spotted Cami sitting in the sand several yards away, her arms wrapped around her legs and her head on her knees.

Abby paused for a moment to catch her breath, then kicked off her shoes and walked barefoot through the warm sand toward the girl. As she approached, she could see Cami's slender shoulders shaking, and the sound of her sobs mingled with the waves crashing on the sand. Sinking down next to Cami, she reached over to put her arm around the girl's shoulders, but then withdrew, unsure if that was the right thing to do or not.

"I'm sorry Beth said that," Abby said softly. "She didn't know."

Cami lifted her head and turned to look at Abby. Tears ran down her face, and her eyes were red and puffy. "I-I miss h-her," she sobbed, her breath coming in gulps. "I m-miss her s-so much."

The girl blurred as Abby's eyes filled with tears. This time she didn't hesitate and pulled Cami into her arms. She held her tightly to her chest. Cami clung to her as sobs ripped through her and shook her small frame. Abby gently swayed back and forth, stroking her hair, while tears streamed down her face. She felt completely out of her depth. This poor little girl had lost everything, and she had no idea what she was doing.

Abby continued to hold her, the waves providing a soothing backdrop, until Cami's sobs eventually quieted into occasional hiccups.

"I'm not very good at this," Abby admitted, her voice just above a whisper. "I don't know what I'm doing most of the time, and I'm probably making a lot of mistakes."

Cami pulled back slightly, wiping her nose with the back of her hand. Her hazel eyes, still wet with tears, studied Abby's face.

"I want you to know something," Abby said softly, choosing her words carefully. "Your mom was special, and no one can ever take her place. Not me, not anyone."

Cami nodded, her bottom lip trembling.

"But I promise I'll do my best to take care of you," Abby continued. "And maybe someday, when it doesn't hurt so much, you'll feel happy again. It's okay if that takes a long time. But it's also okay to feel happy sometimes too. That doesn't mean you love your mom or dad any less."

Cami wiped her eyes with her small fist. "I felt happy when we were shopping," she whispered. "And then I remembered my mom, and I felt bad."

"That's normal," Abby said softly. "But your mom would want you to have happy moments."

Cami looked up at Abby with wide eyes. "You really think so?"

"I know so."

The little girl was quiet for a moment, then asked in a small voice, "You won't leave me too, will you?"

"I'm not going anywhere," Abby promised, her heart aching at the innocence and vulnerability in Cami's question.

"Do you think my mom is mad because I like the new markers you bought me?" Cami asked, her voice small and raspy from crying.

Abby brushed a strand of hair from Cami's forehead. "No. I think your mom would want you to have fun. Being happy doesn't mean you've forgotten her."

"Really?"

"Really," Abby said gently. "She'll always be right here." She lightly touched Cami's chest, directly over her heart.

Cami seemed to accept what Abby said and leaned back into her embrace. They sat together watching the waves until Cami's breathing returned to normal.

"Ready to head back?" Abby asked gently.

Cami nodded, and Abby helped her to her feet, brushing the sand from their clothes. On the way back to the bungalow, they stopped at a small grocery store. After the heavy conversation they'd just had, Abby didn't feel much like shopping. They picked up some cereal, bread, and a few other essentials to get them by until they could make a bigger trip later.

Back at the bungalow, Abby ordered pizza for dinner. They ate in the living room while watching a Disney movie that made them both laugh. Cami fell asleep on the couch before the movie ended, and Abby carefully carried her to bed, surprised at how light she felt in her arms.

As she tucked the blanket around the sleeping child, Abby felt a strange mix of emotions. Responsibility, fear, and something else . . . a fierce protectiveness she hadn't expected. She brushed a gentle kiss on Cami's forehead before turning off the light.

CHAPTER 22

The next morning, Abby woke feeling more optimistic than she had in weeks. Yesterday's conversation at the beach had been difficult, but it felt like she'd reached a turning point with Cami. For the first time, she believed they might actually be okay.

Her goal for the next couple of weeks was to keep Cami as busy as possible. She'd ordered several of the books that Julie had recommended on dealing with grief in children, and one of the common pieces of advice was to keep them busy.

She spread out a map of the Outer Banks on the counter in the kitchen. "What would you like to do while we're here?" she asked Cami, who sat at the table with Lola, eating a bowl of cereal.

Cami's eyes widened. "I get to pick?"

"Of course. It's your vacation too."

Cami slid off the chair, climbed onto the stool next to Abby, and leaned in to view the map, her finger tracing the coastline. "Can we see the wild horses you told me about?"

"Absolutely," Abby said, writing it down in her notebook. "What else?"

Cami's face lit up with genuine excitement as they planned their adventures together—something Abby had seen only rarely since they'd met. By the time they finished breakfast, they had an itinerary filled with activities that had Cami bouncing with anticipation.

They visited the Maritime Museum, where they learned about and saw artifacts from the wreckage of one of Blackbeard's ships. Another day they took a ferry and spent the day exploring Roanoke Island. A few days later, they walked the boardwalk at Emerald Isle and did plenty of shopping, adding little personal touches to the bungalow.

Cami beat Abby soundly several times at mini golf, giggling uncontrollably when Abby's ball went sailing into a decorative pond. "You're supposed to hit it into the holes, not the water!" she'd exclaimed, doubled over with laughter.

But the highlight of their adventures was the guided horseback riding tour they went on to see the famous wild horses of Corolla. They rode along the beach at sunset, and their guide led them to where a small herd played in the surf. Cami watched in awe, rattling off facts about the mustangs that impressed everyone, including their guide.

"You sure know a lot about horses," Abby whispered to her.

Cami beamed with pride. "They're my favorite."

"Do you think we can go horseback riding again sometime?" Cami asked over a spoonful of cereal, a couple of days after their trip to Corolla.

Abby finished buttering her piece of toast and sat next to her at the breakfast counter. "The same ones?"

Cami shrugged. "Are there others?"

Abby considered the question for a moment. "I'm not sure. I would imagine there would be other places to ride horses here." She recalled the horse trophies and ribbons she'd seen displayed in Cami's room in California. Maybe getting her involved in a hobby for the summer would be a good outlet for her. "Did you ride a lot in California?"

Cami swallowed a bite of her cereal while her head bobbed up and down. "Me and Ava did. Julie took us to the Riding Academy for lessons, and we even got to go to a competition once at the Los Angeles Equestrian Center. That place is *huge*." She spread her arms wide.

"What kind of competition?" Abby had grown up loving horses, but her mother had wanted no part in allowing her daughter around "those stinky animals." Marilyn had also been terrified Abby would fall and break an arm or worse. Abby loved that Cami had been given the opportunity to cultivate her interests.

"Dressage and jumping," Cami answered around another mouthful of cereal.

"Dressage?"

"It's like dance—but only with horses instead of people." Cami jumped from the stool and demonstrated, prancing around the kitchen with exaggerated steps. "The horse has to do the special moves, and you have to sit really straight and proper."

Abby laughed as Cami continued to demonstrate several dressage moves, complete with sound effects. It was the most animated she'd seen the little girl since buying her the art supplies. It felt like they were making real progress.

"Do you think there are equestrian classes here?" Cami asked.

"How about when we go into town for lunch, we stop at the Blue Magnolia and see if Beth knows?" She knew she could just look it up on her phone, but Beth was a local and might have better information on the best place to take her. They hadn't been back to the quaint little shop since that first day, but Abby had thought about Beth's invitation to visit several times.

Cami's eyes clouded over for a moment, but then she gave a small nod. She took a couple more bites of cereal, then turned to Abby and tilted her head. "Why do we always go out to eat or get pizza, except for breakfast?" She held up her empty spoon.

"I thought you liked eating out."

"It's fine, I guess. At my house, we didn't eat out much. I mean, before."

Abby gave her a sheepish look. "I'm not a very good cook," she admitted.

Cami pursed and twisted her lips, her brows furrowed. "How bad can you be?"

"Pretty bad, I'm afraid." Abby grimaced. Truth be told, she couldn't even boil eggs.

"Didn't your mom teach you how to cook?"

Abby chuckled at the thought of her mother in the kitchen. "No, we had a chef that made our meals for us."

Cami's eyes grew wide. "Like in a restaurant?"

"Kind of, except he worked just for our family. In our house."

Cami frowned. "What about at your fancy apartment? Didn't you cook there?"

Abby shifted in her seat. "No, Muriel used to do the cooking."

"She wasn't very nice." Cami scooped up another spoonful of cereal. "I bet I'm a better cook than you," she said, giggling through a mouthful of food.

"You know how to cook?" Abby was amazed. Cami continued to surprise her, and Abby found herself enjoying discovering these different sides of the girl's personality. She hadn't spent a lot of time around children and was learning that eight-year-olds were far more capable than she'd imagined.

"Yep. My mom taught me," she said. "Plus, I watched a lot of Food Network. Me and Ava love to play *Chopped* kitchen. Well, we *did*." Cami's gaze dropped for a moment, and the corners of her mouth sank into a frown. "Do you think Ava can come visit sometime? You said she could."

Cami and Abby had had several video calls with Ava and Julie since Cami had left California. Cami would say hi to Julie and then take Abby's phone into her room, where she and Ava would talk and giggle for as long as the adults would let them. Abby and Julie continued to keep in regular contact. They'd been trying to coordinate a visit, but Julie had just started a new round of cancer treatments and Ava was away at summer camp.

"That would be fun," Abby said. "Julie is going to call me when Ava gets back from camp. How does that sound?"

"Okay!" Cami brightened. She rinsed her cereal bowl and put it in the dishwasher before padding through the French doors into the living room. A few seconds later, Abby heard the TV turn on.

Abby finished her toast and climbed off the stool. They didn't have anything planned for the day, but maybe Cami would want to go and find something to do. She walked into the living room where the little girl was sprawled on the sofa, completely engrossed in a cooking show. Abby sat on the chair and curled her feet underneath her. "What are you watching?"

"*Chopped*." Cami's eyes remained glued to the screen.

Abby raised her eyebrows but said nothing. She focused on the show, and soon, she was just as absorbed as Cami. She'd never seen anything like it. They gave contestants a basket of random ingredients, and they had to make a dish using every item from the basket within a set amount of time. Many of the ingredients Abby had never heard of. Most of the dishes the contestants came up with looked delicious.

"You and Ava do this?" she asked Cami during a commercial break.

"Mmm hmm." She nodded. "Julie is great at picking ingredients and being the judge."

Abby wasn't sure if she could pick the ingredients out to make pancakes, let alone anything close to the complex dishes created on the show. She glanced at Cami and watched her eyes gleam with interest as she watched.

"Who do you think is going to win?" Cami asked, her eyes remaining focused on the screen.

"Hmm." Abby chewed on her bottom lip while she deliberated. "I think the girl with the red bandana," she finally said.

"Me too, if she doesn't mess up the dessert round."

Abby felt a small thrill at having chosen the same contestant as Cami. It was a tiny thing, but it felt like progress. She watched the last round of judging intently. "These judges are brutal," she said with a laugh when one of them made a particularly harsh critique.

"I know, right? It's awesome!"

They both cheered when the girl with the red bandana was declared the winner.

"Let's get ready and head to town," Abby suggested, as she got up to stretch. "We can ask Beth about the horses."

Cami's face lit up, and she leaped off the sofa. "Cool!" She smiled and skipped out of the room.

Abby pulled out her phone and sent Julie a text.

Hey Julie, do you have any easy recipes I could try making with Cami?

Sure, how easy? Cami's a pretty good cook.

Easy. I'm not.

LOL, I'll email you some.

Abby smiled and looked around the room. While the bungalow had seemed too small at first, Abby now loved its coziness and charm. Sharing a bathroom had proved to be somewhat of a challenge, but she and Cami had settled into an easy routine. She had to admit she felt content here.

Chapter 23

The door to the Blue Magnolia was propped open to let in the early summer breeze. A chalkboard sign on the sidewalk in front of the store advertised a summer sale on tank tops. Abby stepped inside and Cami followed, choosing to hang near Abby this time. Beth came from behind the fitting rooms and broke into a wide grin when she saw them.

"Hi there! I was hoping you'd come back," she called out. She gave Abby a quick once-over, nodding in approval at her casual teal sundress and flip-flops. "Well, look at you. Bluefin Bay has been good to you. You could almost pass for a local now."

Abby flushed at the compliment. Her friends in New York wouldn't consider going out in public in such casual attire, yet Abby felt at ease and natural. She'd even piled her long curls into a messy bun on top of her head, which allowed the breeze to tickle the back of her neck. There was a sort of freedom in dressing this way—one she hadn't realized she was missing.

"And you." Beth smiled at Cami. "You look like you've been spending a lot of time in the sun."

Cami smiled shyly and half-hid behind Abby, peeking around her arm. "We saw the wild horses," she said in a soft voice.

"Did you? That's wonderful!" Beth's warm response seemed to put Cami at ease. "What can I help you ladies with today?" Beth asked. "We have a new shipment of children's clothes that I think you might like. It's Cami, right?"

Cami bobbed her head and slid a questioning glance at Abby. Abby agreed with a short nod, and the girl ran off in the direction of the children's department. She knew she'd have to curb the spending at some point, spoiling Cami would only backfire later, but until she had everything she needed, Abby was enjoying splurging on someone other than herself.

"I actually stopped in because I was hoping you might be able to help us," Abby said, shifting her gaze back to Beth.

Beth glanced at her watch and turned toward a young salesclerk who was leaning against the counter at the register, a bored expression on her overly made-up face. "Misty, I'm going to take a quick break. Will you keep an eye on the store?"

"Sure, whatever," the girl replied, snapping her chewing gum.

Beth let out an exasperated sigh and glanced over to where Cami was flipping through dresses on a sale rack.

"Cami, do you want to color while we talk for a minute?" Beth asked, pulling a coloring book and some crayons from behind the counter. Cami nodded, and she set her up at a small table near the register where Misty could keep an eye on her. "We'll be right over there if you need anything," Beth said, pointing toward a door marked "Employees Only."

"Okay," Cami replied, already reaching for a blue crayon.

Beth nodded to Misty. "Could you keep an eye on her for a minute, please?"

The salesclerk nodded, and Beth led Abby into a large

room, where they could still see Cami through the open doorway but had a bit more privacy for their conversation. Abby had never been in the employee section of a store before and gave a curious glance at her surroundings. A door along one wall led to a small bathroom. Shelves with bins of merchandise and boxes lined the walls, and larger boxes and racks of clothes filled the rest of the room.

"Sorry it's such a mess," Beth said, gesturing around the room. "I've had such a hard time finding good help."

"It's fine," Abby reassured her.

"So how are you both doing? Are you settling in okay?" Beth asked as they sat at a small table near the door.

Abby was surprised by the genuine concern in Beth's voice. Back home, conversations rarely went beyond what event was coming up, or who was seen where. People didn't ask how you were actually feeling. It was a nice change.

"We're doing . . . better," Abby said, happy to be able to answer that honestly. "It's been a difficult adjustment, but being here has helped. Cami lost her parents in a car accident recently. I—I was named her guardian."

Beth reached across the table and squeezed Abby's hand. "I'm so sorry. That's a lot for both of you."

Abby nodded, unexpectedly moved by the simple gesture of compassion. "Thank you."

"Are you enjoying your stay in town so far? Have you been to Two Scoops yet?"

"Yes, and no. I mean yes, we are enjoying it here, and no, we haven't been there yet. That's the ice cream shop, right?"

"Only the best ice cream in the entire Outer Banks," Beth said. "My friend Colleen owns it."

"My grandfather took me there when I was a kid. Well, same location, different name. We'll have to check it out."

"Oh, right. Yeah, Colleen bought it a few years ago, but it's always been an ice cream shop. You won't be sorry. Well, your waistline might be." She chuckled. "Tell her I sent you over."

"I will, thanks." Abby smiled, moved by how everyone seemed to know and support each other in this small town. It reminded her of her childhood visits here with her grandparents—that sense of community had always been present, though she hadn't fully appreciated it as a child. She was grateful to find it mostly unchanged, exactly what she'd hoped for—a place where both she and Cami could begin to heal.

"So, what can I help you with?"

"I was wondering if you know any places that rent horses in the area. Not a trail ride, but maybe lessons. Cami took dressage lessons in California, and she'd like to get back into it. I'm wanting to keep her as busy as possible. You know, keep her mind off things. She loves horses."

"Piper loves horses too! If we could get the two of them together, Piper will talk her ear off." Beth reached across the table for a pen and pulled a sticky note out of a black dispenser. She pulled her phone out of her pocket and scrolled through it for a minute, then wrote a name and phone number on the piece of paper. "Logan Taylor gives lessons out at the Seabreeze Ranch," she said, handing the paper to Abby. "He's great and will be able to help you figure out what will work best for Cami. Piper takes lessons there."

"Thanks." Abby smiled. "I'll give him a call when we're done here."

Beth drummed her fingers on the table, then looked at Abby. "You know, Piper has a lesson tomorrow afternoon. If you want, I can call Logan and see if it's all right if you and Cami come along. That way I can introduce the two of you, and Cami will have a friend to go with. It's a win-win."

Abby let out a sigh of relief. She knew nothing about horses, let alone what would be appropriate for an eight-year-old girl. "That would be amazing, thank you. You're sure it's not too much trouble?"

Beth rose to her feet and waved her hand in a dismissive gesture. "Not at all. I have to go anyway. Besides, this way I'll have someone to talk to while Piper has her lesson, and the girls can get to know each other. I better get back up front, though. Misty isn't exactly the most motivated employee."

Cami looked up from her coloring book when she saw them emerge and quickly put down her crayon, running over to Abby with an excited smile.

"Can I show you something?" she asked, tugging at Abby's hand and leading her toward a display rack. "Look!" She pointed to a T-shirt with horses galloping across the front.

"Oh, good." Beth grinned at the girl. "I'm happy to see you found something you like. I'll be ready at the register when you're done."

Cami carefully took the shirt from the rack and held it up against herself. "Can I get this? Please?"

"That's perfect," Abby said, nodding. "I think it's just what you need for our visit to the stables tomorrow."

Cami's eyes widened. "We're going to see horses tomorrow?"

"We are," Abby confirmed, loving the way Cami's whole face lit up with excitement. "Beth's daughter, Piper, will be there too." They paid for their purchases, and Beth confirmed their meeting time and place for the following day, handing Abby a business card with her cell phone number written on the back.

"See you then." Abby grinned and walked out of Blue Magnolia with Cami beside her. Another step forward.

They dropped the bag with Cami's new shirt in the car and strolled down the sidewalk. It was mid-afternoon, and the stores were busy. Abby wondered what the small seaside town was like once the summer was over and the out-of-towners like her left. Up ahead, she spotted a colorful sign that read "Two Scoops" and remembered Beth's recommendation.

"Want to get some ice cream?" she asked Cami, who was skipping alongside her, occasionally slowing to peek into shop windows.

"Yes, please!" Cami grinned, grabbing Abby's hand.

They stepped inside the busy shop. The sweet, warm aroma of freshly made waffle cones filled the air, making Abby's mouth water instantly. Cami stood beside her in the long line, bouncing on her toes with excitement as she peered at the colorful tubs of ice cream behind the glass. Abby smiled, remembering her own childhood visits here. If the ice cream was as good as it had been then, it would be well worth the wait.

The shop was clean and decorated with the same bright red stripes she remembered. The addition of several small bistro tables with red chairs in the store was a charming, nostalgic touch. There had only been a handful of flavors to choose from when her grandfather had brought her here. Now, a huge glass case ran along the entire front of the store that contained more varieties of ice cream than Abby had ever dreamed possible.

They made their way to the counter, where a middle-aged, heavyset woman with short, bright pink hair greeted them. "Good afternoon. What can I get for you today?"

Abby glanced at the woman's name tag and returned her smile. "Hi, Colleen. I'm supposed to tell you that Beth sent us," she said. "I'm Abby, and this is Cami."

"Oh, wonderful," Colleen said. "I'd offer to shake your hand, but mine's a bit sticky. Are you new in town?"

There was something about Colleen's open, friendly manner that immediately put Abby at ease—it was the same quality she'd first noticed in Beth. People here didn't seem to have the practiced politeness of New Yorkers; they were genuinely interested in connecting. "Yes, we're here for the summer." Abby glanced at the line behind her. She didn't want to take up too much of the woman's time, as busy as they were. "I'll have a single scoop espresso chip cone. What do you want, Cami?"

"I'll try the Three Amigos," Cami said, standing on tiptoes to see into the glass case.

Colleen scooped two giant scoops of each flavor into homemade waffle cones and carefully handed them to Abby and Cami. "Second scoop's on me," she said as she rang them up at the register. "Welcome to Bluefin Bay. Maybe next time you stop by, we won't be quite as busy, so we can have a proper introduction. Any friend of Beth's is a friend of mine."

"Thanks, that would be nice." Abby smiled, and they both thanked Colleen on their way out.

As they stepped back into the sunshine, Abby found herself marveling at how easily people offered up their friendship here. In New York, making friends required calculated moves—joining the right boards, attending the right fundraisers, cultivating relationships over months or even years. Here, it seemed as simple as walking through a door.

"Let's eat these down on the beach," Abby suggested, and they headed down the boardwalk.

"This is amazing!" Cami squealed, licking her cone.

"Mine is pretty amazing too." Abby licked the top of her cone. "What flavor is yours again?"

"Three Amigos. It's vanilla ice cream with chocolate sandwich cookies, peanut butter cups, and toffee. It's the best ever!"

CHAPTER 24

They found a bench at the edge of the boardwalk and kicked off their shoes. Large, colorful umbrellas dotted the sand, and a group of teens played volleyball farther down the shore. Huge waves rolled in, dissolving into foam on the shoreline. Streamers of seaweed littered the sand, and crabs skittered in and out between them. Boats dotted the surface of the water off in the distance, and people walked and fished along the long wooden pier that jutted far out into the ocean. A few puffy clouds offered bits of shade from the afternoon heat.

Abby had never felt more relaxed.

"How many do you think there are?" Cami asked.

Abby followed her gaze. She appeared to be looking along the shoreline, but Abby had no idea what she was talking about. "How many what?"

"Seashells," Cami said between licks of her ice cream cone. "How many do you think there are?"

Abby squinted her eyes. Shells of all shapes and sizes were scattered across the sand as far as she could see. She laughed. "Way more than I can count. Why?"

Cami shrugged, ice cream dripping down her fingers. "My mom used to say that there are as many dreams as there are seashells on the beach."

"She sounds like she was a very wise woman," Abby said. Cami had talked very little about her mom since they had been together, and Abby wanted to encourage her to feel comfortable talking to her about Lucy. It was important to her that Cami keep those memories alive, even if it was a painful reminder of Michael.

"Do you think it's true?"

Abby considered the question for a moment and let out a long breath. "I remember hearing once that a dream is a wish your heart makes."

"Yeah, it's from *Cinderella*."

"Yes! That's where I remember it from. If dreams really are wishes that your heart makes, then I would like to believe there are as many dreams as there are seashells."

Cami tilted her head in agreement but stayed silent. They watched the waves roll in as they ate their ice cream cones. Talking about Lucy made Abby think about her own mother and how much she wished they were closer. She had sent Marilyn a text when they had arrived in Bluefin Bay, to let her know where they were staying, but received no response. She knew Marilyn didn't approve of their trip, and she certainly wouldn't approve of Abby eating a double scoop of ice cream, but it felt good to make her own decisions. Even if she had no idea what she was doing.

As she watched Cami lick her ice cream cone with childish abandon, Abby found herself thinking about what kind of childhood she wanted to give her, even if they were only together for a short while. Something vastly different from her own rigid upbringing—something with more freedom, more joy, more seashells, and lots of ice cream and hugs. A childhood where dreams were encouraged rather than dismissed as impractical.

"What's that?" Cami pointed to a large clump of tall beach grass, pulling Abby from her thoughts.

Abby peered at the clump but didn't see anything out of the ordinary. "I don't see anything."

"I thought I saw something move," Cami said and rose to her feet, leaning forward to get a better look. She took a couple of steps toward the clump, and Abby saw a slight movement near the bottom of the grass.

"There!" Cami took several more steps toward the clump of grass.

"Cami, wait!" Abby stood and rushed to hold Cami's arm, gently pulling her to a stop.

Cami flashed her an impatient look and yanked her arm back. "I just want to see what it is."

"We don't know what it is. You could get hurt," Abby said, more firmly this time. "At least let me come with you."

Cami tilted her brow, looking uncertain for a moment, then agreed. "Fine."

They slowly made their way toward the clump. Abby heard the grass rustle. Whatever it was seemed to be moving toward them. She reached out her hand and was about to grab Cami's arm again when a small dog peeked its head out from between two clumps of the tall grass.

"It's a puppy!" Cami squealed as she dropped to her knees and crawled toward the animal, who blinked back at her in surprise.

"Cami, wait! You don't know if it will bite," Abby warned. She didn't have any experience with dogs. As a child, she had desperately wanted a dog, but her mother had refused to entertain the very idea of owning a pet, and Michael claimed to be allergic to animals.

The small animal crouched low and flinched as Cami got closer. She gently coaxed it the rest of the way out from the grass clumps and carefully picked it up. It wasn't actually a puppy, Abby noticed, taking a closer look at the animal. It was light brown with matted fur, and it looked to have white—or what were once white—feet and huge upright ears. The fur around its mouth was tangled and dirty, but Abby thought it might also be white. The dog was quite small, easily fitting in Cami's arms, but it was also very skinny. Abby glanced around, checking to see if anyone might be searching for a lost pet, but didn't see anyone.

"Oh, Abby," Cami said, hugging the dirty, skinny animal to her chest. "He's so cute."

Abby raised a brow. "Cute" wasn't the word she would have used to describe the dog. Interesting, maybe.

"He looks like he's starving." Cami frowned. "Can we feed him?"

"Oh, I don't know. I'm sure he must belong to someone around here," Abby said, even though another glance around the beach confirmed that no one was looking for him.

Cami's eyes made the same track, and she must have come to the same conclusion as she threw Abby a skeptical glance. "I don't see anyone. Oh!" She frowned, and a look of distress crossed her features. "He's shivering." She pulled the dirty little dog closer to her.

Abby cringed and hoped it didn't have fleas. "Maybe they just haven't looked here yet," she reasoned. She felt bad for the little dog but wasn't about to take someone else's pet. Although, she had to admit, it didn't look like anyone had been caring for it.

"We can wait and see," Cami bargained. "Oh, I know!" Her hazel eyes brightened. "We can take him to the vet and see if he has a chip. I saw that on TV. They scan them with a price scanner, and if it beeps, they have a chip. Then it shows who they belong to."

Abby frowned. "A price scanner?"

Cami rolled her eyes. "Well, it *looks* like a price scanner. Can we?" Her wide eyes pleaded with Abby. "Please, please, please?"

Abby groaned inwardly. A third scan of the beach produced no dog seekers. The poor little thing looked neglected, and there was no doubt the dog was quite content in Cami's arms as it relaxed against the child's chest. Abby wrestled with herself over what the right decision was, but finally caved when the tiny dog looked at her with its sad brown eyes.

"All right," she said with a sigh. "We can take him to the vet to see if he has a chip."

"Yay!" Cami cheered and gave the dog a hug. "You hear that?" she said. The dog's ears perked up as it lifted its gaze. "We're going to help you," Cami promised. She glanced from the dog to Abby. "Thank you."

Abby's heart swelled two sizes from the look she saw in Cami's eyes, and she instinctively knew she was doing the right thing. "Let's go." She smiled and tucked a loose strand of the girl's hair behind her ear. "And while we're there, we will have them check him for fleas too."

"Ewww, gross." Cami scrunched her nose as they walked up the boardwalk and back to their rental car.

Abby used her phone to look up the number for a local vet and was pleasantly surprised when they told her to bring the dog in right away. The vet's office wasn't located too far from where they were parked, and it would only take them a few minutes to make the short drive.

Cami held tightly to the small dog, securing it against her chest as Abby drove, following the GPS. She had a feeling

Cami was already getting attached, and her stomach sank at the thought of breaking the news that they couldn't keep him.

She parked the car in a vacant spot right outside the front door of the vet's office and tossed her keys into her purse. Cami was already unbuckled and out of the car before Abby got her door open. Once inside, a young woman took the dog into an exam room while Abby and Cami waited in the lobby.

"Why would someone just leave a helpless little dog on the beach all alone?" Cami asked, her hazel eyes filling with tears.

Abby frowned. "I don't know. Maybe he went exploring and got lost and his owners couldn't find him."

"If he were my dog, I wouldn't stop looking until I found him. He's too little to be out there all by himself."

"He is pretty little. Let's hope he has a chip so we can find his family for him."

A short time later, the vet tech returned and handed the dog back to Cami. "No chip," she said.

Abby stood silently, weighing her options. Taking on a dog was a huge responsibility, especially when she was still figuring out how to take care of Cami. She already felt over-whelmed most days—how would she take care of a pet too?

When Abby didn't say anything, the vet tech continued. "He's malnourished, and from the looks of it, he hasn't been well taken care of." She frowned and patted the dog on the head. "Poor little guy. Do you want me to notify the shelter?"

"No!" Cami cried, pulling the dog tight against her.

Abby let out a long breath and rubbed her temple. Getting a dog definitely wasn't part of her summer plan.

"We can't send him to a shelter. They'll kill him," Cami cried.

"Oh, sweetie, I don't think they do that."

"Uh, actually the shelters here are pretty crowded," the vet tech said. "You'd be surprised how many people get a dog while they're vacationing because they think it'll be fun to have them on the beach. But then they ditch them when they leave. It's a real problem here. The shelter will hold him for seven days to see if someone claims him, but that's it."

Cami and Abby gasped in unison.

Tears pooled in Cami's eyes. "You can't let them kill him," she cried. "He's so cute. And he's so little. He won't be any trouble. Can't we keep him?"

"What if someone is looking for him though, Cami? They won't find him if we have him."

"I can put up a notice here and at the shelter." The vet tech smiled, clearly playing devil's advocate.

"See?" Cami perked up. "If someone is looking for him, they can still find him. Please, Abby. I'll take care of him, and you won't have to do anything."

Abby closed her eyes and let out a long breath. When she opened them, she met Cami's pleading gaze. The girl certainly knew how to tug at her heartstrings. Looking at the small dog, Abby had to admit he was rather endearing, with those big ears and expressive eyes. Maybe having a pet would be good for Cami. Give her a sense of responsibility . . . an emotional outlet. She'd read about therapy animals and emotional support animals in some of the books that Julie had recommended. Maybe having the dog around wouldn't be such a bad idea.

Abby looked from the hopeful little girl to the skinny dog with the big ears. She thought about the excitement Cami had shown about the horses, and now this dog—her love for animals was clear. Maybe this was something they could share, something that would help them bond. "Fine," she said. "We can keep him for now and see if anyone claims him."

"Yay!" Cami threw an arm around Abby in a quick hug, being careful not to crush the dog she held in her other arm.

Abby's eyes stung, and she blinked back the tears threatening to form from the unexpected display of affection. She turned her attention to the vet tech. "Would you have time to give the dog a quick exam to make sure he doesn't have fleas and give us recommendations on food and care?"

"Of course. I'll take him back into the exam room and have the vet look him over." The young woman smiled. "We will give you a discount too because you're not sending him to the shelter."

"Thank you." Abby smiled and watched Cami hand the little dog back to the young woman. The last thing she'd expected to come home with today, or any day, for that matter, was a dog. Her life had changed so much since Cami came into it. As much as she hated to admit it, she was a little excited about keeping the small dog too. Maybe this little stray was meant to be theirs. There had been something about the way he looked at her on the beach that told her they needed him as much as he needed them.

Cami happily rattled off a lengthy list of things they would need to get for the dog while they waited for the tech to come back out of the exam room.

"How do you know so much about dogs? You didn't have one, did you?" Abby didn't recall seeing any pet-related items in their apartment.

"No, but I wanted one. I love animals—dogs, horses, cats, bunnies, everything! But horses are my favorite. Well, maybe now it's dogs!" Cami grinned. "Ava's teacher at school had a class hamster, and she got to take care of it on weekends some-times. I helped."

Abby suppressed a chuckle as the exam room door opened, and the vet tech emerged.

"Well, good news and bad news," she said, handing the dog back to Cami. "The good news is that except for being a little underweight, he seems healthy. Right now he weighs six pounds, but ideally, he should weigh around seven or seven and a half."

Cami nodded. "What's the bad news?" Abby could hear the concern in her voice.

The vet tech looked at Abby and grimaced. "He has fleas. You should pick up some flea shampoo to wash him up today, and I'll prescribe a monthly treatment to keep them from coming back."

Abby sighed. How on earth had she gone from a simple trip to the beach for ice cream to committing to a flea-ridden stray dog? But seeing the look of pure joy on Cami's face as she cuddled the little animal, Abby couldn't bring herself to regret it.

They stopped at the pet store on the way back to the bungalow. She and Cami had agreed before they went into the shop that they would only get the essentials, just in case the pup's owner appeared to claim the little dog. They ended up leaving the shop with a trunk full of supplies, including a bottle of flea shampoo.

Back at the bungalow, Abby helped Cami give the little dog a bath, rinse, and repeat just to make sure the fleas were gone and he was squeaky clean. They were both surprised to see that he was not light brown, but almost yellow, and he did have white feet, along with a full white beard. The vet had guessed him to be a mix of Chihuahua and some kind of terrier because of his coarse coat. Abby didn't think either of those breeds had beards, but on him it was endearing.

They gave the little dog a bowl of food, which Cami carefully measured according to the instructions from the vet. Cami's brow furrowed in concentration as she leveled off the measuring cup. Abby felt a surge of pride watching her careful attention to detail.

The vet had warned them that if he tried to eat too much at one time, he would end up getting sick. Until he was back to a normal weight, they would have to do smaller feedings several times a day. They watched the tiny dog as he ate his kibble. The decision to take him in felt more right by the minute.

"What should we name him?" Cami asked, bouncing a little on her toes, her eyes never leaving the dog.

"I don't know that it's a good idea to name him right away," Abby warned. "What if his owners come back?" The thought of Cami getting attached only to have the dog claimed by someone else made Abby's stomach tighten.

Cami frowned and twisted the hem of her shirt. "But we gotta call him something, don't we? What if . . ." Her voice dropped to a whisper. "What if nobody comes looking for him?" She knelt beside the dog, gently stroking his back. "Look how skinny he is, Abby. If somebody really, really wanted him, they would've found him before we did. He was all alone and scared."

Abby didn't think anyone would claim him either, but she didn't want to give the girl false hope. She'd been through so much already. "The vet tech said his previous owners had seven days to claim him. Let's just wait and see for now."

"If they don't, can I keep him?" Cami made her best puppy dog face and folded her hands in front of her chest. "Please? I'll feed him and walk him and everything."

Abby glanced down at the dog, who had just licked his new bowl clean. He turned his little head up and met her gaze, holding it as though he knew she was the one he'd have to win over. *He sure is cute.*

"Let's take it one day at a time," she finally answered.

Cami scrunched up her face, and Abby prepared herself for an outburst, but the girl's expression softened. She bent and picked up the small dog, cradling him in her arms. "Well, he's here now." She smiled at him. "And I think we should call him Chance."

Abby glanced at the dog again, who stared back at her expectantly. "Why Chance?"

"Because there's a chance I can keep him." Cami grinned.

"Silly girl." Abby smiled at Cami and ruffled the fur on the top of the dog's head. "Chance it is." The name did seem to fit. A second chance. Wasn't that what they were all getting in Bluefin Bay?

Chapter 25

The next morning, Cami was a giant ball of nervous energy as she waited for their trip to Seabreeze Ranch. She had changed her outfit three times already and must have asked Abby a dozen times if it was time to leave yet.

"Take Chance outside, then we'll go," she finally said. "I need to finish this email."

"All right," Cami said and bounded out the door with Chance right on her heels.

Abby finished the email and snapped the lid on her laptop shut. She had let the landlord know they had a dog in the bungalow and hoped it wouldn't be an issue. Chance had been really good so far and hadn't had any accidents inside. It was obvious someone had once loved the little guy, and it was getting harder not to love him back.

After Cami got Chance settled in his crate, they left to meet up with Beth and Piper. Seabreeze Ranch was just outside the Bluefin Bay city limits, nestled between rolling hills and a stretch of pine forest. As they got closer, the landscape opened to reveal sprawling green pastures dotted with horses.

A wooden sign with "Seabreeze Ranch" burned into it marked the entrance, where a long gravel driveway led to a collection of well-maintained buildings.

Abby's stomach did a little nervous flutter as she pulled into a parking spot in front of a split-rail fence that ran along the front of the property. She glanced over at Cami, who stared out the window with wide, bright eyes. There was no doubt she was impressed with the ranch.

"Wow," Cami whispered, her face nearly touching the window as she strained against the seat belt to see everything. "It's so big."

"Remember," Abby said gently, "we're just here to meet the trainer and watch Piper's lesson today. I should have made that clearer—you probably won't be riding yet."

Cami's face fell. "Oh. But maybe next time?"

"If the trainer thinks you're ready, absolutely," Abby said, feeling a twinge of guilt for not explaining better before they'd left the bungalow. She'd been so focused on giving Cami something to look forward to, she hadn't thought to manage her expectations. Plus, there had been the distraction of the dog.

"Oh look! That's Beth." Cami pointed to a gray SUV pulling into the parking spot next to theirs.

Beth waved.

Abby smiled and waved back, then turned to Cami. "You ready?"

"I'm a little nervous," Cami admitted, fidgeting with the hem of her T-shirt. "What if they ride differently here than they do in California?"

Abby hadn't given that much thought. As far as she knew, a horse was a horse, and there was only one way to ride them —on top. "I'm not sure, but that's what today is for—to see how they do things and if you like it."

"Okay," Cami murmured, rubbing her forearms. "You

won't leave me alone, right?" She looked up at Abby, her forehead creased with worry.

Abby put her arm around Cami's slim shoulders and pulled her close for a moment before letting her go. The little girl's vulnerability tugged at her heart. "No, I'll be right here."

"Thanks, Aunt Abby."

Aunt Abby.

The words hit Abby like a punch to the stomach. It was the first time Cami had called her that since they'd left California. While she should have felt pleased at this sign of growing trust, instead she felt a twist of guilt deep in her stomach. She'd reluctantly agreed to go along with the lie Michael had crafted. It seemed necessary, the kindest option at the time. But now, hearing the title spoken with such innocent trust, Abby wondered how she would ever find the right moment to tell Cami the truth. Every day that passed, every small step forward in their relationship, only made the eventual revelation seem more impossible, more potentially devastating. She forced a smile. "You're welcome, sweetie. Let's go meet everyone."

"Hi, I'm glad you made it." Beth smiled. "Cami, you remember Piper, right?"

Cami slid a quick glance toward the other girl and nodded, suddenly shy.

"Hi, Cami," Piper said, a huge grin on her face. "You'll love it here. Mr. Taylor is the best."

Cami gave a small, hesitant smile, her eyes bright with anticipation.

They walked up the path together and stepped inside the huge barn. Abby looked around, surprised to see that it was cleaner than she'd imagined. A small office was situated near the large sliding double-doors they'd entered through, and several areas were sectioned off that held a huge number of saddles, blankets, reins, and other items that she didn't recognize. Large fans were evenly spaced on the ceiling and slowly rotated, circulating the air, and there was a strong scent of sweetgrass and horses. The rest of the barn consisted of two double rows of stalls, and a large stack of square hay bales ran along one wall.

"I'm going to get Bella ready for my lesson. Do you want to come with me?" Piper asked Cami, tucking her hair behind her ear with a hesitant smile.

"That's a great idea," Beth said before Cami had a chance to respond. "That is, if it's okay with Abby." She gave Abby a sheepish grin.

Cami's cheeks flushed pink with excitement, and she looked at Abby. "Can I?"

"Yes, have fun." Abby smiled as the two girls ran toward the other end of the barn and disappeared into one of the stalls.

"I'll introduce you to Logan while they get Bella ready," Beth said. She walked over to the office and pulled the door open. "Hey, Logan, you in here?"

There was no response.

"He's probably in the other barn." Beth turned and motioned for Abby to follow her. "You'll like Logan. He can come across as being a bit . . . gruff, but he's a good guy. We went to high school together. I've known him forever."

Abby considered that for a moment while they walked the dirt path from one barn to the other. She hadn't stayed in touch with anyone she knew in high school. It had been an all-girls school, and she'd had a few good friends while she attended, but they just sort of lost touch after graduation. The one time she'd attended a reunion, the conversations had been primarily a competition of achievements, marriages, and career milestones.

"He got divorced a few years ago," Beth continued. "Has no kids, but he's great with Piper. His brother, Luke, works here too, but you likely won't see him. He mostly works the cattle."

"Sounds interesting," Abby said, trying to navigate the uneven path in her wedge heels. She'd chosen a light floral summer dress and decided to wear her long hair down, but was now regretting her choices. Her curls were starting to frizz in the humidity, and she felt very overdressed next to Beth's jeans and lace-up ankle boots.

"Have you lived here your whole life?" Abby asked.

"Yes, I can't imagine living anywhere else," Beth replied as they stepped into the barn. It was nearly identical to the other, except this one had no office. A long flatbed trailer loaded with hay bales was parked in the center of the aisle. Several men were busy unloading it, stacking the bales neatly along the wall. "There he is." Beth gestured toward one of the men unloading the trailer and headed in that direction.

The men stopped working as the two women approached. Abby avoided looking at them but felt their stares on her, and she could feel her cheeks grow warm. Why had she worn a dress?

A deep, somehow familiar voice called out, "The trailer won't unload itself. Get back to work."

Abby's brow furrowed as she tried to place where she'd heard it. A knot formed in her stomach as realization dawned on her. It was the same man she'd collided with in town—the one with the intense blue eyes who had not-so-nicely told her to watch where she was going. He stepped out from behind the trailer and walked toward them.

Abby watched him approach, unable to take her eyes off him. His long legs were clad in faded denim over a pair of scuffed cowboy boots. He wore a plain green T-shirt that hugged his broad shoulders, and his short, dark hair was covered by the same straw cowboy hat he'd worn when she first saw him. He had to be well over six feet tall, even without the hat.

"Logan, this is Abby." Beth smiled as he came to a stop in front of them.

Abby flushed as she realized she'd been staring at him.

Recognition flashed in his eyes as they met hers. "Abby," he said, extending his hand. "We've met before, I believe."

"Yes," she admitted, placing her hand in his. His grip was warm and strong and a hot second hung between them until he pulled his hand back. "Sorry about running into you in town."

"No harm done," he said, though his tone suggested he hadn't forgotten.

Beth glanced between the two of them and quirked a brow. "You two have already met?" Her lips twitched into a knowing grin as she glanced at Abby. "You can fill me in later."

Abby's face flushed deep red again as Beth turned back to Logan.

"Abby has a girl about Piper's age and she's wondering about riding lessons for the rest of the summer."

"Summer's almost over," he grunted, crossing his arms over his chest.

Beth put her hands on her hips. "Logan Taylor, you know as well as I do that you have room in your schedule. It's barely mid-July; there's still a good month and half left."

Logan turned to Abby and her flush intensified. Why was he having this effect on her? She couldn't remember the last time a man had made her flush, including Michael. It was something about the way Logan looked at her—as if he could see right through her.

"Does she have any experience with horses?" Logan asked, his gaze holding hers.

"She took dressage lessons while she was in California."

Abby placed a hand on her purse and gripped it tightly in an effort to steady herself.

Logan grunted.

Beth shot him a glare, then said, "Cami's in the other barn with Piper. They're getting Bella ready for Piper's lesson. I'm sure Piper wouldn't mind if she got on Bella afterward, so you can see what she knows, if that's okay with you, Abby?"

"Sure, if you have time in your schedule, that is." She flashed Logan an innocent grin.

The corners of his mouth twitched, but his expression remained neutral. "I'll give her a look-see."

"All right then," Beth said with an approving smile. "Abby and I will watch from the bleachers and check in with you after."

Abby held Logan's gaze for just a moment before she turned and followed Beth out of the barn toward a large outdoor arena. The scent of fresh-cut grass mingled with the earthy aroma of horses and sun-warmed dirt as they approached the riding area. A stand of bleacher seats lined one side of the arena, and they climbed the stairs and sat about halfway up. From there, they had a clear, unobstructed view.

Cami and Piper were already in the arena. Abby smiled at the sight of the two girls laughing and chatting as they led a beautiful chestnut-colored horse around the perimeter. Cami was gesturing animatedly with her free hand while Piper nodded, both of them seeming to have forgotten their initial shyness with each other.

Abby turned to Beth. "I hope it's not an imposition for him to assess Cami's skills," she said, fidgeting with the hem of her dress. "He didn't look too happy about it."

"Oh nonsense, he's just cranky. Been that way since his divorce." She waved her hand dismissively. "He'll be fine with her."

Abby found herself wondering how long ago the divorce had happened and what the story was behind it. Even though people here seemed more open than in New York, she didn't feel comfortable asking about it. Not that it really mattered. They were here for just a few more weeks anyway. She pushed the thought aside.

"Thanks again for setting this up. Cami was so excited I don't think she slept a wink last night."

"Is she doing okay? Poor kid, losing both of her parents at the same time." Beth frowned and shook her head.

"She has her moments." Abby sighed. "I think this will help. The book I'm reading about kids and grief says to keep them busy."

"Good idea. Gives her something to focus on and look forward to." Beth gave a quick glance at the girls, who were now talking with Logan. "The girls seem to be getting along well. You know, if Cami wants, I'm sure Piper would love to hang out with her. Most of her friends are away at summer camp, and she's been pretty lonely."

"That would be great. Cami's friend from California is at camp right now too, and she's missed her. I was hoping she could come for a visit this summer, but nothing has been planned yet."

While Julie and Abby had tentatively planned a visit for after Ava returned from summer camp, it was contingent on how Julie was doing. She'd been struggling with the stronger treatment and wasn't sure if she'd feel up to traveling. Abby had been reluctant to commit to a visit to California too. She was concerned that any progress she'd made with Cami would be derailed if she was back in the same building where she'd lived with her parents.

Abby also worried, though, about how much time Cami spent with just her. The pressure of being the child's sole companion sometimes felt overwhelming, especially when she still wasn't sure how to connect with her. It would be good for Cami to spend time with someone her own age.

"Does Cami like those dreaded video games too?" Beth wrinkled her nose.

Abby laughed. "Yes, she's either playing those or watching cooking shows on TV."

"*Chopped*?"

Abby's eyes widened. "Yes, how did you know?"

"Piper is addicted."

"I'm hoping having the dog now will get her outside a little more," Abby confided.

"You got a dog?"

Abby grimaced. "No, the dog sort of got us." Beth listened attentively as Abby explained how they'd found Chance and ended up taking him home.

"It's so wonderful that you're fostering him," she said. "You must be a nurturer, fostering Cami and a dog."

Abby never thought of herself as a nurturer, but it made her feel good to hear Beth say it. "I'm just trying to help," she said.

"Well, the dog sounds like a real keeper. Piper loves dogs, but Joe, my husband, is allergic. She even tried to persuade him to have allergy shots, but if you want to see a big man faint dead away, just show Joe a needle." She laughed.

"Yeah, my husband was allergic to them too," she said before she could stop herself. She squinted her eyes shut, knowing the question was coming.

"Was? Is he not allergic anymore or not your husband anymore?"

There it is. Abby hesitated, trying to decide how she should answer. How do you explain to someone you've just met that your dead husband had another family? That everything you thought you knew about your life was built on lies?

"You know what?" Beth touched Abby's hand for a

second before continuing. "You don't need to answer that. I can see there's a story there, and I'm just being nosy. Maybe we can talk about it another time. You said you were here for the summer. Where do you live? In California?"

A wave of relief washed over Abby at Beth's insightful change of subject. "No, I'm from New York. Manhattan, actually. Cami lived in California."

"New York." Beth whistled. "I've always wanted to go there, but we've never made it. Is Central Park as big as it looks on TV?"

"Bigger, actually," Abby said.

They chatted about New York and Bluefin Bay while Piper had her lesson. When she was done, Cami climbed onto the horse. True to his word, Logan had Cami take Bella into the arena. Abby knew she could ride from seeing her on their horseback tour of the beach, but watching her effortlessly follow Logan's commands filled her with an unexpected sense of pride. The girl and horse moved as one, and even Piper stared in amazement.

"The girl is a natural on that horse!" Beth exclaimed. "Logan's going to love working with her."

"We don't have a horse, though." Abby wrinkled her brow. "Will we need to get one?" She was still waiting to connect with Benny—his last message had said they needed to talk about her finances—and she hadn't wanted to deal with it. A horse would be expensive. Plus, there was boarding and equipment, and she'd have to figure out what to do with it after the summer. It's not like she could bring a horse to Manhattan. And what if Benny's investigator actually found a relative of Lucy's who was willing to take Cami? He'd said the search was nearly exhausted, but still. She couldn't bear to bring more loss to the little girl.

"Logan can lease one to you," Beth said and turned to look at Abby. "Say, do you read much?"

Abby blinked, taken aback by the sudden change in topic. It had been a long time since anyone had asked her about her interests. Most conversations in her group revolved around the next big event. "I guess I do. Yes," she stammered.

"My girlfriends and I meet once a week for book club. We're meeting this evening. If you don't already have plans, I'd love to have you join us. It's at my house this week, so Piper and Cami can hang out together. You can even bring the dog if you want. Joe won't be back for a couple more weeks, and we'll have the evidence gone by then." She wiggled her eyebrows.

"Yes." Abby smiled. A warm feeling spread through her as she realized how welcome she felt here in this little seaside town. "I would like that very much."

CHAPTER 26

"Oh my gosh!" Piper shrieked. "That's the cutest dog ever!"

Cami beamed as her new friend rushed up to the car to meet them. Abby watched the two girls walk up the sidewalk, their heads practically touching as they fawned over the small dog, and disappear into the two-story colonial-style house. She grabbed the bottle of wine from the backseat—she'd splurged on a good Zweigelt, hoping to make a good impression—and walked to the front door. She hesitated for a moment, trying to settle the butterflies in her stomach. She wasn't sure why it was so important to her that these women liked her. It wasn't like she was staying beyond August, when the lease on the bungalow was up. She took a deep breath, knocked. To her surprise, Colleen opened the door and invited her inside.

"Hi, Abby," she greeted. "We're glad you could make it."

"Hi, Colleen, it's good to see you again." Abby held up the wine. "I wasn't sure what book you were reading, so I brought this instead. I hope that's okay."

"We don't actually talk a lot about the books, but don't

tell anyone." She snickered and motioned for Abby to follow her. "Book club with the girls rolls off the tongue so much smoother than wine drinking with the girls, don't you think?"

Abby laughed and followed Colleen down a short hall into the living room. Beth and two other women were seated on an overstuffed white sofa. Two matching chairs were arranged across from it, with a large whitewashed wood and glass coffee table in between. The room, tastefully decorated in a rustic farmhouse theme, was warm and inviting.

"Hi, Abby." Beth stood and took the bottle of wine Abby held out for her. She glanced at the label and raised her eyebrows. "Fancy! Hey, girls, we're having this first!" She laughed and gestured toward the two women seated on the sofa.

"Abby, let me introduce you. This is Tara Dalton and Diane Holloway," Beth said, then dipped her chin in Colleen's direction. "And Colleen Merritt, I think you two met yesterday at Two Scoops. Girls, this is Abby. She and Piper's friend Cami are visiting Bluefin Bay for the summer."

"Hello," Abby murmured, her fingers fiddling with the slender gold bracelet on her wrist.

"Hi, Abby," Tara and Diane said in unison. Tara sat in the middle of the sofa, and Diane sat next to her on the left. The two women were complete opposites in their appearances. Where Diane was tall and lithe, Tara's feet barely touched the floor, and she had ample curves.

Diane's toffee-brown hair was streaked with caramel highlights and carefully curled and styled. A pair of startling red glasses perched on her thin nose. Bold black eyeliner rimmed her large eyes, and she wore bright red lipstick on her thin lips. She met Abby's gaze with interest, but not judgment, which was a refreshing change. Her friends in New York, even those she'd known the longest, continuously assessed one another for flaws and weaknesses.

"Pop the cork, I'm dry." Tara giggled, holding up her empty wine glass. Her sandy blonde hair was cut into a sleek bob with a side part that curved along her jawline. Her deep-set eyes sparkled with mischief, and a spray of freckles covered her nose and cheeks.

Abby turned to Beth. "Can I help with anything?"

"No, it's a fend-for-yourself situation here." She grinned and walked over to an off-white credenza that held a large charcuterie board, a cheese and cracker tray, several bottles of wine, and a stack of small plates and napkins. "If you like cheese and crackers, you'd better get some now before Tara cleans it out." She tossed a wink at Tara, who broke into a fresh fit of giggles.

"I can't help it." She shrugged. "Cheese and crackers are my kryptonite. It's the only thing that keeps me going between washing soccer uniforms and driving to hockey practice."

"Don't forget the baseball cleats that somehow always smell like they've been marinating in old cheese," Beth added with a laugh.

"And the basketball shoes that I have to keep in the garage because they make my eyes water." Tara giggled.

Abby couldn't help but smile at the good-natured ribbing between the friends. It was obvious that these women were close—not the calculated social connections she was used to, but real friendships. The kind she often saw in movies and wondered if they really existed.

"I picked up a pizza for the girls," Beth said, handing Abby a wine goblet. She grabbed a corkscrew and opened the bottle Abby brought. It was her favorite brand of Austrian Zweigelt, a richly colored red with a deep, bright core of spiced cherry and raspberry flavors. She filled Abby's glass, then refilled her own empty goblet before handing the bottle to Colleen. By the time it made its way to Tara, and she'd refilled her glass, the bottle was empty.

"Another one bites the dust," Tara declared, holding the bottle high in the air before setting it on the coffee table in front of her.

Beth nudged Abby lightly with her elbow and leaned toward her. "She doesn't get out much," she whispered loud enough for Tara to hear.

Tara's infectious laughter filled the room. "It's true," she said, grinning. "Between running after the boys and Matt, wine night out . . . I mean, book club night, is my one luxury."

"Tara has five boys." Beth raised her eyebrows and widened her eyes. "Can you imagine?"

"It's not so bad," Tara shot back. "If you like football, basketball, baseball, hockey, and every other sport you can think of. Oh, and stinky feet."

They all broke out in laughter. Abby sat in one of the large white chairs and felt the muscles in her shoulders relax.

The women pelted Abby with what seemed like an endless barrage of questions about New York City. What is Broadway like? Is the Statue of Liberty really green? Does FAO Schwarz really have the floor piano like in the Tom Hanks movie? Abby didn't mind. She was grateful the topic stayed off the train-wreck that was her personal life. And as she answered their questions, she began to realize that she didn't miss it. Her life in New York. Not the crowded streets, not the social obligations. None of it. The realization was both liberating and unsettling.

Colleen opened another bottle of wine, the women filled their plates with snacks, and conversation turned toward work. Abby learned that Tara was a stay-at-home mom, and Diane was an office manager at the doctor's office in town. Both Colleen and Beth lamented about the lack of good help available these days, and Beth shared that Misty had failed to show up for her shift that afternoon, so would have to be let go.

"It puts me in a real bind, though." Beth shook her head. "The kids all have summer jobs by now, and I haven't had any new applicants."

"Too bad you don't have any nieces or nephews in the area," Colleen said. She came from a large family, and most of the employees at Two Scoops were related to her. "If I have trouble, I just call their parents, and the problem is solved."

The seed of an idea began to form in Abby's mind while she listened. Beth had been so kind to her and Cami, introducing them to friends, helping with riding lessons. Maybe this was a way she could give something back. Plus, the idea of having something meaningful to do each day, a purpose beyond just existing, suddenly seemed very appealing. She'd always dreamed of working in fashion, and while this wasn't quite following that dream, it was something.

But what about Cami? The girl was only eight—it wasn't like she could stay by herself at the bungalow. And they were just starting to build a bond. Would taking time away to work disrupt that progress? Still, the opportunity felt right. "I can help you," she blurted out. "For the rest of the summer, anyway. I don't have any experience, but I can learn, and I'd work cheap."

Beth blinked back at her as if she had misunderstood. She furrowed her brows. "You? Work at Blue Magnolia?"

Abby felt her cheeks grow warm, and she shifted her gaze down to the plate that rested on her lap. Of course, Beth wouldn't be interested in hiring her—she'd never worked a day in her life. What had she been thinking? Plus, what would she do with Cami while she worked?

"Yes, before you change your mind. Yes!" Beth exclaimed, gleefully clapping her hands. "We could work around Cami's riding lessons, and she could hang out with Piper some days.

Or even spend time at the store—I've got that little reading nook in the back where she could stay if needed."

Abby's pulse quickened, and a lightness spread through her chest as she met the other woman's sparkling eyes.

"I told you things would work out." Diane flashed Abby a grateful look and popped an olive into her mouth. "God always provides."

"Amen," Colleen said and waved her hand in the air.

Beth cleared her throat and raised her glass. The rest of the women followed suit. "To new friends." She lifted her glass toward Abby. "And old friends." She waved her glass toward Colleen, Diane, and Tara. "It's not where you are in life but who you have at your side that matters!"

"Cheers!" the women chorused.

As their glasses clinked together, Abby felt something shift inside. All her life, she'd surrounded herself with the "right" people—those who could advance her social standing or Michael's career. But she'd never had friends who would stand by her through the hard times, who would welcome her into their homes and lives without expecting anything in return. Maybe that was what had been missing all along.

Chapter 27

"Did you have fun?" Abby asked Cami as they pulled up in front of the bungalow later that night. It was already dark outside, and Chance had curled up in Cami's lap during the ride, fast asleep.

"Yes, Piper has a new game. It's so much fun," Cami said, gently nudging the small dog awake.

"Good. I'm glad you and Piper seem to get along."

"She's pretty cool." Cami reached for the door handle and slid out of the car, setting Chance on the grass. The night breeze was cool and refreshing, and they stood together in the small yard and waited for Chance to do his business before going inside.

Abby kicked her shoes off at the door and stretched. Cami and Chance padded through the living room and disappeared around the corner. The little dog followed Cami around like a shadow. The words Diane said earlier in the night played through Abby's mind. *God always provides.* Maybe they *were* meant to find the little dog. Cami giggled in her room, and Abby felt grateful that she'd found a friend in Piper. She missed Ava so much, it was good for her to have someone her age to connect with.

Abby padded barefoot into the kitchen, pulled a glass out of the cabinet, and filled it with water. She brought it to the breakfast counter, sat down on one of the stools, and turned on her phone. She checked her email for a message from Julie, but there was nothing.

Her mind wandered to her life in New York, where everything had felt polished on the surface but empty underneath. Even the friends in their circle, she was beginning to see, hadn't been hers at all. Not really. They'd all been carefully selected either by Michael or her mother to serve a specific purpose. Nothing like the eclectic group of women she'd spent the evening with, each with her own unique style and personality. Friends you could count on, not friends who vanished the minute things went sideways.

The back of her throat burned as she remembered that not one of her New York *friends* had called her after Michael was killed. Not one. Only Marcia, Benny's wife, had reached out a few times, and even that had seemed more like an obligation to Benny than genuine concern for her. She couldn't imagine Julie or Beth and her friends abandoning each other that way. They'd all welcomed her into their lives without hesitation, even knowing she was only going to be there temporarily.

Abby lifted her head, scrubbed her hand down her face, and stared into the inky blackness through the window over the sink. Somewhere along the way, she had lost control of her life. Or maybe she never had control in the first place. She'd let fear take root. Fear of standing up for herself, fear of making her own decisions, fear of being herself, and it had plunged down deep, holding on with a death grip. Did she even want to go back to "normal"?

"Abby!" Cami's strangled cry broke through Abby's thoughts. Her stomach clenched at the terror she heard in the child's voice. "Aunt Abby! Come quick!" Cami sobbed from the bedroom.

Abby's heart skipped as she slipped off the stool and sprinted to the girl's room. Cami sat cross-legged on the floor, her eyes so wide Abby could see the whites around her hazel irises. Tears streamed down her face, and Abby's chest tightened as she tried to figure out what had happened. Then she saw it.

Chance was on the floor, nestled between Cami's legs at an awkward angle. His little body was stiff, and his front legs moved in a rhythmic paddling motion. His eyes were open but had a dazed look about them, and his head moved in an erratic, circular motion. She could see his tiny jaw clenching and unclenching. *He's having a seizure.*

"What's wrong with him?" Cami wailed, her breath coming in short gasps. "Make him stop," she cried. "Please make him stop."

Abby dropped to her knees in front of the child and gently put her hands around the middle of the seizing dog, careful to avoid his mouth. "Okay," she said as calmly as she could. "I've got him, get up."

Cami scrambled away and climbed onto her bed. "Don't let him die, Aunt Abby," she sobbed hysterically. "Don't let him die."

Abby felt the burn of tears as they welled in her eyes, and she tried to think. When she went to the girls' academy as a child, one of her fellow classmates had frequent seizures. Some of the other girls made fun of her, but Abby always felt sorry for the girl as she lay helpless on the floor, twitching and writhing. She remembered how the teachers had rushed in, fumbling to help,

Now, with the little dog convulsing at her feet, Abby knelt beside him, keeping her hands lightly on his back so he wouldn't thrash into anything and hurt himself. Several

minutes passed before his body began to relax and the movements slowed and then stopped.

"Is he d-dead?" Cami asked, her voice hoarse and
wavering.

"No, honey." Abby shook her head. "He's just tired.
Come down here and hold him so I can call the vet."

Cami climbed off the bed and cautiously knelt next to
Abby, but made no move to touch the dog. Her eyes were red
and puffy, and the grief Abby saw reflected in them tugged at
her heart.

"What happened to him?" She sniffled. "Why did he do
that?"

"I think he had a seizure."

Cami put her small hands on her face and scrunched her
eyebrows. "What if he . . . What if it happens again? I don't
want him to die."

Abby brushed a stray strand of hair behind Cami's ear. "I
don't want him to die either. If you don't want to hold him,
will you please run and get my phone from the kitchen so I
can call the vet?"

Cami nodded and rose to her feet, wiping her eyes. She ran
out of the room and returned a few seconds later with Abby's
phone. Chance, now alert and happy, wagged his tail frantically when Cami stepped back into the room. He wriggled
from Abby's grip to greet her.

Cami's face lit up. "Look! He's okay! He's okay!" She
handed Abby the phone and sat next to her on the floor.
Chance climbed into her lap. He licked her face with his little
pink tongue and then settled comfortably in the nest Cami
made with her legs. She glanced back up at Abby, concern
etched across her forehead.

"Did I do something wrong to make him have a seizure?"
she asked. Her bottom lip quivered, and she looked back
down. "Me and Piper gave him some pizza," she confessed. "I

know the vet said he shouldn't eat people food. I didn't mean to hurt him." Fresh tears rolled down her face, and she bent over and buried her head in the little dog's neck.

Abby rubbed her hand up and down Cami's back. "You didn't hurt him," she reassured the child. "I promise. Let me call the vet and see what they want us to do." She tapped her screen and brought her phone to her ear, a sudden wave of doubt washing over her. She hadn't expected Cami to bond so deeply with the dog as quickly as she had. What if Chance's real owners showed up now and Cami had to give him back?

She pushed the thought away as the call connected. She had programmed the phone number for the vet clinic, as well as the after-hours emergency number, right after they'd come home with Chance. Now she was glad she'd taken the time to do it. The vet answered almost immediately, and Abby explained what happened.

"What did they say?" Cami asked as soon as the call ended, her eyes searching Abby's for answers.

"They want us to bring him to the clinic in the morning so they can run some tests to make sure he's okay." Abby ruffled the fur on the little dog's head.

"But he'll be okay, right?" Cami stared at Abby as if willing her to heal the dog, her eyes shiny with tears.

The vet had told Abby that seizures were not uncommon in dogs, but there were several different causes. Until they ran blood tests, they wouldn't know the best way to treat him.

"I'm sure he'll be fine. They'll tell us more tomorrow after they examine him. Right now, we all look pretty tired." She glanced down at the dog, who was now dozing in Cami's lap. "Why don't we get ready for bed?"

"But what if he has another one?"

"If he has another one, we'll call the vet again and she'll meet us at the clinic," Abby said. "She said it was unlikely that he would have another one tonight."

"But he still could?" Cami sniffed.

"Let's have faith that he won't."

"I'm scared." Cami's bottom lip quivered. "I don't want him to die too. Can we sleep in your room so we can both watch him?"

Abby gazed at the distressed girl and the tiny little dog in front of her. Warmth spread through her chest, but she resisted the urge to pull the girl into a hug. Her instincts told her that she needed to let Cami come to her, and she was beginning to trust them.

Forty-five minutes later, Abby rolled onto her side. Outside, the night sky was clear, and the moon cast just enough light through the window for her to see. She propped her head on her hand and stared at the two figures who were fast asleep beside her. Cami's dark hair was spread across her pillow, her long eyelashes rested on her cheeks, and soft breaths fell from her slightly parted lips. Her arm was curved protectively around Chance, who sprawled out between them. As Abby watched them sleep, she was filled with the quiet satisfaction that she was exactly where she was meant to be.

Chapter 28

A bby pulled into the parking lot of Seabreeze Ranch a little faster than she should have and checked her watch. She was fifteen minutes late. Again. They'd fallen into somewhat of a routine over the past couple of weeks, but it always seemed like there was a customer at Blue Magnolia that needed help right when she was supposed to leave. While Beth reassured her it was fine to let one of the other clerks handle those customers, Abby didn't want to make anyone feel like they were being brushed off. She'd experienced that too many times in New York.

Abby loved working at Blue Magnolia. She had a knack for designing creative displays, and the customers really seemed to like her and her suggestions. She got along well with the other salesclerks, and she and Beth were becoming close friends. For the first time in her life, Abby felt like she had a purpose beyond just looking good at Michael's side or hosting the perfect dinner party.

She'd also been welcomed as a regular at book club, and she and Cami both looked forward to those evenings with their friends. Abby had laughed when Beth confessed they'd been "reading" the same book for almost two years. Cami had adjusted surprisingly well to Abby's work schedule, often spending time in the store's nook reading and coloring, or playing with Piper when their schedules aligned.

Abby swung her legs out of the car and hurried toward the barn where Scout, the horse they'd leased, was stalled. After dropping Cami off earlier, she'd promised to return on time to pick her up, but the last customer had taken longer than expected. She knew Cami wouldn't be upset about her being late—she loved being around the horses—but Abby didn't want to impose on Logan. Their interactions since their first meeting had been strained at best. He'd been brusque and dismissive with her from the start, making her feel more like an unwelcome intruder than a paying client.

Aside from the usual nickers, foot stomps, and curious glances from the stalled horses as she strode through the center of the barn, it was quiet. Scout's stall was empty, and Abby glanced at her watch again to make sure she hadn't read the time wrong. No, Cami should have been done by now.

Abby made her way to the arena. Cami was astride Scout, and they were gliding across the ring, horse and rider perfectly in tune with one another. She spotted Logan leaning against the railing near the center of the arena. Aside from the day she'd made arrangements for Cami to have lessons and agreed to lease Scout, they hadn't spoken to each other unless it was a quick "hello" or "see you later." She had tried making conversation with him a couple of times, but got the distinct impression he didn't like her much. His curt responses and the way his shoulders tensed whenever she approached made her feel awkward and unwelcome. She hesitated for just a moment before joining him at the rail.

He slid a glance at her and tipped his hat. "New York," he greeted, then turned his attention back to Cami and Scout.

Abby raised an eyebrow but didn't respond. She watched

as Cami approached the first set of verticals at a canter. Abby held her breath as the large bay easily cleared the jump. "Wow," she breathed.

"She's a gifted rider," Logan muttered, not taking his eyes off Cami and Scout.

Abby's heart swelled with pride as she watched Cami and Scout effortlessly clear the rest of the jumps, Cami's helmet bobbing each time they landed. They trotted across the arena and came to a stop on the other side of the fence from them.

"Did you see us, Abby?" Cami's eyes sparkled with joy.

"I did! You were amazing. When did you start jumping?" Abby knew Cami had been trying to talk Logan into letting her jump, but he had balked, wanting to make sure she was ready.

"Today." Cami beamed. "That's why I'm late. Sorry." She shrugged, not looking the tiniest bit sorry.

"That's all right, she was late too," Logan grunted before Abby could reply.

Abby felt her cheeks grow warm, and she clamped her lips into a thin line, not wanting to take away from Cami's moment. Still, she felt a flicker of annoyance at how easily he undermined her in front of Cami, especially when she'd been working so hard to establish boundaries and routines with the little girl.

"You did a good job today, Cami. Take Scout back to the barn, and don't forget to brush him down good," Logan directed, patting Scout on his neck.

"Can't I go one more time? Pleeeease?" Cami pleaded, her voice rising to that particular pitch eight-year-olds had perfected for maximum persuasion.

"Nope, I have another lesson."

Cami stuck out her bottom lip in a dramatic pout. "Fine," she said and made a clicking sound with her mouth. Scout's ears perked up, and they began walking toward the exit.

"I didn't know you were going to start her on jumps," Abby said, wanting to discuss Cami's progress and next steps.

"Neither did I." Logan stepped away from the rail and began walking toward the barns.

Abby followed, frustrated by his dismissive attitude. "Are you sure she's ready?"

Logan stiffened, then turned and frowned at her. "You were watching, right?"

"Well, yes," Abby stammered, instantly feeling foolish for questioning his expertise. Why couldn't he just have a normal conversation with her?

"She's ready." He turned and continued walking, making it clear the discussion was over.

Abby watched his back as he walked away from her. She hurried after him as fast as her heels would allow, catching up to him near the barn door. She needed to talk to him about some upcoming competition Cami had been chattering excitedly about all week. "Logan!"

"What?" he grunted without stopping or looking at her.

She clenched her jaw. "Will you please stop?"

Logan stopped walking but didn't turn around. Abby huffed out a breath and walked around him. She crossed her arms over her chest and stuck out her chin. He met her gaze, annoyance etched on his face.

"You know, you aren't going to keep clients around if you treat them this way," she blurted out.

"Thanks for the business lesson." He continued walking, then stepped into the barn.

Abby huffed out a breath. Something about his attitude just rubbed her the wrong way—maybe because she'd spent too many years letting people dismiss her without standing up for herself. Or maybe it was the inconvenient flutter she felt whenever he did look at her, a reaction she was determined to ignore. She had to make this work, for Cami's sake.

"Logan, wait," she called and walked up to him. "I'm sorry," she said, her tone softening. "It's been a long day. I didn't mean to snap at you."

He raised an eyebrow and gave her a glassy stare. His gaze lingered just long enough to make her pulse quicken, and Abby had to resist the urge to fidget under his scrutiny. She tucked a loose strand of hair behind her ear, suddenly self-conscious.

"Look, I don't know much about horses," she began.

"Obviously." He folded his arms across his chest and leaned back on the heels of his boots.

Abby rubbed the back of her neck and gave a slight shake of her head before she continued. "I know she has a lot of trophies from horse—" She paused as she tried to think of the right word, but it didn't come. "Events." She waved her hand back toward the arena and felt her face and ears grow warm. "Are there events here that she could participate in? She was talking about some competition the other day and I thought maybe . . ." Cami seemed so happy the days she was at the ranch, and Abby wanted to do whatever she could to encourage the girl to pursue her interests.

"There's a regional competition in September," he said, his voice flat. "But you'll be long gone by then." He let his arms fall to his sides and walked away from her.

September. Abby felt a twinge in her chest. Their lease on the bungalow was up at the end of August. She hadn't thought beyond that deadline. She'd been living in this strange limbo where the future didn't exist. Summer people—that's all they were to him. Tourists who'd disappear with the warm weather, not worth investing in. The realization stung more than it should have.

Abby narrowed her eyes at his retreating back. Three months ago, she would have lowered her head and gone home, but not anymore. She had done nothing wrong and didn't deserve to be treated like that. He acted like he couldn't wait to be rid of her and Cami, and after all the progress the little girl had made, that she'd made, it stung. Her chest tightened, and a flicker of anger surged through her. How could he be so oblivious, so... dismissive?

"What's your problem?" She snapped.

He turned and slowly walked back to her, stopping just inches away from her face. Close enough that Abby could smell the faint aroma of sweat and the woodsy scent of his aftershave. Close enough to notice that his blue eyes had flecks of gray in them.

"You're all the same," he said. "You rich, bored city folks come vacation at the beach for the summer and expect to be treated like royalty. You sashay in here with your fancy dresses and your high heels, and you sign your kids up for lessons and then have completely unrealistic expectations of what they can accomplish before the end of the summer. Or you sign them up to simply get them out of your way, and then can't even be bothered to pick them up on time. Then, at the end of the summer, you go back to your big city life and stick your kids in boarding schools, and they won't see a horse again until next summer when you come back expecting the same thing. That"—he poked a finger at her—"is my problem, New York."

Abby's jaw hung open. *So that's why he calls me New York.* She felt a sudden wave of heat rush through her body, and she clenched her fists at her sides. "You know nothing about me or my life! For your information, I was late because I had to finish up with a customer, not because I was having my nails done! Not that it's any of your business." She was yelling at him, but she didn't care. It felt good to speak her mind for a change, to finally push back against someone who had already decided who she was without bothering to get to know her.

"And you don't know anything about that girl"—she pointed toward the stalls—"or what she's been through. You don't care. You saw me come in here and you had your mind made up about me before we'd even talked. That, Mr. Taylor, is called being a hypocrite. Don't worry about looking for any competitions for her." She poked her finger back at him. "I'm sure there are plenty of other ranches that would be happy to help us." She turned on her heel and stomped toward the stall where Cami stared at her, open-mouthed.

"Let's go, Cami," she said, barely slowing down as she passed Scout's stall. Already, guilt was starting to build. She'd let her frustration with Logan override her thinking about what was best for Cami. After weeks of things going so well, of Cami adjusting to their new routine and seeming happy, she might have just ruined it all because she couldn't hold her temper with this . . . this impossible man.

"But . . ." Cami's voice was small and confused.

"We can talk about it in the car. Let's go," she said in a clipped tone, immediately regretting her sharpness. This wasn't Cami's fault.

Cami gave a quick glance at Logan before hurrying after her, her small shoulders slumped. Abby climbed into the car and slammed the door shut. She pressed the button to start the engine and gripped the steering wheel so tight her knuckles turned white. She waited until Cami fastened her seatbelt, then threw the transmission in reverse and backed out of her spot. Cami sat in stunned silence on the short drive back to the bungalow.

Abby was still fuming as they got out of the car. The nerve of that man. Something about Logan just pushed all her buttons, and clearly, she pushed his too. Granted, she could have handled it a little better, but she was tired of having people run her life for her and make assumptions about her. Her only regret was that Cami had been there. Would this derail all the progress they'd made together over the past couple of months? How would this affect Cami's riding lessons? The little girl had been thriving at the ranch, coming out of her shell more every day. Abby hated that her outburst might take that away from her.

"Cami, I'm sorry you had to see that," she said once they were inside the house.

"You ruined it, didn't you?" Cami's mouth twisted and her face turned red.

Abby's mouth went dry. "No, we can find a different ranch."

"I liked *that* one!" Cami shouted. "Piper and Scout are at that one." She pounded her fists on her thighs. "I knew you were going to ruin it," she cried.

"Cami, it's—"

"No! I don't want to hear it!" Cami clamped her hands over her ears. "I knew you would ruin it. First you took me away from Ava and my home, and now you're taking me away from Piper and Scout. You ruin everything! I hate you! I hate you!" She ran through the living room, and seconds later came the all too familiar slam of her bedroom door.

Abby collapsed onto the sofa and bent over, trying to catch her breath. She and Cami had come such a long way in recent weeks, and she'd undone everything in one conversation. She closed her eyes and felt a hot tear escape her eyelashes, followed by a soft plunk as it landed on the floor by her feet. She felt something warm and damp brush against her ankle, and her eyes snapped open. Chance.

The small dog looked up at Abby with dark brown eyes and blinked. He looked confused, and she reached down to pat him on the head. He dodged her hand and ran out of the room, glancing at her over his shoulder. Even the dog was mad at her. A few seconds later, he returned and looked from her to the hall and back. He wanted Cami.

"I'm sorry, little man," Abby said and picked him up. "I think she needs some alone time right now." She planted a kiss on the top of his head and held him close while she cried, but the warmth of his small body against hers was comforting. She gave him another kiss and sniffed, pulling herself back together.

Weeks ago, when no one had claimed the dog, they had officially adopted him, celebrating by making a trip to the pet store. Cami had carefully selected a blue collar, and they'd had a bone-shaped tag engraved with his name and Abby's phone number. The look on Cami's face when they'd fastened it around his neck had been worth every penny.

All of Chance's bloodwork had come back normal, but because of the severity of the seizure, the vet had diagnosed him with idiopathic canine epilepsy. She'd prescribed an anti-seizure medication for the little dog, and Cami had taken it upon herself to make sure he had his two daily doses, right on schedule. She'd even figured out that if she put the capsules in a spoonful of plain yogurt, Chance didn't mind taking them. Cami spent hours researching canine epilepsy and sharing what she'd learned with Abby. Cami and Chance were insepa-rable. She took the little dog with her everywhere but the stables.

The stables. Logan's face flashed through her mind. The jab of his finger, his angry words. Abby felt anger and indig-nation build inside her. She took a deep breath and slowly released it, her fingers softly stroking Chance's wiry fur. She wished she could change how she'd reacted to Logan's words. That's all they were, words. But words had bite sometimes.

She'd been on the receiving end of her mother's irrational accusations her entire life. She should be used to them by now. Her mother would even go so far as to insist that Abby not waste money buying her Christmas gifts, saying that she should just make a donation to whatever the charity of the moment was instead. Then, she'd spend the next month complaining about how ungrateful and selfish her daughter was for not getting her anything.

Since she'd been in Bluefin Bay, away from her mother—away from her old life—Abby was becoming more confident and sure of herself. Just yesterday, Beth had commented on how much more assertive she'd become at the store, confidently helping customers and making decisions without constantly seeking approval. She'd even stood up to a difficult customer the other day—something she would have never done in the past. Maybe that's why Logan's words had affected her so strongly. Regardless, she knew she owed the man—and Cami—an apology, and hopefully he'd agree to let Cami return to the ranch for the few weeks they had left of the summer.

She glanced around the comfortable room she'd begun thinking of as home, and her throat tightened. The thought of returning to New York turned Abby's stomach. She had no desire to return to the sterile, empty apartment she'd shared with Michael, or sit through any more stilted lunch conversations with her uppity friends. More than that, the idea of uprooting Cami again, when she was finally settling in and making friends, seemed cruel. She'd heard nothing from Benny since his investigator had gone down to Mexico. What if no family were found? Could she keep Michael's daughter? Would she?

CHAPTER 29

Michael. Abby hadn't thought about him much since they'd been in Bluefin Bay. Part of that, she knew, was avoidance. If she didn't think about the situation, she didn't have to deal with it. But she had to admit that she didn't really miss him like she thought she would, like a wife ought to miss her husband. Now when she thought about him, the only things she felt were betrayal and anger.

She'd discovered parts of herself that Michael had always discouraged—her desire to work, her creativity with the displays at Blue Magnolia, her newfound love of cooking. He'd always insisted they eat out or have meals catered, dismissing her occasional interest in learning to cook.

"That's what we pay people for, darling," he'd say with his condescending smile. She wondered if that was just another way he'd kept her dependent and diminished. She held up her left hand and stared at the bare finger where her wedding ring used to sit. She couldn't even see the indentation from the band anymore.

A knock at the door interrupted her thoughts, and

Chance scrambled off her lap. He rushed to the door, his tail curled up like a spring, his bark as menacing as a seven-pound dog could muster. She wasn't expecting anyone and glanced at her phone as she stood to see if she'd missed a text or call from Beth. The screen was blank. She slowly turned the handle and opened the door. Logan stood on the porch, his straw cowboy hat in his hands and a sheepish, crooked grin on his face.

Abby's hand tightened on the doorknob. "Logan."

"Hi, Abby," he said, and glanced down at his hat, his fingers aimlessly turning the band. "Mind if I come in for a minute?"

Abby raised her eyebrows. She'd just been thinking about how to approach him to smooth things over for Cami's sake—and there he was on her doorstep. "I—uh, of course, come in," she said, stepping back to let him in.

Logan cleared his throat. "I actually came to apologize."

Abby tilted her head to the side and stared at him for a moment. She decided he looked sincere. He stood just inside the door, and Abby could tell he was uncomfortable. She was suddenly aware of her tear-stained face and the tension that still lingered between them. She padded across the room and perched on the arm of one of the chairs, trying not to notice how handsome he was without his hat covering half his face.

"Chance, that's enough. Stop barking," Abby said, and the small dog became silent and focused on sniffing Logan's boots. Deciding he was perhaps a friend instead of a threat, Chance put his front feet on Logan's legs and gazed up at the tall stranger.

Logan stooped and held his hand in front of Chance's tiny black nose.

"Watch out, he'll take your fingers off if I tell him to," Abby warned, then couldn't help but smile at the absurdity of her tiny dog being threatening. "He's our fierce protector."

Logan chuckled, and the tension in the room eased a bit.

"I can see that," he said, then picked up the small dog, who rewarded him by licking the side of his face. "I think I'm more in danger of being licked to death than having my fingers taken off." His mouth curved into a smile. "But I deserved that."

Despite her lingering frustration, Abby found herself smiling at the sight of this tall, rugged man holding the tiny dog so gently. She met Logan's gaze, waiting to hear what he had to say. For Cami's sake, she hoped they could resolve this.

Logan looked down and shuffled his feet before meeting her gaze again. "I was out of line," he said. "I was reacting to something that had happened earlier and took it out on you. I shouldn't have insulted you. It wasn't fair, and you're right, it's no way to run a business. I'm sorry."

Abby toyed with a lock of her hair while she considered what he'd said. The man did know how to give an apology. She rubbed an itch on the side of her nose and nodded. "I'll accept your apology on one condition."

He quirked a brow. "Oh? What's that?"

"That you accept mine. I shouldn't have said what I said the way I said it." She felt her cheeks flush. "Plus," she hedged, "there might have been some truth behind your words—at one time in my life anyway."

He gave Chance a pat on the head and set him on the floor before closing the distance between them. "Deal." He held his hand out in front of her.

She slipped her hand into his large, calloused one and they shook. They stared at one another for a long, drawn-out moment, and Abby felt a strange warmth beginning to flood her. She averted her gaze and cleared her throat. "So we, uh, I mean Cami, can come back?"

"Yes." Logan rubbed the back of his neck and took a few steps backward. "You, and she, are welcome anytime, and she can finish out her lessons if you still want to bring her."

"She'll be happy to hear that." Abby could feel the tension leaving her shoulders. "Would you like something to drink?" The invitation came naturally. She wanted him to stay—to get to know this side of him.

"Sure, thanks." He set his hat on the arm of the sofa.

She padded into the kitchen, and he followed, sitting on one of the stools at the breakfast bar.

He glanced around the room. "Where's Cami?"

Abby pulled a glass out of the cabinet. "Soda or water?"

"Water is fine."

"She's in her room." Abby added a few ice cubes to the glass, filled it with water, and set it in front of him. "I can tell you she wasn't very happy with me when we got home." She lifted her hands in a helpless gesture, then turned and filled a glass for herself. She leaned against the counter across from him and took a sip of the ice-cold water. "I'm actually glad you stopped by."

Logan leaned forward, resting an elbow on the counter. "That so?"

Abby nodded. "Saved me a trip out to the ranch to grovel." They both laughed. "So tell me what happened earlier that had you so upset."

Logan scrubbed a hand down his face. "It happens every year." He shrugged. "Summer people—tourists—come and expect me to turn their kids into Olympic-level riders before the end of the summer, then want to blame me when they can barely trot."

Abby frowned. "They really do that?"

Logan nodded and took a sip of water. "Yeah, happened right before you got there, which is why I was so angry. The woman couldn't understand why I wouldn't let her child use the jumping course." He shook his head. "She wanted to make a video to show her friends, and apparently, Junior simply walking his horse across the arena wasn't showstopping enough. I tried to explain to her that the child wasn't ready. That it was a safety issue. But she wasn't happy and threatened to sue the ranch for false advertising. So when you showed up late again, I . . ." He trailed off.

"Completely overreacted," she finished for him. That was something her mother would have done—had done—only with Abby, it was with volleyball. When she didn't make the varsity team and was relegated to the junior varsity squad, her mother had pitched such a fit that Abby had quit because she was too embarrassed to face the coach again.

"You okay?" Logan asked.

Abby glanced at him and felt her face flush. *How long have I just been standing here?* "I'm sorry." She gave a slight shake of her head. "What you said brought back a memory, and I guess I was woolgathering."

The door to Cami's room opened, and the girl stepped out and looked at them with an incredulous stare. Abby couldn't have timed her entrance better if she tried, and she let out a long breath.

"Mr. Taylor," Cami said, her eyes wide with surprise. "What are you doing here?"

Logan, who was oblivious to the fit that Cami had thrown earlier, smiled warmly at her. "Hey, Cami, I was just apologizing to your—" He glanced at Abby, who gave him a nearly imperceptible shake of her head. "Uh, Abby."

"She's the one who should apologize," Cami said, her voice small and uncertain as she twisted the hem of her shirt between her fingers.

Heat stained Abby's cheeks as Logan's forehead creased. He threw Abby a confused look, then turned back to Cami. "She did, actually."

Cami's mouth fell open. "She did?"

Logan nodded.

"Does that mean I can still ride Scout?" Cami asked, looking first at Abby, then at Logan.

"I'm sure he'd be upset if you didn't come back," Logan said.

Cami's face brightened, and a smile danced on her lips. "Yay!" She clapped her hands. Chance jumped up and down at her feet, unsure why his person was so happy, but determined not to miss out on the excitement. Cami scooped him up and gave him a quick hug before she lifted him toward Logan. "Did you meet Chance?"

"I did, but not officially." He looked at the dog. "Chance. That's a great name."

"I thought so too." Cami grinned. "Abby, can Logan stay for dinner?"

Abby glanced at the clock. She didn't realize it was so late. She looked at Logan and gave a half shrug. "You're more than welcome to join us if you want."

Logan lifted his hands. "I don't want to impose. I'll just pick something up on the way back to the ranch." He slid off the stool.

Cami's forehead puckered, and she stepped around the counter so she was standing directly in front of him. "You can stay. Abby said you could stay, and I think you should stay. Chance wants you to stay too."

"Well, if Chance thinks I should stay . . ." Logan glanced at Abby and raised his eyebrows.

"Sit back down, cowboy." She laughed.

Abby pulled a wooden cutting board from the cabinet while Cami dragged a chair to the counter to kneel on.

"Can I chop the strawberries?" Cami asked, bouncing slightly on her toes.

"Sure," Abby said, handing her a plastic knife. "Just be careful with your fingers."

Logan sat at the counter and watched as they worked in

surprising harmony. Cami's tongue poked out between her teeth as she concentrated on slicing the berries into perfect pieces.

"This is going to be big salad," Cami announced, glancing at Logan. "It's the best thing we make."

Cami was quite an accomplished cook for her age and took great pride in teaching Abby various cooking techniques. Abby found she rather liked working in the kitchen and enjoyed selecting recipes that were challenging. She and Cami pored over recipes on the internet, along with the ones Julie had sent. Several nights a week, they worked together in the kitchen, creating culinary "masterpieces," as Cami liked to call them.

"Sounds serious," Logan said with a smile.

Abby tossed chunks of rotisserie chicken into a large wooden bowl. "It's become our Friday tradition," she explained, sprinkling feta cheese over the romaine. "Cami's the official berry expert."

"And Abby does the dressing," Cami added, carefully transferring her strawberry slices to the bowl. "You have to put the blueberries in last, or they get squished."

When the salad was assembled—a colorful mountain of greens, berries, chicken, and cheese—Abby drizzled it with raspberry vinaigrette while Cami watched with critical eyes.

"Perfect," Cami declared, carrying silverware to the table with exaggerated care.

Logan took his first bite and closed his eyes. "This might be the best salad I've ever had," he said, his expression genuine.

Cami sat up straighter in her chair, her face glowing with pride.

———

Abby insisted on cleaning up the kitchen herself. She listened with interest while Cami sat on one of the stools and told Logan about her dressage trophies and the stable where she had lessons in Los Angeles. She was surprised to learn that Cami hadn't shared much about her riding experience with Logan during their lessons. Watching her chat animatedly with Logan, Abby couldn't help but feel a surge of pride. The child who had barely spoken when they first arrived was now confidently talking away, building relationships with the adults in her life. It was wonderful to see her coming out of her shell.

Cami told Logan it had been her dad's idea that she take lessons in the first place, which was another side of Michael that Abby didn't know. It was almost like he'd been two entirely different people. How could she not have seen it? She'd gone through it in her head over and over and still came up with nothing. There was an ache in her chest that she didn't think would ever go away.

The strains of a melody Abby couldn't quite place filled the room. "Is that . . .?" She snapped her fingers, trying to pull the name from her memory.

Logan grinned and fished his cell phone out of his pocket. "The theme from *The Magnificent Seven*? Yep." He glanced at the screen. "Sorry, I need to take this. Excuse me for just a minute." He stood and walked into the other room.

"I'm glad he came over." Cami swung her legs back and forth, and there was a look of contentment on her face.

"Me too," Abby agreed, and they exchanged smiles.

Logan stepped back into the room, hat in his hands. "That was my brother, Luke," he said. "There's a problem at the ranch. I need to get going."

Abby frowned as they walked him to the door. "I hope it's nothing serious."

"No, there's a fence down and he needs help getting the cattle back on the right side of it."

"You have cows too?" Cami's eyes grew wide.

"Yep, we sure do. Quite a few of them. Thanks again for the dinner and the company." He placed his hat on his head and looked at Cami. "We'll run the jumping course again next time you're there, all right?"

"Thanks, Mr. Taylor." Cami's mouth curved into a smile.

Abby followed Logan onto the small porch. He turned back, the light casting shadows across his features as he tipped his hat and flashed her a crooked smile. "Have a good night, New York." This time, the nickname sounded almost affectionate.

Abby felt her cheeks tinge pink at the way his eyes lingered on hers, and she returned the smile. "You too, cowboy."

CHAPTER 30

The afternoon sun warmed Abby's shoulders as she reclined in the Adirondack chair on the bungalow's small deck, watching Cami and Chance play in the yard. The little dog darted back and forth across the grass, his tiny legs pumping furiously as Cami tossed a small tennis ball for him to chase. Each time he returned with the ball, Cami would erupt in delighted giggles that made Abby's heart swell.

"Did you see that, Abby? He caught it in the air!" Cami called out, her face flushed with a combination of excitement and heat.

"I saw! He's getting really good at that," Abby replied, smiling at how the girl's entire face lit up with joy.

These peaceful moments had become more frequent over the past week, especially since Logan's visit two days ago. The tension in the bungalow had dissipated, replaced by an easy companionship that surprised Abby. She'd never imagined herself in this role—caring for a child, making a home in a seaside town, working in a small boutique—but somehow, it felt more natural than the carefully curated life she'd left behind in New York.

"Can we go down to the beach?" Cami asked, flopping down on the grass beside Chance, who immediately climbed onto her lap.

"Sure," Abby said, checking her watch. "We have a couple hours before dinner."

Cami jumped up, nearly dislodging the small dog. "Can I bring my shell collection bucket?"

"Of course. And don't forget Chance's leash—we don't want him running after seagulls."

As Cami darted inside to gather their beach things, Abby's phone vibrated in her pocket. Benny's name flashed on the screen, and she felt a familiar knot form in her stomach. She'd been avoiding his calls and emails for the past few days, not ready to hear whatever new revelation about Michael might be waiting. For now, she just wanted to enjoy this fragile peace they'd found. She silenced the phone and slipped it back into her pocket. She'd deal with it later.

———

Their afternoon at the beach had been perfect. They'd collected shells, built a sandcastle that Chance promptly trampled, and waded in the shallows until their toes were numb from the cold water. Afterwards, they stopped at Colleen's ice cream parlor on the boardwalk, where they ran into Beth and Piper.

"You two look like you've had a good day," Beth said, noticing their windblown hair and sun-kissed cheeks.

"The best." Cami grinned, oblivious to the chocolate ice cream dripping down her cone and onto her fingers. "We built this huge sandcastle with two towers, but then Chance ran right through it! He thought he saw a crab hiding in there."

"He was determined to dig it out," Abby said, adjusting the tired dog in her arms where he nestled against her.

"Did you find any cool shells?" Piper asked, pointing to Cami's collection bucket. "I found a perfect spiral one yesterday."

"Yeah! We got tons today!" Cami held up the bucket to show her friend. "Maybe we can trade some tomorrow?"

Piper nodded. "Cool. I'll bring mine."

Beth shifted the rectangular box she was carrying. "We were just picking up an ice cream cake. Joe's back for a few days, so we're having a little celebration tonight."

"That's wonderful," Abby said, understanding all too well what having a husband who frequently worked away from home felt like. "It must be nice having him home."

"Piper's been counting down the days," Beth said with a warm smile. "Speaking of which, we're still on for lunch tomorrow at the café, right?"

"Absolutely," Abby confirmed. "Noon?"

"Perfect." Beth nodded. "Well, we should get this cake home before it melts. See you tomorrow!"

As Beth and Piper walked away, Abby and Cami headed back to the parking lot where they'd left their car for the drive home to the bungalow.

Now, with the dinner dishes cleared, Cami freshly showered and tucked into bed with a book, and Chance snoring softly beside her, Abby finally had a moment to herself. She curled up on the couch with a cup of tea and pulled out her phone. Three missed calls from Benny, and a text asking her to call him back as soon as possible. With a deep breath, she dialed his number.

"Abby, finally," Benny answered on the second ring. "I've been trying to reach you."

"I know, I'm sorry. Things have been . . ." She paused, searching for the right word. "Busy."

"How's it going with the girl?"

"Cami," Abby corrected gently. "Her name is Cami. And it's going well, actually. Really well."

"Good, good," Benny said, though he sounded distracted. "Listen, Abby, that's not why I've been calling."

The knot in her stomach tightened. "What's going on, Benny?" She clutched her mug of tea more tightly, her fingers tensing around the warm ceramic. She didn't know how much more news she could deal with.

"It's your trust account."

Abby's hands started to shake, and she set her tea down on the coffee table before she spilled it. Her grandfather had set up that trust account for her. After she and Michael were married, it seemed natural to let Michael oversee it. He was, after all, a financial advisor—and her husband. Her throat tightened and heat rose from her chest, up her neck, and across her face. How could she have let this happen?

"Abby? Are you there?"

"Y-yes, Benny. I'm here," she murmured. "How bad is it?"

"It's not good. He didn't empty it, there were safeguards built into the trust to prevent that, but there is a substantial loss."

A sharp prickle ran through Abby's fingers. Her chest tightened and hot tears stung her eyes.

"There's more," Benny said.

She squeezed her eyes shut. Who had she been married to?

"There's an active criminal investigation into Michael's business practices."

Her eyes snapped open. Her jaw went slack. "Am I . . . What . . ." Tears spilled down her cheeks, her throat constricted. "W-what does this mean?"

"I'm not done going through everything yet, but I've spoken with the investigator and we're meeting tomorrow."

"Do I need to be there?" Her voice was barely more than a whisper.

"No. Stay there. After I meet with the investigator and get a clearer picture of what we're dealing with, I'll call you back. I just wanted you to know in case you hear anything." He paused for a moment. "Abby, the press picked it up."

The air left Abby's lungs in a whoosh. She felt as though someone had punched her in the stomach. Her mother would have a field day with this. "What am I going to do, Benny? How could I be so stupid?"

"You aren't stupid, Abby. I was friends with him too, and I had no idea about any of this. You trusted him, and you had no reason not to. You can't blame yourself."

"But I should have seen—I don't know. Maybe if I had gone with him to California more often or paid more attention . . ." Her voice cracked and she trailed off.

"Listen to me," Benny said, his voice soft but firm. "This is not your fault."

Abby shook her head, refusing to believe that she didn't have some culpability. She'd spent her entire life blindly doing what everyone told her to do. Maybe if she'd been more independent, or assertive, she would have noticed something, anything. "I was oblivious to everything. Completely oblivious."

"He fooled everyone," Benny reminded her.

"What do I do now?" She hated that she had to ask.

"Just try your best to relax."

Abby snorted. Relax? How was she supposed to relax, knowing her husband had not only been a cheat but also a criminal?

"I know," Benny said. "But there's nothing else you can do right now. I'll be in touch after my meeting with the investigator tomorrow."

"Will I be investigated too?"

"No, I don't think so. Thankfully, it doesn't appear that he used any of your joint accounts, and you clearly had no idea what was going on. Your name isn't on any of the paperwork I've seen. I'll know more tomorrow and can give you a better picture of your finances then."

Abby let out a shaky breath. "Thanks, Benny," she managed, trying to steady herself.

"You're going to be okay, Abby. You're stronger than you think."

"I'm not feeling very strong right now." She half-laughed, half cried, willing herself to hold it together.

"It's there," Benny said gently. "I've known you for a long time. You'll be just fine."

"Thanks, I don't know what I would do without you."

"I'm more than happy to help," he said. "Oh, and the private investigator is still looking for any of Cami's relatives, but so far hasn't found anything promising. And Marcia wanted me to tell you you're supposed to let her know if you need anything."

"Tell her thank you. That's very kind of her. I'll keep that in mind." Abby always had the impression that Marcia didn't care for Michael and only socialized with them as a favor to her husband. Maybe that would change now that Michael was gone. Abby had a feeling a lot of things would change now that Michael was gone.

"I'll call you tomorrow," Benny promised, then ended the call.

Abby sat for a long while in stunned silence. Everything just seemed so surreal. She glanced around the brightly decorated room and felt like she was living someone else's life. Or maybe it was more like starting a new one.

"Who was that?" Cami's sleepy voice interrupted her thoughts. Abby turned to see the little girl standing in the hallway, her pink pajamas rumpled and her hair slightly mussed. She clutched an empty water glass in one hand while rubbing her eye with the other.

"I thought you were asleep," Abby said gently, trying to mask the panic she felt. How much had Cami overheard?

"I got thirsty." Cami padded across the room in her bare feet. "Was that your lawyer again?"

"Mmm hmm."

"What did he want? He sure calls a lot."

Abby hesitated, unsure how much to share with the child. She didn't want to taint Cami's memory of her father, but she also didn't want to add more lies to the already complicated situation. "Some financial stuff I need to figure out," she said carefully.

Cami yawned and settled on the far end of the couch, tucking her feet underneath her. "Is it bad?"

Abby sighed. "It's complicated. But we're going to be okay."

"Promise?" Cami's voice was small.

"I promise," Abby said, surprised by how much she meant it. Despite everything—the dwindling funds, the investigation, the uncertainty of her future . . . their future—she felt strangely determined. They would be okay.

Cami scooted closer on the couch. "Today was fun," she said. "Can we go to the stables tomorrow? Mr. Taylor said we could try a new jump."

Logan. The thought of seeing him brought an unexpected flutter to Abby's stomach that she quickly tried to dismiss. "Of course," she said. "We're meeting Beth and Piper for lunch at the café at noon, remember? We can go to the stables after that. And maybe we can stop by Blue Magnolia afterward. Beth has a new shipment of those hair clips you liked."

Cami's face brightened. "The butterfly ones?"

"Those are the ones."

"Cool." Cami yawned and leaned her head against Abby's shoulder. "I like it here," she said softly. "I don't want summer to end."

Abby rested her cheek against the top of Cami's head, breathing in the scent of her strawberry shampoo. "Me neither," she whispered, realizing how much she meant it.

Their lease ended in August, but not for the first time, Abby found herself wondering if they might stay longer. The thought of returning to New York—to the sterile, empty apartment, the whispers and stares, the reminders of Michael—made her stomach churn. They'd found peace here. Happiness.

Cami's breathing had deepened, and Abby realized she'd fallen asleep. Carefully, she shifted to look at the girl's face, peaceful in sleep, long eyelashes fanned against her cheeks. Something fierce and protective welled up in Abby's chest, catching her off guard with its intensity. This child—who'd been thrust into her life through the most unimaginable circumstances—had somehow worked her way into Abby's heart. The realization both terrified and exhilarated her.

"We're going to be okay," she whispered again, more to herself than to the sleeping girl. Maybe it was time to stop avoiding the hard decisions and start figuring out what their future might look like. With no relatives of Cami's being found, she needed to seriously consider what was next.

CHAPTER 31

"Cami, you about ready to go?" Abby called from her room. She checked herself one last time in the dresser mirror before grabbing a thin gold bangle and slipping it on her wrist. Beth had been right. The sand-colored capris paired perfectly with the simple, pale blue blouse she wore.

She glanced at her watch. They were supposed to meet Beth and Piper for lunch, and Cami wanted to stop at the tack store in nearby Swansboro first. They hadn't packed any of Cami's riding clothes when they left New York, and she wanted a pair of jodhpurs. Abby wasn't sure what those were, but Cami explained they were the short riding pants she'd seen Piper wear at her lessons.

"Cami?" Abby called again, stepping into the hallway. The bathroom door was still closed and there was no response. She'd been in there for quite a while, and it wasn't like her to not answer. Frowning, Abby approached the door and knocked lightly. "Cami, is everything okay?" Concern quickly turned to panic as she heard the muffled sound of crying from inside the room. She twisted the knob and exhaled in relief when it turned and the door swung open.

Cami stood at the sink, holding a pair of scissors, staring at her reflection in the mirror with a mixture of horror and regret while tears flowed freely down her cheeks. Chunks of long, dark hair lay in a pile on the rug around her bare feet, and what was left framed her delicate features in a short, uneven bob. Abby sucked in a breath and cupped her mouth with her hands. In the mirror, Cami's eyes met hers, and the scissors fell out of her hand onto the floor. She covered her face with her hands.

"I'm sorry," she sobbed, her body trembling.

Abby's heart ached, and she pulled Cami into her arms and let her cry. Abby could feel the pain in her sobs, and her own eyes filled with tears. She held her until the sobs subsided, then pulled a couple of tissues out of the box on the bathroom counter and led Cami into her room. Soft pastel walls were dotted with seashell decals, and the quilted bedspread was patterned with tiny shells in soft blues and pinks. They sat on the bed, and Abby handed her a tissue. Cami's breath hitched as she tried to stop crying.

"I'm sorry." She sniffed, looking at Abby, her eyes red and puffy.

Abby put her hand on Cami's arm and gave her a light squeeze. "Shh, no more apologies, sweetie. Tell me what happened."

Cami closed her eyes and took several deep breaths before opening them again. She entwined her fingers with Abby's and stared at their hands. "I . . . I wanted to French braid my hair," she said and sucked in a few short breaths. "My m-mom always braided my hair like that for . . . for r-riding."

Tears streamed down Cami's cheeks, and Abby pressed her lips together as the back of her throat began to sting.

"But—but I couldn't do it." Cami's face crumpled, and she began to cry again. Abby wrapped her arm around the girl's slim shoulders and pulled her close.

"So I got mad and I—" She sniffed and wiped her nose. "I cut it off." She sobbed for a few minutes, then looked at Abby. The sadness and pain in her eyes were almost more than Abby could bear.

"It made me so angry! It's not fair! She's never going to be able to do my hair again." She buried her head in Abby's shoulder and wailed.

Abby held her tightly, tears streaming down her own cheeks as she murmured into the little girl's hair. "I'm so sorry, honey. I'm so sorry."

Cami pulled back and looked up, tears drenching her dark eyelashes. "I'm never going to see her again. What if . . . what if I forget her?"

Abby felt an ache in her throat and hugged Cami close, planting a kiss on her temple. "You won't. Not ever."

"But how do you know?" She sniffed.

"She made you, and that means you carry a part of her with you always."

"Really?"

"Really. And Cami? Remember what we talked about before? I'll never try to replace your mom. But I want you to talk about her all the time. Tell me stories about her, what she liked, what made her laugh. That way, we keep her memory alive."

Cami wiped her eyes with the back of her hand. "You won't mind?"

"Of course not. And you can talk about your dad too," Abby added. Whatever Michael was or did, he seemed to have genuinely loved and cared for this little girl. Even knowing how complicated her feelings about Michael were, she needed to set those aside and focus on Cami. "And if you ever want to talk to someone else about her too, like a counselor, we can find someone. Sometimes it helps to have different people to talk to."

Cami threw her arms around Abby's neck and hugged her tight. "Thank you, Aunt Abby."

Abby's eyes burned, and she tried to swallow the lump in the back of her throat as she hugged the girl back. *No, thank you.*

———

Abby slipped into the bathroom and grabbed her phone. She sent a quick text to Beth.

> Minor emergency. Can we bring lunch to your place at 1 instead of meeting at café? Will explain when we get there. Nothing serious, promise.

> Of course! Hope everything's OK. See you then.

Next, Abby called Tangled, a highly rated salon located near the tack shop, and explained the situation to the receptionist. She promised to fit Cami in as soon as they were able to get there. Satisfied she was handling the situation as well as any parent could, Abby returned to her room.

Cami sat hunched on the edge of her bed, fingers nervously touching the uneven ends of her newly shortened hair. "I can't go out like this," she whispered, fresh tears threatening to spill.

"I have an idea," Abby said gently, kneeling in front of her. "I found a salon near the tack shop that said they could fit you in. They could even it out, make it look intentional."

Cami looked up hesitantly. "Do you really think they could fix it?"

"I do." Abby nodded, offering her hand. "And I bet you'll look absolutely adorable with a proper bob. What do you say? Ready for an adventure?"

After a moment's consideration, Cami took Abby's hand and stood up. "Okay," she said quietly. "But can I wear my baseball cap until it's fixed?"

"Absolutely." Abby got up and retrieved a bright purple cap with rainbow sequins from the hook on the closet door where Cami had left it the day before.

––––––––

When they arrived at Tangled, the receptionist greeted them warmly. As they settled into the waiting area, Cami fidgeted nervously with the hem of her T-shirt.

"What if they can't fix it?" she whispered.

Abby squeezed her hand. "They will. And you know what? I think I'm going to get my hair cut too."

Cami's head jerked up, her eyes round. "Really? But your hair is so pretty!"

"The heat and humidity here are making it so frizzy," Abby said, tugging at a long curl. "I've never had short hair before." Her mother and Michael had always insisted she keep it long. Michael had once told her that men preferred women with long hair, and somehow that had become an unspoken rule in their marriage.

"You'd really do that?" Cami asked incredulously. "For me?"

Abby smiled and tucked a piece of Cami's uneven hair behind her ear. "Us girls need to stick together, right?"

An hour later, they stepped out of the salon, both sporting fresh new hairstyles. Abby loved her shoulder-length, layered bob, and thought Cami looked adorable in her short pixie cut. It framed her heart-shaped face perfectly. After a quick stop at the tack shop, they picked up takeout and brought it to Beth's house.

"Oh my goodness, look at you two with your new hair!" Beth exclaimed as she ushered them inside. "I was wondering what your emergency was this morning."

Cami glanced at Abby with wide, scared eyes. Abby smiled reassuringly at her. She'd promised not to say anything about the incident in front of Piper.

"We decided to have an impromptu makeover before we went to the tack shop." Abby gave Cami a wink.

Relief washed over the girl's face, and she smiled gratefully at Abby.

"Oh my gosh," Piper squealed, running up to Cami and touching her short locks. "I love your hair!"

Cami's cheeks tinged pink, but her eyes sparkled. "Thanks." She self-consciously brought her hand up and touched the tapered back. "You don't think it's too short?"

"No! It's amazing!" Piper turned to Beth. "Can I get mine cut too?"

Beth rolled her eyes and winked at Abby. "Monkey see, monkey do." She tugged playfully on one of Piper's braided pigtails. "If you still want to have it cut tomorrow, then yes."

"Yes! Thanks, Mom. Can we eat in my room? I promise we won't make a mess."

Beth hesitated.

"Please, Mom." Piper folded her hands into a steeple and batted her eyelashes at her mother.

Abby bit her lip to keep from laughing. It was comforting to see that Beth struggled with boundaries too.

Beth leaned toward Abby and whispered loudly. "See what I have to put up with?" She turned to Piper. "I suppose," she said. "Not one crumb on the floor, though. Chance isn't here to clean up after you this time." Her expression was stern, but her eyes twinkled.

The girls rummaged through the take-out bags and took what they wanted, then walked out of the room with their arms full.

"Did your mom call us monkeys?" Abby heard Cami ask Piper as they disappeared down the hall.

CHAPTER 32

Abby and Beth made eye contact and burst out laughing. Beth took what was left in the take-out bag and Abby followed her into the living room. They divided up the food and sat next to each other on the sofa.

"I hope you don't mind burgers. It's been a bit of a rough morning." She held up a cheeseburger. "And this was the first place we passed on the way here that Cami approved of."

Beth took a bite of her burger and nodded. "Been there," she said around her mouthful of food.

Abby pulled a fry out of its carton and took a bite, chewing thoughtfully. While she'd only known Beth a short while, they had spent a lot of time together, here at Beth's house, at Blue Magnolia, and with Colleen, Tara, and Diane on book club nights. She felt closer to Beth in that short amount of time than any of her New York friends, and she'd known most of them for years. Beth seemed like someone she could actually open up to about everything.

"What's on your mind, Abby?" Beth asked. "You look like you're a million miles away."

Abby focused her gaze on Beth and set the carton of fries on the coffee table. She let out a long breath. "I don't know what I'm going to do about Cami." She pulled up her knees and wrapped her arms around them.

"What's wrong with Cami? Is she in some sort of trouble? I heard you and Logan had words in the barn the other day. Is there trouble there?"

Abby's eyebrows shot up. "How did you hear about that? Did he tell you?" Had Logan been talking about her around town? Just when she thought they'd smoothed things over . . .

Beth shook her head. "Small town. The locals know pretty much everything that goes on. I also heard he was at your place later that night." She wiggled her eyebrows. "For several hours."

Abby's cheeks grew warm. "It wasn't a big deal. We had a misunderstanding, and he came over to apologize."

Beth raised her eyebrows. "He apologized? Whoa, that's not like Logan to go out of his way to do that. Must have been some apology if he was there half the night."

Abby gave Beth's shoulder a playful shove. "He wasn't there half the night, Miss Nosy. Cami talked him into having supper with us, then he left. It really wasn't a big deal."

"He's single, you know." She slid Abby a knowing glance.

Abby felt her cheeks flame. The thought of dating again made her stomach flutter. She'd been with Michael since she was nineteen—what did she know about flirting or dating as an adult? The idea was terrifying. "It doesn't matter, and even if it did, there's no way he'd . . ." Abby rubbed her forehead, blew out her cheeks, and hugged her legs closer. "Besides, we have to go back, so . . ." Abby knew she wasn't making any sense. She was full of so many conflicting emotions, she couldn't think straight, let alone form a coherent sentence. "It's complicated." She put her forehead on her knees and drew in a deep breath, trying to collect her thoughts.

Beth slid closer and rested her hand on Abby's arm. "Abby, what's going on? What's wrong?"

Abby picked up her head and met Beth's clear blue eyes. "Do you remember when you asked me if I was married?"

Beth nodded. "Yes."

"Well, I am. I mean, I was. I'm not—" Abby shook her head and sighed. "I'm a widow."

Beth gasped. "Oh, Abby, I'm so sorry." She rubbed Abby's arm. "When?"

"It's not like that, though." Abby frowned, and before she knew it, the entire story tumbled out. All of it. The call about Michael's accident and then his death, discovering his double life, the other wife, Cami, the guardianship, Julie and Ava, the financial troubles, everything.

"And the worst part is . . ." Abby glanced down the hall, making sure there was no sign of the girls before she continued. "Cami thinks I'm her aunt," Abby confessed, her voice low. "Michael told her I was his sister. Julie thought it was better to let her believe that, but now I don't know how to tell her the truth. It's been so hard because I don't want to continue to lie to her, but I don't know what to do. She's already lost so much." It felt like a dam breaking, the words pouring out in a rush of relief. She hadn't realized how much she'd been holding in until that moment.

Beth stared at her in shocked silence, and the longer it stretched, the more Abby's stomach twisted. She bit her lip. Maybe she'd shared too much.

"Wait—so Michael had a whole secret family, and when he died, you just . . . took in his daughter with another woman?" Beth finally asked, her voice a mix of disbelief and admiration. She reached for Abby's hand. "That's . . . I don't even know what to say. I can't imagine being in your position. No wonder you've been struggling."

Relief washed over Abby as she nodded. "I said I would

keep her until they could locate any family, but they haven't found anyone. Her mother was from Mexico, and they haven't been able to track down any relatives there. It's been nearly three months now."

"You're a much bigger person than I am." Beth sniffed, wiping under her eyes with her fingers. "If I found out Joe had a child with someone else? I honestly don't think I could handle it the way you have."

"If you would have asked me that a year ago, I would have said the same thing, but . . ." Abby paused and squinted her eyes while she thought. "I don't know, Beth. There's just something about her. She didn't ask for this any more than I did. She's as much a victim in all this as I am, probably more—she lost her mom too. And honestly, I think she's the only truly good thing Michael ever created—the only part of him worth saving." She gave a sad smile. "Sometimes I look at her and wonder if maybe this was his one honest relationship, the one place he wasn't living a lie."

"What are you going to do?"

"I don't know. The lease on the bungalow is up in two weeks." She felt her lips tremble, and a tear escaped from the corner of her eye and ran down her face. She thought about what Benny had told her the night before about Michael's finances and the ongoing investigation. "The more I think about going back to New York, the less I want to. It doesn't feel like home anymore. It feels . . . contaminated by everything Michael did. But here . . ." She gestured vaguely around her. "Here—in Bluefin Bay—I feel like I can breathe again." Abby's pulse quickened as an idea sparked to life, and she looked at Beth. "Will you still need help at the Blue Magnolia after the summer people leave?"

Beth furrowed her brows. "Yes. You'll be gone, and the other girls will have to go back to school."

Abby straightened her legs and grasped Beth's hands. "What if I didn't go back to New York?"

Beth's eyes widened, and the corners of her mouth curved into a smile. "Are you serious? Because I'd say you have a job as long as you want one! You're really thinking about staying?"

Abby ran her hands through her hair, loving the feel of the shorter style. She'd made so many changes since she'd been here, she didn't fit in New York anymore. *They* didn't fit there. "I think I need to stay." She met Beth's eyes and allowed herself a hopeful smile. "I'm going to try."

"I'm so excited!" Beth flew off the sofa and jumped up and down before throwing her arms around Abby with such force she nearly knocked her off the sofa. Beth pulled back, a line etched between her brows. "Wait—what about Cami? If they don't find any family—would you keep her? You know, permanently?"

Permanently. Abby let the word sink in. She'd been afraid to let herself think too much about keeping Cami, especially with the private investigator still searching. But it had been on her mind, especially since Benny's call the night before. They'd been through so much and come such a long way over the past few months. At this point, the thought of Cami being taken out of her life was . . . unbearable.

"Yes," she said, her voice trembling. "I would." The words felt good coming out of her mouth.

"It's obvious you love the girl."

Beth's face blurred as Abby's eyes filled with tears. "I do. I really do."

Beth clapped her hands together, and her eyes sparkled with excitement. "We need to find you a house!"

Abby laughed and leaned into the back of the sofa. She reached for Beth's hand and gave it a squeeze. "Thank you, Beth."

Beth's face reddened for just a moment. "Thank you! I

need you at the Blue Magnolia." She glanced down at their entwined hands. "Besides, I've kind of gotten used to having you around."

Abby's heart felt full. She gave Beth's hand another squeeze. "Me too. It's nice to have someone I can really talk to."

"Oh my gosh, I just realized that means Piper and Cami will be in the same class," Beth exclaimed. "I can't wait to tell her. She's going to be so excited!"

Abby held up her hand and shook her head. "Don't say anything yet, please."

Beth frowned. "Why not?"

"I need to talk to my lawyer first and make sure I can do this. I don't want to say anything to Cami until I know for sure that she can stay with me."

Beth squeezed her eyes shut, wrinkled her nose, and did a little excited wiggle. "Okay, I'll wait, but it's going to be hard. I'm so excited, Abby!" She paused and her smile faded. "But what about the whole 'aunt' thing? I mean, if you're going to keep her permanently, how are you ever going to tell her you're not really her aunt?"

"I honestly don't know," Abby sighed, rubbing her temples. "I've been tying myself in knots about it for months. I'm just . . . terrified it will destroy everything we've built. She's already lost so much—her mom, her dad, her home. Finding out I'm not who she thinks I am . . ." She shook her head, words failing her.

"That's really tough. Maybe with a counselor?" Beth suggested, her voice gentle. "Someone who specializes in kids, who could help guide that conversation?"

"That's . . . actually a really good idea." Abby nodded slowly. "I just know I can't keep living with this lie between us forever. It's eating me up."

A sudden patter of footsteps interrupted them, and Abby

quickly wiped her eyes as Piper appeared in the doorway, her head tilted with curiosity.

"Mom, where's Cami?" Piper asked, looking between the two women.

Beth frowned. "Isn't she upstairs with you?"

"No." Piper shook her head. "She came downstairs to get a napkin like ten minutes ago, but she never came back up."

Abby and Beth looked at each other, horror dawning on them simultaneously. Abby felt the blood drain from her face as her stomach plummeted. Her hand flew to her mouth, her whisper barely audible. "No."

CHAPTER 33

"Oh no, Abby," Beth whispered as she gripped Abby's wrist. "When we were talking . . . She must have heard all of it." She glanced anxiously toward the hallway. "We need to find her. Now."

"Piper, did you check the backyard?" Beth asked, already moving toward the front door.

"No, but I don't think—"

"Stay here in case she comes back," Beth instructed her daughter. To Abby, she said, "She couldn't have gone far."

"What if she . . ." Abby broke off, unable to continue. Her breath was coming in short gasps, and her throat felt as though it was closing.

"Abby, don't worry. We'll find her." Beth grabbed her upper arms.

Abby struggled for air.

"Look at me," Beth demanded, giving Abby a little shake and holding her gaze. "We will find her. She needs you."

That snapped Abby back into the moment. They ran outside. The clear summer day had vanished. Dark clouds had gathered overhead, the air thick with the scent of an approaching storm. A rumble of thunder rolled in the distance. The wind picked up, sending leaves swirling across the lawn.

Abby scanned both sides of the street, heart pounding, but Cami was nowhere in sight. "I don't see her."

"She might have headed for the beach," Beth suggested, pointing toward the path that cut through the dunes.

"Let's go!" Abby shouted, and the two women ran behind the house and hurried toward the beach path. Abby's heart pounded and her lungs constricted with every step.

Once they cleared the dune, the beach stretched out before them, nearly empty as other beachgoers had fled from the approaching storm. The two friends stood at the edge of the sand, scanning the coastline for any sign of the girl. The wind churned up the water, sending enormous waves crashing onto the shore.

If Cami had tried to go into the water, she'd have been swept away in an instant! Abby frantically grabbed Beth's arm. "What if we don't find her?"

"We will," Beth reassured her. "God didn't bring the two of you this far to separate you now."

A violet light flashed across the sky, followed by a loud clap of thunder. The air felt charged, and a drop of rain hit Abby's arm. She closed her eyes. *Please, God, I know I have no right to ask, but please show me where to look. Please help me find her.* A strange sense of calm washed over her as the rain began to fall in earnest. She turned to Beth. "Get some towels and a blanket."

Beth nodded and turned back to the house.

The first heavy raindrops began to fall as they separated. What had Cami overheard exactly? Had she learned the truth about who Abby really was? The thought made Abby's heart clench with fear. The wind picked up as Abby made her way along the dunes, sending sand swirling around her ankles.

"Cami!" she called out, her voice barely carrying over the growing roar of the wind and waves. "Cami, where are you?" Abby ran along the dunes toward the pier. The rain now fell in sheets. She could hardly see where she was going, but still she ran. Her toe caught on a clump of beach grass, and she fell hard on her knees. Heart hammering, she scrambled upright and kept going. "Cami!" she screamed over the noise of the storm. Thunder rolled overhead, mixing with the relentless roar of the ocean, and she strained every sense for any sign of the little girl. Every step was a fight against the wind, every heartbeat a plea that Cami would be found safe.

Then she heard it. The faintest cry of a child. Abby peered through the pelting rain, trying to pinpoint the direction the sound came from. There it was again, faint but unmistakable. She stumbled through the wet sand, calling, "Cami!" Finally, she crested a dune. There, huddled at the bottom, was Cami. Her arms were wrapped around her knees, and she was pressed against a clump of grass.

"Cami!" she shouted and raced down the dune toward the girl. Her legs felt like gelatin, and she nearly fell again.

Cami lifted her head, and her eyes grew wide as she scrambled to her feet and stumbled through the wet sand toward Abby. She barreled into Abby with such force, she knocked them both off balance, and they tumbled to the ground, clinging to each other in a desperate, trembling hug.

Abby pulled her upright, tears mingling with the rain on her cheeks. Both of them were crying, trying to talk at the same time until Abby lifted her hand, forcing a shaky breath.

"Slow down, sweetheart. Are you hurt?" She looked her up and down, searching for blood, bruises, anything, but saw nothing obvious. She said a quick prayer of thanks.

Cami shook her head. "I'm scared," she cried, her body trembling. "I got turned around, and then it started to rain, and I couldn't see anything." A clap of thunder sounded overhead, and Cami jumped. She was shaking, and her lips had taken on a blue hue.

Abby took Cami's hand. "Come on, let's get you back to Beth's. We need to warm you up." They started to walk back the way she'd come, but Cami stumbled back a step, digging her heels into the sand.

"No. You lied to me," Cami shouted, her voice breaking.

Abby froze. Rain pelted her face as guilt washed over her. How much had Cami heard? Her stomach twisted. "Cami, please. Let me explain."

"I thought Mommy was Daddy's wife," Cami continued, her voice rising with confusion and distress. "But Beth said you were his wife too. How could Daddy have two wives? That doesn't make sense!"

"I don't understand it either, sweetheart," she said softly. Rain streamed down her face, mingling with her tears. "Your father made some very complicated, and very wrong, choices. He kept secrets from all of us—from your mom, from me, even from you. I only found out about all of it after the accident."

"Why did he do it?" Cami's breath hitched, her words tumbling out in a sob. "Why did Daddy lie to everyone?"

The million-dollar question. Abby swallowed hard. "I don't know, Cami. I wish I did."

"But why didn't you stop him?" she cried. "Why did you stay with him? He was my dad, and he loved my mom. Why would you do that?"

"I didn't know," she said simply.

Cami blinked and her brow furrowed. "What do you mean, you didn't know? How could you not know?"

Abby shook her head. "I didn't know about you or your mom until the hospital called me after the accident, I promise."

"But you were in our house."

"I was," Abby agreed. "Your address was on the paperwork from the hospital, and they gave me your dad's keys. At the hospital, they told me your mom had been in the accident too, but they kept calling her his wife, and I was so confused because I was his wife, and I wasn't in that car. So I went to the address on the paperwork, your house, to find answers. That's when I found out about you."

"You really didn't know?"

"I really didn't know."

Cami studied her through wet lashes, suspicion clouding her young face.

"Did you or your mom know about me?" Abby asked gently. She didn't want to upset her even more, but the truth mattered.

Cami chewed her lip while she thought, then shook her head, her gaze dropped to the sand. "I don't think so. I didn't. I think my mom would have been really mad."

Abby nodded, her throat tight, as the rain poured down around them. Thunder cracked overhead, sharp and sudden, and Cami flinched.

"So Mommy wasn't really married to Daddy?" Cami's lower lip trembled.

"I don't know all the details, sweetheart," Abby said gently. "But I do know your dad loved you very much."

"Then why did he tell me you were my aunt when you weren't?"

The question struck Abby silent for a moment. How could she explain Michael's deception in a way an eight-year-old could understand when she barely understood it herself? She whispered a quick prayer for wisdom, asking God to give her the right words to comfort the little girl. "I think . . ." Abby paused, choosing her words carefully. "Sometimes grown-ups make really big mistakes. Your dad made a mistake by not telling the truth." Another crack of thunder boomed overhead, and they both jumped.

"We need to get out of this rain," Abby said and reached out her hand. "Please, Cami. Come back with me."

Cami hesitated. "Are you going to send me away now? To those foster people?"

Abby dropped to her knees in front of Cami. "No, no, sweet girl," she said, but Cami wouldn't look at her. She gently cupped Cami's chin and raised it until their eyes met. "I'm not sending you to foster care."

"But I heard you and Beth talking. You said—"

"If you heard everything, then you know I told Beth I don't want you to go to foster care, Cami. I want you to stay with me."

"You really want me? For keeps?" Cami asked, her voice barely audible over the storm.

"Yes, I do," Abby assured her. "More than anything. If you want to stay with me, that is."

"Forever?"

"Forever."

Cami was quiet for a moment, her eyes searching Abby's face. Then she stepped forward and wrapped her arms around Abby's neck, burying her face in her shoulder. "I want to stay with you too," she whispered.

Abby held her close, relief washing over her. "No more secrets, okay? From now on, we tell each other everything."

Cami nodded against her shoulder. Another flash of lightning illuminated the sky, followed by thunder that seemed to shake the ground beneath them.

"Let's get home," Abby said, standing and keeping an arm around Cami's shoulders.

As they turned toward the dunes, they saw Beth hurrying toward them, a large umbrella in one hand and towels in the other.

"Thank goodness!" Beth called out, her face breaking into a relieved smile. She rushed forward, draping a large towel around Cami's shoulders and another around Abby. "I was so worried!"

"We're okay now," Abby said, giving Beth a grateful smile.

As they walked back through the rain, Cami slipped her hand into Abby's. They were going to be okay.

CHAPTER 34

Abby woke early the next morning and sat at the breakfast counter, sipping coffee. She sent a quick text to Benny, asking him to contact her when he had time, then opened her laptop and began browsing real estate websites to see what houses were available for sale in Bluefin Bay. A warm lightness filled her chest, along with a confidence that she had never known before. She was doing what *she* wanted for the first time in her life. And it felt good.

She was refilling her coffee when her phone rang. Benny's name flashed across the screen.

"Hi, Benny," she greeted him warmly. "It's kind of early to be returning phone calls, isn't it?"

"Not when my favorite client texts me at the crack of dawn asking me to call her."

Abby laughed. "Touché."

Benny chuckled on the other end. "You have good timing. I actually needed to talk to you, anyway. But first, what can I do for you?"

"Well, you're not going to believe this, but I've decided to stay in Bluefin Bay."

"You seem to have really enjoyed your summer there. How much longer are you going to stay?"

Abby hesitated for a second before answering; she didn't want him to try to talk her out of this. "Permanently."

There was a brief silence on the other end, and Abby held her breath while she waited for Benny's response.

"I think that's wonderful, Abby," he finally said. The sincerity in his voice brought tears to her eyes.

"Thank you, Benny. I really like it here, and Blue Magnolia is going to take me on full time."

"I'm so happy for you. What does your mother think of this?"

Abby cleared her throat. "She hasn't returned any of my messages."

"Probably for the best," Benny said. "Sometimes we have to distance ourselves to save ourselves."

"Wow, Benny, that's pretty deep," she teased, but the words resonated in her soul.

"Thanks. I saw it on a coffee mug," he admitted, and they both laughed. "What are you going to do with your apartment here?"

"I'm not sure. I guess I'll have to go back and go through everything." She sighed. It was not a chore she was looking forward to. "I don't know that I'll keep much. I'm planning to sell it. That will help with the finances."

"That's a good idea. Let me know if you need any help."

"I will. Thank you, Benny. You've been a great friend. I appreciate you."

Benny cleared his throat. "Thank you."

"So, what did you want to talk to me about?"

"Ahh, yes. I pulled the private investigator. The lead in Mexico came up empty. Lucy had no other family, Abby."

Abby's chest tightened. She pressed the phone to her ear

and took a slow, shaky breath. "So . . . Cami has no family at all?"

"No one, except Jack, who's made it perfectly clear he wants nothing to do with her."

Her stomach twisted. "What are the next steps, then?"

"Since there's no other family, you'll need to contact family services and get a caseworker. They'll find a suitable foster family for her. I can make those arrangements for you."

"No, Benny," Abby said firmly. "We're staying here in Bluefin Bay. I want to make this arrangement permanent. Foster care was never an option."

"Well, you are her guardian. You can petition for permanent guardianship," Benny said.

Abby squeezed her eyes shut and firmly gripped her coffee mug to prevent herself from jumping up and down. She let out a shaky breath. "Yes, that's what I want to do."

"Are you sure about this, Abby?"

"Yes, more sure than I've ever been about anything in my life," she assured him. "Can you take care of getting the paperwork together for me?"

"Of course. And Abby?"

"Yes?"

"Congratulations. I'm really happy for you. For you both." His voice softened. "You know, I've known you a long time, and I've never heard you sound this certain about anything. This feels right, Abby. She's a lucky girl to have you, and from what you've told me, you're pretty lucky to have her too. I can't wait to meet her."

Abby swallowed hard. "Thank you." She hesitated for a moment. "Benny . . . about Michael. Have the authorities found anything?"

"There's an ongoing investigation. They had already flagged some irregularities before the accident, and they're still looking into it. But Abby . . . I want you to hear this clearly—

you were never involved, and there's no reason for you to worry about your own legal standing."

Her stomach eased just a little. "So . . . nothing I need to do?"

"Not at this point. Focus on yourself and Cami. That's all you need to worry about right now. I'll keep you updated as I hear more."

Abby set her jaw, nodding even though he couldn't see her. "Okay. Thank you, Benny."

"Anytime, Abby. Take care of yourself—and Cami. I'll be in touch soon."

"I will. Bye."

She ended the call and set the phone on the counter, letting out a slow breath. Benny had made it clear she had nothing to worry about regarding the investigation. There were still unanswered questions, but for now, she could focus on moving forward. The morning light streaming through the kitchen window reminded her that today was a new beginning.

The sound of small feet padding across the floor caught her attention. She looked up to see Cami entering the kitchen, still in her pajamas, hair sticking out in all directions.

"Morning," Cami said, rubbing her eyes. "Who were you talking to?"

Abby smiled, her heart full. "That was Benny, my lawyer."

Cami nodded, climbing onto the stool beside Abby at the breakfast counter.

"Good morning to you too," Abby said, reaching out to smooth a wild strand of Cami's hair. "How would you feel about some breakfast? I think we have everything for toast and eggs."

Cami looked up. "Can I help make it? I'm really good at toast. Even if I burn it a little sometimes."

"I would love that," Abby said, taking another sip of her coffee. "Besides, a little extra crunch never hurt anyone."

Cami beamed and went to get the bread from the pantry. Chance circled around her feet, his tiny tail wagging hopefully. "No, Chance. People food is for people," Cami told him, then giggled when he lay down with a dramatic sigh.

They worked together in the kitchen. Abby making scrambled eggs and Cami carefully toasting and buttering the bread. They settled at the table, and Abby opened her laptop. "I thought we might look at some houses this morning. What do you think?"

Cami's eyes widened. "Really? Like, to buy?"

"Mm-hmm. If we're going to stay in Bluefin Bay, we need our own place. This rental is nice, but . . ."

"It's not really ours," Cami finished.

Abby nodded. "Exactly." She pulled up the real estate website and turned the screen so Cami could see. "I've been looking at these. What do you think?"

Cami leaned in, scanning the listings, her eyebrows scrunched in concentration. She pointed to a blue Victorian with a wraparound porch. "That one has a porch swing. I like that."

"It does," Abby agreed. "And look, it has three bedrooms."

"Why do we need three bedrooms?" Cami asked, taking a bite of her toast.

"Well, one for you, one for me, and maybe one for guests? Or a home office. Or a playroom."

Cami nodded and finished chewing. "Can we go see it?"

"I was thinking about setting up some appointments for this afternoon. I also need to call the rental office and see if we can stay here for a few more weeks until we find something."

"What if someone else buys the house with the porch swing before we can?"

Abby reached over and smoothed Cami's hair. "Then

we'll find another one that's even better. There are lots of great houses here." She clicked through to another listing. "Look at this one. It has a fenced-in backyard for Chance."

Cami's face lit up. "And it's close to the beach! Can we go see that one too?"

"Absolutely," Abby said, adding it to her list. "I'll call the agent after breakfast."

They spent the next half hour scrolling through listings, with Cami offering her opinion on each one. The girl's excitement was contagious, and Abby found herself imagining their life in each property—planting flowers in the garden, decorating Cami's room, sitting on the porch in the evenings watching the sunset.

After narrowing down their favorites, Abby made a call to the real estate agent Beth had recommended, who arranged three showings for that afternoon, including both houses Cami had liked best. Next, she called the rental office, who confirmed that Abby could extend the lease on a month-to-month basis. Now that summer tourist season was nearing its end, they were grateful to have the extension.

"We're all set," Abby said as she ended the call. "We can stay here until we find our new home."

Cami clapped her hands. "Can I have a blue room in our new house?"

"You can have any color room you want," Abby promised.

As Cami ran off to get dressed, Abby stared at her phone. There was one more call she needed to make. She'd been putting it off, but it couldn't wait any longer. Taking a deep breath, she dialed her mother's number.

To her surprise, her mother answered on the third ring. "Abigail? Is that you?"

"Hi, Mother," Abby said, her throat suddenly tight. "Yes, it's me."

"Well, it's about time. I was beginning to think you'd forgotten I existed." Her mother's voice was crisp and clipped.

Abby's shoulders tensed. "I texted several times. You didn't reply."

"I've been busy with the charity gala," she said. "And you know I don't like to text. When are you coming home? This little vacation of yours has gone on long enough, don't you think?"

Abby gripped the phone a little tighter. "Actually, that's why I'm calling. I'm not coming back to New York. Not to live, anyway."

There was a long silence on the other end of the line. "I beg your pardon?"

"We've decided to stay here, Bluefin Bay. Permanently. We're going to look at houses later today."

"Abigail Nicole Whitney, have you taken leave of your senses?" Her mother's voice rose several octaves. "What about your life here? What about your responsibilities?"

"My life is changing, Mother. I have a job here." She hesitated for a moment before continuing. "And I—I've decided to petition for permanent guardianship of Cami."

Abby heard a sharp intake of breath.

"That child is not your responsibility! It's bad enough that we have to deal with rumors and gossip about the investigation the authorities are conducting, but this . . . How am I supposed to explain this to our friends? You don't owe that girl anything. Please tell me you haven't told anyone."

Abby's chest tightened, her pulse quickening. Of course, her mother would make it about her. She wasn't going to back down this time. She straightened her shoulders. "Her name is Cami, Mother. And this isn't about owing anyone anything, or what people will think. I love her."

"Love?" her mother scoffed. "You've known her for what, three months? This is ridiculous, Abigail. You're throwing away everything for some . . . some child you barely know. A child that isn't even yours."

"I'm not throwing anything away," Abby said. "I'm building something new. Something that matters to me. I've got a job I really like, and I'm making friends here, real friends. And for the first time in my life, I'm making choices because they're what I want, not what someone else expects of me. And Cami might not be mine, but I love her."

"I see," her mother said, ice in her voice. "So this is some sort of rebellion? At your age?"

"No, Mother, it's not a rebellion. It's me finally figuring out who I am and what I want." Abby sighed, the corners of her mouth turning downward. Her mother would never understand. "I'd like you to be happy for me, but I understand if you can't be. Either way, this is my decision, and it's final."

There was another long pause. "I don't know what's gotten into you, Abigail. This is not how I raised you."

"Maybe that's the point." Abby's voice didn't waver. "I need to live my own life now."

Cami appeared in the doorway, dressed and ready for the day, her eyes questioning. Abby smiled at her and held out her hand. Cami crossed the room and took it, squeezing tightly.

"Mother, I need to go. Cami and I have appointments this afternoon. I'll call you soon, okay?"

Her mother made a noncommittal sound.

"Goodbye. I—I love you." Abby ended the call before her mother could respond. She set the phone down and looked at Cami. "Ready to go find our new home?"

Cami nodded, eyes serious. "Was that your mom? Is she mad?"

"She's . . . adjusting," Abby said carefully. "Change is hard for some people."

"Is it hard for you?" Cami asked.

Abby thought about it for a moment, then shook her head. "Not anymore."

Chapter 35

Later that week, Abby sat next to Beth at the breakfast counter and took a sip of her soda. "I think Angie showed us nearly every house in Bluefin Bay this week."

Beth laughed. "I told you she was good. Did you find anything yet?"

"We toured some really nice houses, but nothing has really stood out yet." Abby rubbed her brow. Every house they'd looked at had something that made it not quite right—not quite home. "I've got an appointment to meet with her again this afternoon. She says she's found '*the one*.' Apparently, it just went on the market."

Beth's eyebrows rose. "Oh? Where's it at?"

Abby crinkled her nose and tried to bite back a smirk. "It's on Sandpiper Court, right past the intersection with White Heron Lane."

Beth grabbed Abby's arm. "That cute yellow two-story?"

Abby nodded. According to the map, the home was less than a block from Beth's house on White Heron Lane.

Beth squealed and slid off the stool. She danced in a little circle, waving her arms and stomping her feet. "We're going to be neighbors!"

Abby laughed at her friend's antics. "I haven't even looked at it yet." She grinned. If the house looked as good in real life as it did in the photos Angie had sent her, the search would be over.

Beth smiled and sat back down. "I've been inside that house. You are going to love it!"

"Do you know why they're selling?"

Beth scrunched up her nose and tilted her head. "The Millers live there. I didn't know it was for sale already. They used to have an annual New Year's Eve party, but Viola got sick a couple of years ago and they haven't had one since. I think they're moving to Virginia to be closer to their daughter."

Abby nodded. "I'm excited to see it. I have a good feeling about it."

Cami and Piper came stumbling out of Cami's room, giggling hysterically. Chance was swaddled like a baby in Piper's arms.

"Abby, we're going to take Chance outside to play." Cami's eyes sparkled with mischief.

"Stay in the yard," Abby and Beth said in unison. They glanced at each other and laughed.

Piper leaned over and whispered loudly, "They are so weird."

Cami shrugged, and the girls skipped out of the room, the door closing behind them seconds later.

"That poor dog." Abby shook her head.

"He didn't look like he was suffering." Beth giggled. "When are you going back to New York?"

Abby rolled her eyes and let out a sigh. "Next week. Honestly, I'd like to avoid the whole thing, but there *are* some things I need to take care of. We're on a month-to-month lease at the bungalow, but I'm hoping we find something here before we have to go, so I can have my attorney look over that paperwork while we're there."

"How long will you be there?"

"I'm hoping only a few days. Cami wants to enter that equestrian competition next month, so she'll need to spend more time at the ranch training."

Beth waggled her eyebrows. "Which means you'll be spending more time at the ranch with Logan."

Abby's cheeks flushed. "It's not like that. Michael hasn't even been gone six months."

"Not to be harsh, Abby, but it seems to me that he's been gone for a long time." She reached over and gave Abby's hand a gentle squeeze. "Logan is a good man—and a good-looking man." She smiled. "I think he's interested in you too."

Abby considered her friend's words. There was some truth about what she'd said about Michael. And Logan certainly was good looking. No. She wasn't ready to go down that road. Not right now anyway. Maybe not ever. She gave her head a small shake. "I have way too much going on right now to worry about whether or not Logan likes me. I need to focus on Cami right now. Find a home."

Beth leaned back and nodded. "I get it. We'll get you there, though." She gave Abby a wink. "Do you have a lot of stuff in New York to bring back? If you haven't found a place by the time you need to bring it here, we could probably store a few things in the garage for you."

"Thank you. I don't think there's much there I want anymore," Abby admitted. "There are some boxes we brought back from California for Cami, and I'll have to go through all of Michael's things, I suppose." A heaviness settled in her chest as she thought about everything in the apartment. All of Michael's things. It had been easy to avoid thinking about it over the summer, but she knew she needed to deal with it before she could really move on.

"Do you have a friend, or someone you could hire to do that?" Beth asked. "The money you spend might be worth not having to deal with it yourself."

"Yeah, that's not a bad idea. Maybe I can ask my attorney for some recommendations." She smiled. "I might need to take some time off work, though, while I get this all sorted out." Abby grimaced.

"Well, I could put in a good word with the owner." Beth winked. "Seriously, you have done amazing things in the store, and the customers love you. Your job is safe. Take care of what you need to take care of so you can come back."

"Thanks, Beth. I'm really hoping it will go fast, maybe just a few days. I think my attorney can help me with a lot of it. He's been a good friend through all of this."

"It sounds like it." Beth took a sip of soda. "Have you decided what you're going to do about school?"

"Well, I know I'm not going to homeschool her." Abby laughed. "I admire her mother for doing it, though."

"Yeah." Beth grimaced. "I shudder to think about Piper's future if she had to rely on me being her teacher. If you get the Millers' house, you'll be in the same school district as us. We could carpool."

Abby laughed. "Next you'll have me in the PTA."

Beth shrugged. "There are worse things."

———

Abby drove slowly down Sandpiper Court until she spotted the pale yellow, two-story house she'd seen in the photographs on the Realtor's website. She pulled into the driveway behind Angie's now-familiar silver BMW.

"This is it. What do you think so far?" She turned to

Cami, who stared out the window at the charming house with her mouth open.

"It's so pretty!" Cami unbuckled her seatbelt and scrambled out of the car, running up the short walk to the front door before Abby could even turn off the engine.

Angie met them at the door and showed them through the three-bedroom home. The main level had an open floor plan with beautiful wood floors, a huge kitchen, and a large master bedroom. Upstairs were two more nice-sized bedrooms, plus a huge bonus room that Cami declared would be the perfect place for sleepovers with Piper. The spacious yard was nicely manicured with a brick patio in the back. Abby couldn't find a single thing wrong with it.

"The owner is willing to negotiate on the majority of the contents too," Angie added as they walked down the stairs and back into the living room. "They're downsizing and would need to sell most of it, anyway."

Abby looked around the room again. It was tastefully decorated and felt very "homey." She would definitely be interested in seeing what they could work out.

"I'll give you two a few minutes to talk. Feel free to look around some more," Angie said, giving Cami a wink. "I'll be out on the patio when you're done." She stepped through the large glass doors into the backyard.

Abby turned to Cami, who was hopping from one foot to the other with barely contained excitement.

"What do you think of the kitchen?" Abby asked, walking over to the marble countertops. "I bet we could make some really great cookies in here. Maybe even try that chocolate soufflé recipe you've been talking about."

Cami ran her small hand over the shiny countertop. "Can we make pancakes every Saturday? With blueberries?"

"Absolutely," Abby said, smiling. "There's plenty of room for both of us to cook together."

"It's a million times better than the last one we looked at." Cami wrinkled her nose.

Abby laughed. "It wasn't that bad."

"It had polka dot wallpaper in the bathroom!" Cami exclaimed, making a dramatic gagging sound.

Abby put her hands up. "Okay, okay. It's way better than that one," she conceded. She walked back into the living room and ran her hand along the wooden mantle above the fireplace. A flutter of nerves swept through her chest. This was a big step—buying a house without anyone else's input. She'd have a home inspection done, of course, but no parents telling her what neighborhood was appropriate. No Michael insisting on the right address. Just her, making a choice for herself and Cami.

Cami walked over and stood beside her, leaning against her side.

"You really like it?" Abby asked.

Cami nodded. "It feels like home. Chance will love it too."

Abby's throat burned, and she swallowed hard. She took a deep breath, trying to calm her racing heart. This was the right choice. She could feel it. "Go get Angie. Let's make an offer."

A couple of hours later, they walked into Two Scoops and got in line. Abby had made an offer on the house, and it seemed like there was an endless amount of paperwork to fill out. Angie said she'd contact the homeowner with the offer and would have an answer within a couple of hours. Each minute felt like an eternity.

Cami's eyes lit up as they stepped out of the real estate office. "Let's get ice cream and wait on the beach where we found Chance. It's our good luck spot!"

Abby smiled, letting her little hand tug her toward the car. The air smelled of salt and warm sand, and they drove the short distance to Two Scoops.

Colleen greeted them as they came up to the counter. "I hear you aren't leaving us after all."

"Nope, you're stuck with us." Abby grinned.

"Well, ice cream is on me today." Colleen smiled. "What will it be? The usual?"

Abby and Cami nodded in unison. They'd made stopping at Two Scoops a regular habit over the summer.

Colleen filled two cones and handed them to Abby. "See you at book club."

"Thanks, Colleen." Abby waved as they walked out the door.

They sat on the bench at the end of the boardwalk and licked their cones while they watched the seagulls flying overhead. There was just enough of a breeze to keep it from being too hot.

"You know, I heard from Julie earlier today," Abby said, glancing at Cami.

"About what?" Cami asked, ice cream smeared around her mouth.

"They're coming for a visit. Julie and Ava."

Cami's eyes lit up. "Really? When?"

"As soon as we get back from New York. Julie said they could come for the long weekend over Labor Day. That way you"—she tapped Cami on the nose—"don't have to miss any school." She handed Cami a napkin.

Cami wiped her mouth, then looked up at Abby. A wrinkle formed across her forehead. "Do you think I'll like regular school?"

"I do," Abby said. "We've talked about this, remember? You said you were nervous but excited to meet other kids."

"I know. But what if nobody likes me?" Cami's voice was small.

"That won't happen. You're a wonderful girl, and you'll have Piper there with you. And honestly, I'm not cut out for homeschooling. Remember when we tried to double that cookie recipe?"

Cami giggled. "You got all the math wrong, and the cookies got flat instead of puffed up."

"Exactly! This is going to be good for you. You'll make friends, learn new things, and have fun."

Cami was quiet for a moment, then asked, "Can I bring Ava to the ranch to meet Scout?"

"Of course you can."

Abby's phone rang, and her heart pounded as she dug it out of her purse. It was Angie.

"Good news, Abby," she said. "They accepted the offer! You are a new homeowner!"

Abby was speechless for a moment. She was buying a house! She took a deep breath and gripped the phone tighter with her shaking hand while she made arrangements to meet with Angie at the office the next morning to set up a closing date and fill out the rest of the paperwork. She clicked off the phone and turned to Cami, who stared at her impatiently.

"We got it!" she yelled.

"I knew we'd get it!" Cami squealed, jumping up from the bench. She threw her arms around Abby's waist. "We have a house of our very own!"

Abby laughed and lifted Cami up, spinning her around once before setting her back down. They danced in a little circle, holding hands and giggling until they were both out of breath. "I told you this was our lucky charm spot!" Cami said, beaming up at Abby.

"You sure did," Abby said. They linked their arms and walked back up the boardwalk.

"We're going to have to buy a car now too," Cami said as they approached the little red rental car. "Can we get one with a sunroof?"

"We'll see," Abby said. There were so many things that needed to be done. She'd need to make a list.

"Hey, New York," a deep, familiar voice called from behind them. Logan.

Abby flushed before she even turned around. He stood holding a bag from Two Scoops.

"Mr. Taylor!" Cami all but shouted. "Guess what? We're staying here. We just got a house."

Logan lifted his brows, his gaze shifting to Abby. "Is that so?"

Abby nodded. "We just found out that our offer was accepted. We were celebrating with ice cream on the boardwalk." She nodded toward the bag in Logan's hands. "Seems like a popular day for that."

Logan shrugged. "I have my vices." He laughed and turned to Cami. "Now that you'll be staying, I'll have to see what kind of competitions we can find for you and Scout. We might even be able to get you into that one next month. If you're still interested, that is."

"Yes, please!" Cami bounced on her toes. "That would be awesome!"

Logan and Abby laughed, and their eyes met and held for a long moment. Abby felt a small flutter and looked away.

"Well, I better be going before my ice cream melts," Logan said. "Luke won't be very happy with me if I bring him ice cream soup."

"Ice cream soup." Cami giggled. "That's funny."

"I'll see you tomorrow for your lesson, kiddo." He nodded at Cami, then shifted his gaze back to Abby. "Guess I'll be seeing you around then, New York."

Abby raised an eyebrow. "You know, you can't call me that anymore. I'm a local now."

Logan's crooked grin appeared. "You might live here, but you'll always be New York to me." He tipped his hat at her.

"Whatever you say, cowboy."

They watched him walk across the street and climb into his truck. He waved at them as he drove past.

"I think he likes you," Cami said with a knowing smile as they got into the car.

"You do, huh?"

"Yep, he looks at you the way Prince Charming looks at Cinderella in the movie."

Abby glanced at the girl beside her out of the corner of her eye but didn't respond. There was something about that crooked grin of his and the way he'd looked at her that filled her with hope for something more to come.

Cami turned the radio up and sang along to a pop song as they drove back to the bungalow, bouncing to the music and looking like she didn't have a care in the world.

Abby thought about how far the girl had come over the summer and realized how much she herself had grown as well. No one expects their life to change in an instant. She'd known what she'd be doing every day for the next month, the next year, until suddenly she hadn't known what was happening at all. Everything was normal until it wasn't. Yet, somehow, in all the chaos that had followed Michael's death, she had found who she really was and where she belonged.

———

Later that afternoon, they walked along the beach, paper grocery bags in their arms, toward the bungalow. They'd stopped at the local market to pick up ingredients for a cele-bration dinner—fresh fish, lemons, and the makings for Cami's favorite chocolate chip cookies.

The sun angled west, casting the waves in glimmering silver and bathing the shore in warm, golden light.. Chance trotted ahead of them, occasionally stopping to investigate something in the sand.

"Can we eat dinner on the patio tonight?" Cami asked, skipping alongside Abby.

"Sure, why not? It's a special occasion."

"And can I help make the cookies?"

"I'm counting on it."

Cami beamed up at her, and Abby felt her heart swell with affection. She thought about how afraid she'd been that first night in the hospital, how lost and confused she'd been when she discovered Michael's secret life. She'd been terrified of taking responsibility for this child she didn't know.

Now, she couldn't imagine her life without Cami in it.

They stopped to watch Chance chase after a small crab scuttling across the sand. Cami's laughter rang out, pure and joyful, carried away by the ocean breeze.

"I love it here," Cami said, her small hand finding Abby's.

"Me too," Abby replied, squeezing Cami's hand gently.

As they turned to head back to their bungalow, Abby realized that for the first time in her life, she truly felt like she belonged somewhere. Not because someone had chosen it for her, but because she had found it herself. Bluefin Bay, with its charming streets, friendly faces, and endless ocean views, wasn't just a place to escape to anymore. It was home.

A Note from Laura

Dear reader,

Thank you for spending time with Abby and Cami, and for joining them on a journey of heart, hope, and self-discovery. Watching Abby find her wings, and embrace the unexpected joys and challenges along the way, has been a tender reminder that even in seasons of change, hope and grace are never far from reach. My prayer is that their journey has touched your heart and perhaps even encouraged you in your own.

If you'd like to stay connected, and find out when my next book is out, I'd love to invite you to join my newsletter. Subscribers get exclusive updates, sneak peeks at upcoming books, and little extras I only share with my readers. You can sign up here:

www.harpethroad.com/laura-ashwood-newsletter-signup

Finally, if this story resonated with you, would you consider leaving a review? Your words not only help other readers discover the book, but they also mean the world to me as an author.

With heartfelt thanks,
Laura

Acknowledgments

Writing a book is a solitary endeavor, but there is really a team behind it.

To my husband, thank you for putting up with all my endless chatter about my "imaginary friends." Your patience, encouragement, and steady support mean more than I can ever say.

To Gus, my faithful furry writing companion, who is always by my side and willing to give endless hugs and kisses.

A huge thank-you to Jenny at Harpeth Road for taking a chance on me, and to the entire team there for helping make Abby and Cami's story the very best it could be. I'm deeply grateful for your insight, hard work, and belief in this book.

To the Ladies of the Lakes—you are an inspiring, generous group, and I'm so blessed to know you.

And to my morning writing crew: Kari, Laina, and Carolyn. Thank you for the motivation, the prayers, and all the laughter along the way. I truly couldn't do this without you.